The vampyre stood upon the black branch now, its back still to the vanishing sun. The heron put her eye to the keyhole. The stink of rotten matter grew smothering. The icarus fanned and flexed its pinions. Aeriel wondered wildly where her gargoyle had gone, and where was the strange beast the old gatherer had spoken of?

Solstar sank lower, barely a fingernail above the hills. Oceanus peered, pale blue through the curled, black trees. She heard a scratching sound. The staff tipped in her hands. She saw the heron giving her neck an odd, lunging twist. The tip of her beak in the keyhole turned. The painted girl tore the shackle from her wrist.

Solstar set. The sky above turned black as nothing. The orchard around them was drenched in shade. The vampyre upon the far tree turned, lit now with the ghostlight of Oceanus and the stars. Aeriel had only one glimpse of pale garments on a young man's form, a face savage with hunger, and blank, colorless eyes.

Look for this other TOR book by Meredith Ann Pierce
THE DARKANGEL

MEREDITH ANN PIERCE

A GATHERING OF GARGOULES

A TOM DOHERTY ASSOCIATES BOOK

This is a work of fiction. All the characters and events portrayed in this book are fictional, and any resemblance to real people or incidents is purely coincidental.

A GATHERING OF GARGOYLES

Reprinted by arrangement with Little, Brown and Company, in association with the Atlantic Monthly Press

A TOR Book

Published by Tom Doherty Associates
8-10 West 36 Street
New York, N.Y. 10018

Cover art by Kinuko Craft

First TOR printing: July 1985

ISBN: 0-812-54902-3
CAN. ED.: 0-812-54903-1

Printed in the United States of America

To Joy

Contents

A
GATHERING
OF
GARGOYLES

1

ISTERNES

Aeriel sat on the low windowseat.
The stone was warm from the light of Solstar. That
sun lay on the far horizon, two hours from setting.
Heaven above spanned black and star-pricked. The
spires of the city fanned out before her, beyond the
palace walls. Men with plum-colored skin and long head
veils, women in full sheer trousers that gathered close
at the ankles passed in the streets below. Aeriel listened
to the criers' long, wavering wails, calling the people to
prayer.

Dusk wind rose, bringing the scent of myrrh. The
city had always smelled of that to her, ever since the
first day — even the dust blowing in off the Sea. They
called their city Isternes, though in the far place she had
come from, Aeriel had known of it as Esternesse.

Was it only three daymonths ago that she had come?
Three leisurely passes of Solstar overhead, two long
fortnights of dark. The fair-skinned girl closed her eyes
and tried to picture again the great throw she and
Irrylath had woven from the feathers of a darkangel.

They had taken that throw and spread it to the winds. Like a sail, it had borne them away over the white plain of Avaric. And the scream. She remembered the scream of the White Witch sounding far and shrill from the distance behind, turning the feathers of their sail from night-dark to white as Aeriel and the young prince sailed out of her grasp. The memory of it made her shudder still.

They had drifted east, she and Irrylath, over the Sea-of-Dust. High above that dryland Sea, they had watched dust whales spouting and sounding hugely below, seabirds like specks bathing and pouting in the fine, rolling powder — till they saw the city upon the far shore of the Sea: Isternes. All its buildings of white stone.

Horns sounded from the watchtowers as the wind swept them near, lifted them high over the city gates and dropped them gently within the main square. Palace guard and city guard came at a run. Strangely garbed women, men with almond-shaped eyes pressed close.

The Lady came toward them from the palace. She was tall, and wore a robe of grey satin. The turban upon her head was silk. Aeriel could not see her hair, but her lashes were the color of flaxcorn fiber. Her eyes were violet.

"Are you Syllva?" said Aeriel, clad still in her wedding sari. She put her hands together and bowed as she had been taught to do in the syndic's house — so long ago. "The queen of Avaric?"

The turbaned Lady nodded. "I am she, that was the king's wife in Avaric, a score of years and more ago.

4

But now I am Lady again in Isternes. What are you, that have fared all this way across the Mare?"

"I am Aeriel," the girl replied, "and I have come from Avaric to bring you back your son."

Irrylath stood close to her, not touching, but she felt his hold upon the throw. Wind tugged at the sail as it settled behind them. He said nothing. The Lady's eyes had not left Aeriel.

"My son in Avaric fell into a desert lake and drowned."

Aeriel shook her head. "Not drowned. That was a lie his nurse told you." Her skin grew cold at the thought of Dirna: she who had been the young prince's nurse in Avaric — then was later sold into Terrain, became a servant in the syndic's house, where Aeriel had known her. The Terrainean girl turned her gaze back to Syllva again. "Not drowned. In the desert, your son's nurse, Dirna, gave him up to the lorelei, a water witch who kept him ten years prisoner beneath the lake, then . . ."

She faltered there. What could she say? Lady, your son has been a darkangel. The White Witch of the Mere steals children to make them her icari: pale bloodless creatures with a dozen dark wings — then sends them out to prey upon the world. I undid that sorcery on him, made your son mortal again, but in the years he was the witch's "son," he stole the souls of thirteen maids, and drank their blood, and murdered them.

How could she say it? The Lady watched her. Aeriel cast down her eyes.

"Ten years the witch's prisoner in the lake," she said, "then fourteen more under enchantment in Avaric."

Not a lie — but not the whole truth either. Coward, she reproached herself. She found the Lady's eyes again. "But I have undone that enchantment." Truth now. "Your son is free."

The Lady studied Aeriel for a long moment. She drew a deep breath then, turned her eyes to Irrylath — and started. She had not really looked at him before. Aeriel felt her young husband move past her now. He knelt. The Lady stared.

"You have the gold skin of the plainsdwellers," she breathed, "and their straight black hair. Your eyes are the eyes my Irrylath had." She stopped herself. "But my son died when he was six, a double dozen years ago. Had he lived, he would be thirty years by now, and you are a youth no older than sixteen."

Aeriel could see the young man's face only a little, from the side. Syllva had dropped her eyes. Irrylath reached suddenly, catching her hand as she made to turn away. The guards started, lifting their bows, but though the Lady drew back a bit, surprised, she did not pull away.

"Lady," the prince began, "when I lived with the White Witch under the lake, I changed from boy to youth and grew older. But when . . ." He drew breath then, and Aeriel saw he could not say it, any more than she, not the truth — not all of it. "But when I was in Avaric, I was under a sorcery, and did not change."

The Lady eyed him, hesitating. Aeriel bit her breath. If they could get no harbor from the White Witch here, then there was none for them in all the world.

"Mother," the young man kneeling before her said,

6

"much in you has changed since last I saw you, but still I know you. Look at me."

She saw the Lady sigh once, silently, as one taken by a great longing. Aeriel shivered. Still the other did not speak.

"Say it then," Irrylath cried suddenly, casting off the Lady's hand. He tossed his head toward the guards. "And bid them shoot. Say that I am not your son, not Irrylath."

She stood off yet. Aeriel felt light-headed; she feared she might fall. The young man was kneeling perfectly still. Then the Lady drew breath again, and moved nearer. She touched the sark hanging clawed to ribbons at his shoulder, then his cheek, tracing the five long scars.

"I cannot say it," she answered, soft. "For you are he. My son. My Irrylath."

Aeriel leaned back against the windowseat. Even in the light of Solstar she felt cold. The criers from the temple continued to wail. She balanced the instrument of silverwood across her lap and tried to stop remembering. But she was alone in the high palace room, and the memories came.

She remembered the outer chambers of her and Irrylath's apartments: dark, hangings drawn against the light of stars. Only the inner room was shadowy light, for the Lady's son could not sleep, even fitfully, in darkness. Twelve-and-one lampstands surrounded his bed.

Aeriel stood in the doorway, watching him. It was a daymonth since the two of them had come to Isternes.

His long hair, neither plaited nor fastened now, lay loose about the pillowcase. The lamps were burning very low.

Aeriel held a pitcher of oil in her hands. She had meant to be there before he came, refill the lamps and be gone. But she had misjudged the time. He had been sleeping some while now, by her guess.

Aeriel entered the inner room and knelt beside him. The feather throw on which they had sailed to Isternes cascaded in great rumples from the bed, spreading as far as the lampstands' feet. Aeriel ran her hand over the soft white feathers.

She knew that she should go away. The young man's breathing had grown uneven. His eyes fluttered beneath their lids: he dreamed. She touched his cheek. It was hot. Her hand fell to his shoulder, and his fingers upon the covers twitched. Aeriel leaned near.

"Husband," she said softly, "awake." Then softer still, a whisper now, "Irrylath, Irrylath, come back to me."

The young man shuddered, moved beneath the counterpane. A rush of longing overcame her. Aeriel bent and brushed his eyelids with her lips.

"Irrylath," she said. "Husband, wake."

His lids tremored, and for a moment she was certain he must rouse — but no. She closed her eyes, remembering him as he once had been: the darkangel, white-faced wingèd fiend who had borne her away from her home in Terrain to his keep on the plain of Avaric.

He had married her at last, when he was yet the witch's son, for expedience's sake, because he needed a final bride. And he had lain just so, that last fortnight, poisoned by their wedding toast.

She had held a dagger above his breast, ready to kill him, but could not strike. He was so fair. So she had rescued him instead, giving him her own heart, cut from her breast, and laid in his, to replace the one of lead the witch had given him. His heart, made flesh once more, became her own.

He was mortal now, the Lady's son, the prince of Avaric, no more the darkangel. He had sworn to fight the witch, to find a winged steed to ride against her and her other "sons," his former "brothers," the icari. Aeriel gazed at Irrylath: husband to her, but only in name. She dared touch him only when he slept.

Aeriel put her lips to his. His breath was warm against her skin. A drop of oil fell from the pitcher that she held. She felt it strike her cheek and his. Startled, she drew back, and two more drops fell. The young man caught his breath between his teeth, and woke.

He sat with a start, blinking, staring at her. One hand was at his cheek. The oil there smeared. He ran the back of his hand over his lips, his eyes.

"Something touched me," he muttered, his breathing harsh. His eyes found Aeriel's again. "Did you touch me?"

Aeriel felt all her boldness vanish now. "I came to re-fill the lamps," she stammered, and drew back, holding the pitcher before her in both hands now.

The other stared after her. "Did you kiss me?" he whispered.

Aeriel shook her head. She could not think. "No," she told him. "No."

He caught the bedcover about him suddenly, rose and

quit the room. Aeriel set the heavy pitcher on the floor, ran after him. In the dimness of the outer chamber, the white throw swirled about him like a robe. It dipped low in back. Aeriel could see the marks down his back where wings once had been. I did that, she told herself, took away his wings.

At the window, Irrylath tore the hanging aside. He stared out over starlit Isternes, breathing in the pure night air in gasps. He shook the hair back from his eyes without turning to look at her.

"Why?" he said. "Why did you come?"

Aeriel put both hands to her forehead. She wished that she might wake from this. She wished that she might run away. "Your dreams," she started.

He did turn then. "They are my dreams," he almost shouted at her. "They are none of your affair."

And then for a moment it almost seemed his face changed, the fierceness of his gaze turning to something else. He said something, so soft she barely caught it. What had he said? "You cannot help me," or "No one can help me." Aeriel put down her hands. She could barely see him for the dark.

"You cannot sleep two hours together but you wake, shaking from your dreams," she began. "Let me call for the Lady's priest-physician...."

"No."

"Then let me tell the Lady...."

"No!" His voice was hoarse. "Tell her nothing."

Aeriel went toward him, to see him better. His face wore a hunted look in the dim starlight. He drew away from her. She began again, softly, daring:

"Tell me what you dream."

He turned hard and would not look at her. The cords of his arm were drawn so tight the flesh looked like stone. "Go. Can you not leave me?" he whispered. "I did not ask you to come."

Aeriel stopped herself, for she had failed, again. It seemed he stood leagues, half a world away from her. She could not touch him, could not make him speak. He brushed by her. The feathers of the white robe rustled and sighed.

And he was gone, into the inner room. She could not see him anymore. The doorway there was very dim. The lamps within were burning out. Aeriel put her hands back to her eyes. Her limbs trembled.

She wanted to weep, but could not manage it. Dry as dust, her eyes, her mouth. No sound save the sputter of lampwicks dying. Aeriel turned from the inner room, and fled.

The criers in the temple spires had ceased, foot traffic in the streets below grown much less. Aeriel opened her eyes. From where she sat on the smooth stone bench, she fingered the neck of her bandolyn, the four tune-strings and heavy drone. Three daymonths she had been in Isternes.

Hearing movement, she turned toward the door. The Lady Syllva entered. Aeriel smiled, a little wanly. She had wanted to be alone. The Lady wore no turban now, her pale hair set with combs and thickly plaited. Aeriel moved to give her room upon the bench.

"All's still," the Lady said, gazing past her across the square. "All gone to the great kirk to hear the tales."

Aeriel set down her bandolyn. "Will they not be needing you in the kirk?" she asked.

Syllva shook her head. "Not till Solstar sets. There is time. Play me your bandolyn."

Aeriel lifted the instrument again. She had learned to play a long time past, in Terrain. Her mistress, Eoduin, had taught her. Aeriel's lip trembled. They had been more companions than mistress and serving maid, like sisters almost — until the darkangel had stolen Eoduin away.

Darkangel. Irrylath. The fair-skinned girl bit her lip till she stopped thinking. She fretted the strings of the little instrument.

> *"The world wends weary on its way;*
> *The haze hangs heavy on the Sea.*
> *If only there would come a day*
> *When you would not turn from me. . . ."*

The words wound on, with runs and ornaments, as Aeriel plucked and thrummed.

"That is a sad song," the Lady Syllva said, when she had done, "for one so young and lately wed to be singing."

Aeriel looked down and said nothing. The Lady seemed to be watching her. After a time, the other said carefully, "Tell me, if you will, how things lie between you and my son."

Aeriel felt her throat tighten. The knuckles of her one hand about the instrument grew white. She toyed with the hem of her wedding sari.

"You do not sleep in the same chamber," the Lady said, very gently.

Aeriel turned, gazed out the window. She wanted desperately to fly, fly away from Isternes, but she could not leave Irrylath, for she was drawn to his beauty still. She had chosen to love him, rather than destroy him, a choice which bound her yet.

Solstar lay partially hidden by mountains to the east. Aeriel found herself speaking, without meaning to; the words were low.

"He will not enter a chamber where I am sleeping, or lie where I have lain. So I have left him the inner room of the apartments you gave us, and sleep without."

Syllva said nothing for a little. "My attendants say his dreams are troubled."

Aeriel shook her head, not quite sure what she meant, save she felt that she must answer somehow, and her voice had deserted her. The Lady sighed.

"When you first came, three daymonths past, I bade the two of you tell what had befallen to bring you here. But Irrylath would not speak, left you to tell it all."

Aeriel would not look at her.

"You did not give us the whole tale, then," said Syllva gently. "Some parts, I think, you did not tell. What was the enchantment upon my son? How came he by the scars upon his shoulder and cheek?"

The lyon did it, thought Aeriel. The lyon of Pendar, rescuing me. The darkangel would have killed me if the lyon had not come. But he is the darkangel no more. He is Irrylath now. My husband is the darkangel no more. Her voice came back to her.

"Lady, I may not tell you. Those things are my husband's to speak of, if he chooses."

Again the other fell silent, eyed her a moment, as if considering, then seemed to change her mind.

"You have such green eyes, child," she said, "like beryl stones. They remind me of my birthsister, who was regent here when I wed the Avaric king and followed him across the Sea-of-Dust into the west." The Lady sighed a little, sadly. "She went merchanting after my return. I have not had word of her in many years."

Aeriel felt her fair skin flush. All during her childhood in Terrain, her mistress Eoduin had teased her unmercifully for her odd-colored eyes. Syllva was speaking again.

"Eryka," she murmured. "My sister's name was Eryka."

She stopped herself suddenly, drew breath and stood, gazing past Aeriel. The Terrainean girl turned and saw Solstar now three-quarters sunk away.

"Time's short; I had not realized," the Lady Syllva said. "I must to kirk, but afterwards, I would talk with you more, dear heart, about my son. I am troubled for him, and for you. Say you will sup with me."

2

IRRYLATH

Aeriel nodded.

The Lady rose and departed. Aeriel sat alone once more in the high palace room. Night's shadow came running, swept over the city. The chamber was suddenly dark. The Sea beyond gleamed, restless by starlight, reflecting its own inner fire.

No Oceanus rode the heavens. That planet, like a fixed blue eye, had slipped beneath the rim of the world before she and Irrylath had reached Isternes. She gazed at the dark between the stars and had an eerie sense of something unfinished, some task left undone. She felt as though she had lost something.

Aeriel arose, leaving the bandolyn, and crossed the smooth stone floor to the hall. Hurrying down the long, empty corridors, she found a door into the garden. Winding paths there lost themselves among hummocks of plume grass, bee's-wing and cat's-toes.

Aeriel found herself at stream's edge suddenly, heard someone calling her name. Glancing up, she spotted the Lady's six secondborn sons under the lacewillow trees. These were the sons she had borne after Irrylath, after the Avaric king had set her aside and she had returned to Isternes.

"Sister!" cried Arat and Nar, "Aeriel!" They were the eldest two, twenty and twenty-one. They stood in their long gowns of black and red, fists upon their hips.

Syril and Lern, birthbrothers, both nineteen, sat before on cushions of pale blue and green. "Come," they cried, rolling up their gilt-edged scroll. "We are weary of tales out of books."

Scholarly Poratun, eighteen, knelt alongside. "Tell us one of your own," he bade her.

"Or we shall die," finished Hadin, the youngest at seventeen, sprawled in his yellow, chin resting on his palms.

Aeriel could not help smiling. Lern and Syril moved apart to let her sit between them.

"Tell us of Ravenna," Poratun said.

Aeriel sighed. Did they never tire of the tale? It had been barely a year since she had learned it herself, how in ancient days Old Ones of Oceanus had plunged across deep heaven in chariots of fire to waken this, their planet's moon, to life, to fashion beasts and herbs and people for it, to bring it moisture and air.

Then after a time, the Ancients had gone away again, back to their blue world of water and cloud — only a few remaining behind, shut up in their cities of crystalglass. Of these, Ravenna had been the last to withdraw, lingering while she fashioned the lons, one great beast for every land: the starhorse Avarclon for the white plain of Avaric, the cockatrice of Elver, the gryphon of Terrain. These lons, the Wardens-of-the-World, were to watch and guard in their maker's stead until some unknown future time when Ravenna promised to return.

But a witch had come into the world since then, a lorelei with darkangels for "sons." Six of these icari were already abroad and six lons besides the Avarclon had already fallen prey to them. Lost — six of Ravenna's wardens lost. Where their bones lay, no one knew.

Yet the seventh, Avarclon, the last to fall, might be brought to life again. Aeriel had found his remains in the desert, brought back a bit of him to Isternes — one hoof. It was enough. Even now the priestesses of the great kirk were working to restore the starhorse to life. It would take them a year — a whole year! — they said, to call back from the void the starhorse's soul, create for him new flesh and blood and bone.

Aeriel felt herself shivering, even in the warm garden air. A useless urgency gnawed at her. There was nothing more she might do to help. She was only an unlearnèd girl, who knew nothing of ancient arts and sorcery. Her defeat of the darkangel had been only by great good chance. Surely now her part against the witch was done. All she could do was wait.

"Yes, tell us of Ravenna," Syril was saying. "That is a tale we never heard before you came."

But Aeriel felt restless still. "No tales, I pray you," she told them. "Another time. But why are the six of you not in kirk?"

Then Arat laughed. "We are going to a revel in the city."

Hadin caught hold of Aeriel's arm. "Come with us, sister. You look in need of cheering."

But Aeriel shook her head, pulled free of him. "No, no. I must find Irrylath," and realized only then that it was true. She had come into the garden in search of Irrylath.

"Our brother is in the kirk," started Lern. "He is always there."

"He waits to see the starhorse reborn," said Syril. "Nothing gives him any pleasure but that, to know he will soon have a wingèd steed."

"If only there were more than one wingèd steed in the world," she heard Nar murmuring, "I would join our brother in his ride against the icari —"

Hadin interrupted them. "He is not there, in kirk. I saw him here in the garden, just lately."

Aeriel arose. "Tell me where I may find him."

Hadin had risen with her. "There," he said, "I saw him through the hedge beyond the lilygrass. I called to him, but he gave no answer, strode away. He had a bow in hand."

Aeriel turned, following the line of his arm. She was wild to be gone suddenly, as if the world hung on her going. She must find her husband, Irrylath. Nodding her thanks to Hadin and the others, she sped away.

He stood, bow drawn, quiver slung from one hip, a target standing a hundred paces from him. The cord of his bow tripped, sang, and the arrows glinted like slips of light. Irrylath turned as Aeriel drew near.

"Your mother came to me this hour," she said softly, "and spoke of you."

Irrylath caught his breath. "What did she say?"

"She asked me to speak of . . . before we came."

She saw him pale, his blue eyes flash. "What have you told her?"

"Nothing," said Aeriel, "I have not said already in your presence. She knows you dream."

He gazed through her, his expression grown suddenly bleak. She felt herself breathe slowly two times, three. It was as if he had forgotten she were there.

"When I was under the witch's spell," he said, softly, "and I heard your tales of mortal things that grew and lived and changed, dreams of those things came to me, drove me half mad, for I wanted them again, and could not have them."

Aeriel gazed at him in slow surprise. It was the most he had said to her at one time since they had come to Isternes. A little tremor stirred in her breast.

"And now," she breathed, "what do you dream?"

Silence. Nothing. Then:

"I dream," he started, stopped. He looked at her, then swiftly off, as though the sight of her eyes somehow frightened him. "No," he whispered. "I will not say."

Aeriel clutched her fingers together, drew nearer. "Do you dream," she began, "do you dream, now that you are among living things again, of the lorelei's house?"

He let out his breath, almost a groan. "Her house is cold," said Irrylath, "so very still. Nothing changes there. No sound but silence there, or din. No music save her strange crooning. Her house is made all of crystal stone, so dry that garments brushed against it cling. It will take the skin from your fingers if you touch it."

He had closed his eyes. Aeriel shook her head. "You are in your mother's house now. You are not in the witch's house anymore."

"When I was young," said Irrylath, "the lorelei called herself my mother. She laid her cold hand on my breast and called me 'son.' " His face looked haggard in the starlight.

"You are no longer hers," cried Aeriel. "I unmade that darkangel."

"There are times," he muttered, "when I wish you had told the Lady Syllva all, at the start — saved her her wondering and me this . . . pretense." He spoke through gritted teeth. "She does not know me."

Aeriel looked at him. She felt as if she were falling endlessly away from him. Her eyelids stung. "You are her son."

"*You* do not know me," he almost spat, gasping as though he were strangling.

"My husband," she managed, her voice a faltering creak. His eyes were fierce and blue as lampwicks burning low and starved for air.

"Am I?" he cried. "Am I that, Aeriel? Do you think a wedding toast can make it so?"

He strode hard away from her then, not looking back. Aeriel held herself very still. Her heart felt suddenly all made of stone, and if she moved too quickly, or breathed too deep, she was afraid it might fall into dust.

She watched him wrenching the darts from the far target. When he swung around, he started, seeing her, and she realized he had expected her to go. He came on after a moment; his garments, pale, gleamed against the night. For a moment she half believed he was the dark-angel again.

A frown passed over his features as he neared her. That broke her from her motionlessness. She whirled.

He cried out, "Wait."

She halted suddenly, from sheer surprise, feeling his hand upon her arm. It was the first time he had touched her since they had come to Isternes.

"You weep."

His tone was much softer now, his breath not steady yet. Aeriel blinked, and only then felt tears spilling warm along her cheeks.

"Aeriel," he said. "Aeriel, don't weep."

She hardly heard. Dismay made all her limbs feel light. She tried to speak, but the words choked her, came out in sobs. She felt the prince's hand upon her tighten. My husband, she thought. What have I done? The witch made you a darkangel once. What thing have I made you, that you are so cruel?

"I meant you no harm," she managed at last, "when I cut out your heart. I meant only to free you from the lorelei's power."

She could not look at him. Her whole frame shook.

"Not your bride," she gasped. "I see that now. What am I then — your tormentor?" He said something. He was bruising her arm. "Is that why you loathe me?" she cried.

She pulled free of him, fleeing, across the huge and starlit garden. Airy and lush it sprawled. She could not find her way, found herself longing wildly for the west, for the pale ghostlight of Oceanus overhead. These

Istern lands to which she had come were altogether a darker and more shadowy place.

If Irrylath called after her, she did not hear him. She did not want to hear. She put her hands over her ears, and ran.

3

MESSENGERS

Aeriel lay on a low, flat couch in the outer chamber of the apartments the Lady had given them. Save for herself, the suite stood empty. She had sent the attendants all away, bade one beg the Lady to excuse her from supping.

The room was dark, completely still, no lampwicks burning in other chambers. Starlight through the windows lit dim squares upon the floor. Aeriel traced the smooth, uneven pattern in the wood of the couch's side. It was wet. Her cheeks were wet. Aeriel sat up, sighing. She blinked, momentarily giddy from having lain so long.

"This is witless," she told herself. "I am worn out with weeping. I should sleep."

She closed her eyes and leaned back against the cool stone of the wall. She felt herself growing very still, and something, some thread, spinning out of her into the night.

The light around her began to change. She perceived, without turning, night sky over Isternes. Low over the west, the ring of yellow stars formed like a crown, or maidens dancing, began to shift and lose its shape. Thirteen pricks of yellow light drifted toward her over the Sea-of-Dust.

Silently, like fireflies they came, and entered the room through the broad windows on either side of her. Golden flickers, each no bigger than a hand, they alighted upon the dark floor in a circle with Aeriel at the head.

Then like someone turning up the wicks of thirteen lamps at once, the little fires expanded, growing brighter, until they stood narrow and tall as women. Aeriel felt a warmth, almost a pressure upon her shoulder. Opening her eyes, she beheld thirteen maidens of golden light.

Only three daymonths ago they had been the wraiths, the vampyre's stolen brides. Aeriel had rescued them, spun thread for their garments on a spindle that drew from the spinner's own heart. Then she had stood with the wraiths in the darkangel's tower, watching their withered bodies crumble, their freed souls ascend. Upon her right stood the first she had saved, the one called Marrea, and upon her left, the icarus' last bride before Aeriel.

"Eoduin," said Aeriel.

The lightmaiden smiled. "Yes, companion."

"You have come back to me."

"For a little," another said. "We followed the thread you spun for us."

She gave a twitch on something Aeriel could not see, though she felt a strange, subtle tugging against her heart. "I spun no thread."

"Who has once mastered that golden spindle," Marrea said, "never loses the knack."

Aeriel shook her head, not understanding. "I have been so alone. Why have you not come to me before?"

Eoduin knelt. "We may come only along the path you make, and until this hour, your heart has spun no strand long enough to find us, or strong enough to hold."

The maiden standing beside her sighed, fiddling with something between her fingers. "Despair's a heavy strand, though very strong."

"Next time you must spin joy, Aeriel," another maiden said.

"Yes, joy."

"There's a thread."

Aeriel put both hands against her breast, against the ache. Her heart felt bruised.

"Leave off," said Marrea suddenly, sternly. The maidens abruptly ceased their fiddling, eyed one another with guilty glances.

"Why have you come?" said Aeriel.

Beside her, Marrea knelt as Eoduin had done. "Deep heaven is a rare place. We like it very well. All there is light and unencumbering, and we may dance together as much as we choose."

"But we saw you were unhappy," another said.

"Here in a strange country."

"With your chieftain's son."

"We never liked him."

Aeriel sat up then, let her hands fall from her breast. "He is not the same creature who stole you away. He is no more the darkangel."

"That is true," one maiden said.

"But still the White Witch whispers to him. . . ."

"In dreams."

"Dreams," breathed Aeriel. "Do you know his dreams?"

"He dreams," said Eoduin, laying her hands on Aeriel's knees, "of a long, narrow hall, all of the cold crystal stone that makes the witch's house."

"The witch sits before him at the far end of the hall," another maiden said, "upon a siege as white as salt."

"She holds in hand a fine silver chain that binds the young man's wrist. 'Come back to me, my love, my own sweet son,' she calls."

"Then she begins to gather in the chain."

Aeriel flinched. "He would not tell me. He has never told me what he dreamed."

None of the maidens spoke.

"Does he go to her?" breathed Aeriel. "What happens in the dream?"

"We do not know," one maiden said.

"He does not know."

"He cannot know, Aeriel."

"Until."

"'Until,'" said Aeriel. "'Until'?"

"Until he finishes the dream," Eoduin replied. "Until you let him."

"Each time he dreams, he wakens — or you waken him."

"You must leave him to his dreams," said Marrea.

Another echoed, "You must leave him."

Aeriel turned her head, dropped her gaze, tried to

look away, but the maidens surrounded her. They burned silently, like pale golden fire, watching her.

"I know it," said Aeriel. "I know."

She said nothing then. The maidens did not speak. At length she said, "Where will I go?"

"Across the Sea-of-Dust," said Eoduin. "A task awaits you there."

"A task?" Aeriel shook her head. "My part in this is done. The rest is Irrylath's."

The maidens shook their heads. All of them were kneeling now.

"You are wrong, love," said Eoduin. Her fingers of golden light still rested on Aeriel's knees. "Tell us again the rime you learned for the undoing of the darkangel."

Aeriel looked at her and thought back. She remembered the duarough, who had taught her the rime. A little man only half her height, with his stone grey eyes and long, twined beard . . . Aeriel turned her head away from Eoduin. The words of the duarough's rime came slowly to her, but she knew them too well to forget.

> *"On Avaric's white plain,*
> > *where the icarus now wings*
> *To steeps of Terrain*
> > *from tour-of-the-kings,*
>
> *And damozels twice-seven*
> > *his brides have all become:*
> *A far cry from heaven*
> > *and a long road from home —*

Then strong-hoof of a starhorse
           must hallow him unguessed
If adamant's edge is to plunder
           his breast.

Then, only, may the Warhorse
           and Warrior arise
To rally the warhosts, and thunder
           the skies."

She paused a moment, drawing breath.

"I broke the spell upon the darkangel using a cup made of the starhorse's hoof," Aeriel said dully, "and hallowed his heart, as I had never guessed to do, by making it mortal again. Irrylath will be the Warrior, and Avarclon the Warhorse that the wise ones are working to restore."

"Listen to this, then," said Marrea. "What does this mean to you?

"But first there must assemble
           those the icari would claim,
A bride in the temple
           must enter the flame,

Steeds found for the secondborn beyond
           the dust deepsea,
And new arrows reckoned, a wand
           given wings —

So that when a princess royal
           shall have tasted of the tree,
Then far from Esternesse's
           city, these things:

> *A gathering of gargoyles,*
> *a feasting on the stone,*
> *The witch of Westernesse's*
> *hag overthrown."*

Aeriel shook her head. "Nothing. It means nothing to me. I have not heard it before." She frowned a little. "It has the same cadence as the riddling rime — but it makes no sense."

"Nor did the first part, when first you heard it," said Eoduin.

"This is the rest," one of the maidens said.

"Part of the rest," her sister amended.

They had all somehow come closer to her, Aeriel realized. She could not recall their having moved. The spirits watched her with their flickering, golden eyes.

"But I thought only the lons knew the riddle Ravenna sang over them at their making," Aeriel began, "and the duarough from the Book of the Dead."

"We can see very far from our vantage point above," Marrea replied, "half the world, and much of the sky."

"See into women's minds."

"And the hearts of men."

"Into locked boxes and closed rooms."

"Into prince's dreams."

"Or Ravenna's book."

Aeriel shook herself, but still the strange lethargy held her limbs. "This is a dream," she murmured. "That cannot be the rest of the rime."

"It is," said Eoduin, "and so the little mage would tell you, had you time to wait upon his coming. . . ."

"But time is short."

"Already the witch has sent her watchers."

"Her searchers."

"Searchers," said Aeriel. "What do they seek?"

The maidens answered, "The lons of those lands that the witch's sons now hold."

"Those lons are dead," said Aeriel. "The icari killed them when they came to power."

"Not killed," the maidens answered urgently. "Not killed."

"Overthrown."

"Made powerless."

"So that her sons might rule and ravage."

"Pillage."

"Feast."

Aeriel shook her head. "How may they live? The witch would not spare them. She is merciless."

"Ah, merciless," one maiden said, "but cunning, too."

"Dead lons are dangerous — they can be reborn."

"Someone must find the lost lons, Aeriel," said Marrea. "Someone must gather them —"

"For they have slipped the witch's grasp."

"Her icari are already searching."

" 'But first there must assemble   those the icari would claim,' " murmured Aeriel. "Where are they?"

"Scattered," said one.

"In hiding."

"You should know that."

"Why should I know it?" Aeriel began.

But Eoduin was already reciting, " 'Beyond   the dust deepsea.' "

"The rime said 'steeds,' " started Aeriel.

"Hist," Marrea said suddenly, and Aeriel realized they all now spoke in whispers. The maidens glanced at one another. "What will your prince ride in a year's time," Marrea was asking, swiftly, "when he goes against the witch?"

Aeriel shook her head. None of it made any sense to her. "The Avarclon."

Eoduin nodded. "A lon. The lon of Avaric."

Said Marrea, "A single rider — against six icari?"

Aeriel felt the weight of weariness upon her limbs beginning to lift. "His brothers," she murmured. "The Lady's secondborn sons have said they would join him, had they only the means. . . ."

"Steeds," Eoduin finished. " 'Steeds found for the secondborn.' "

" 'And new arrows reckoned —' " another began, but Aeriel hardly heard her. She was looking at Eoduin.

"You believe the lost lons are the steeds the riddle speaks of?"

"Yes," the maidens cried, some of them rising.

"Yes."

"Yes."

"How may I find them?"

But the spirits before her all shook their heads, cast down their eyes. "That far we cannot see."

"But what does the rest of the riddle mean," said Aeriel, "the princess and the bride?"

"It is not necessary that you understand it all," replied one maiden.

31

"Only that you depart swiftly across the Sea-of-Dust."

"And find the Ions before the witch does."

The spirits all had risen now.

"Our time is short, our forms too light to hold long in this heavy place."

"Already the strand you spun for us gives way."

Aeriel put one hand to her breast and realized she hardly felt that light, insistent tugging anymore. Strange — her heart felt lighter than it had in daymonths.

"We may not bide," the maidens said.

Marrea smiled and touched her garment. "Though we have come for love of you."

Her sister beside her echoed, "For love of you."

Every maiden of the circle repeated those words, each touching her garment until at last Eoduin touched her own. "For love of you, sweet Aeriel."

And Aeriel saw they had begun both to dwindle and to rise. She watched them losing their maidens' forms, growing dimmer, less yellow and more white. They trailed away from her. Aeriel sprang up, followed them into the inner chamber: Irrylath's.

Surrounding his bed, the dozen-and-one lampstands stood, but they were all dark now, burned out. Some attendant had forgotten to fill them. Already some of the maidens had dwindled enough to light upon the spouts. The maiden on Aeriel's left began to flicker.

"Eoduin, wait," she cried, for a cold fear had begun to fill her. "The poem speaks of 'a feasting on the stone.' In Terrain — in the high temple in Orm — there is an altar they call the Feasting Stone."

"I remember," Eoduin said, half turning, pausing. "My father and I went there once to sacrifice when my mother was ill. You did not come, but I told you of it."

Said Aeriel, "You told me a veiled sibyl sat there."

The maiden nodded. "To answer riddles and interpret oracles."

Aeriel swallowed, for her throat was dry. Must she seek aid from the sibyl then — was that what the rime advised? But once in Terrain, her pale hair and the slight mauve cast to her skin would mark her to any slaver's eye: not freeborn. Fair game.

The memory of Orm's slave fairs rose in her mind: the hoots and jeers and bids from the buyers, shoves from the slavemaster, her fellows in chains. Aeriel shook her head. No, she must not think of it. She must go to Orm. The maidens had said the need was urgent.

"I will go to the sibyl," said Aeriel, "to ask her the meaning of the riddle, and where I may find the lost wardens."

"Take care, dear heart," said Eoduin. Already her outline had grown indistinct, her voice like wind. Her pale golden fingers brushed Aeriel's cheek.

"Don't go — not yet," Aeriel found herself whispering.

But Eoduin drew away, began to fade. Aeriel reached after her, touched nothing solid, felt only what seemed a steady, warm updraft where the figure stood. The other maidens had diminished to the size of tiny flames, alighted on the lampwicks. Eoduin's flame joined the others, grew very small. Then her form, too, vanished.

Aeriel gazed at the lights upon the wicks. They dwindled, grew bluish, and one by one winked out. The room grew darker, shade by shade, until at last the last was out, leaving only a breath of sweet smoke in the air, and Aeriel alone in the dark.

4

THE
SEA-of-DUST

Aeriel opened her eyes.
She found herself sitting in the outer chamber. Outside, the ring-of-maidens burned, low and yellow in the west. She saw by the tilt of the sky it was only a few hours deeper into the long fortnight.

The apartments around her were quiet, still. No attendants had yet returned. It was the custom in Isternes to sup well just after Solstarset, then sleep. Only a dozen or so hours after sundown did city and palace once more awake.

Aeriel rose. She had a little time. All weariness had passed from her and her terror at journeying to Orm receded to a small, dull ache. The sibyl and her temple were yet a long road away. The riddle of the maidens remained clear in her mind, although she did not understand it all:

> But first there must assemble
> > those the icari would claim,
> A bride in the temple
> > must enter the flame,

Steeds found for the secondborn beyond
the dust deepsea,
And new arrows reckoned, a wand
given wings —

So that when a princess royal
shall have tasted of the tree,
Then far from Esternesse's
city, these things:

A gathering of gargoyles,
a feasting on the stone,
The witch of Westernesse's
hag overthrown.

Aeriel unwound the wedding sari from about herself and folded its yards and yards of air-thin cloth. Then she crossed to a great trunk of rose-colored wood, lifting its lid, and drew out the only other garment she owned: the sleeveless shift she had worn among the Ma'a-mbai.

Aeriel threw on the desert garment, surprised again at how light it felt. With great armholes to let the air enter and a wide, uncollared neck, it hung loosely, falling unbelted to her knees.

"All I need now is my walking stick," she murmured to herself, "and I would be a true desert wayfarer again."

She lowered the heavy trunk lid then. Turning swiftly to catch up the folded sari, she quit the room.

Aeriel hurried down the empty halls. The palace attendants had disappeared hours before. The courtiers were all abed. Aeriel fetched her bandolyn from the music chamber, carried it slung by its strap over her shoulder.

"This is mine," she told herself. "The Lady gave it to me — and I must have some means to earn my living."

She ran unseen through the great receiving hall and out again into the garden. There she gathered almnuts from the little orchard, shaking the papery-shelled kernels from the pale-skinned trees, then dark red dates and leather figs. She pulled up the bitter white bulbs of loongrass growing beside the stream. The fisherfolk carried them in lieu of water flasks.

She tied them all into her sari, hefted the bulky load onto her hip and hurried upstream toward the cliff overlooking the Sea. She came at last to the little headland and followed the stone wall till she came to the steps leading down.

Here the dust boats lay moored. All of pale unfinished wood, each rode the rolling dust upon two flat paddles called skates. Suspended in between, each hold hung above the dry waves, not touching them. A single mast with a lateen sail lay shipped in each.

Aeriel searched for Hadin's little craft. The Lady's youngest son had been teaching her dustsea sailing, how to tack and duck the swinging boom. She found the craft, unslung her bandolyn, untied her sari. She stowed her provisions in the hold, lashing the hempcloth cover down to keep out the dust.

"Aeriel!"

The voice startled her. She whirled. Hadin stood upon the headland. Barefoot, his close-toed slippers clutched in one hand, his yellow robe slung over one shoulder, he wore only the knee-length pantaloons that were the undergarb of Istern men.

Aeriel cast off the mooring, tugged the little boat away from the others. Hadin drew near, and Aeriel saw with a start he was sopping. The Lady's youngestborn laughed, slung the water from his hair.

"I fell in the stream carrying Arat home from the revel. The others went on. I was on the bank, wringing my gown, when I saw you go by." Aeriel had reached the end of the pier. "Sister, where are you off to, alone, at such an hour?"

"Hadin, lend me your boat," she said, looking seaward.

"Would you go sailing?" the other began, joining her upon the pier. "I will come with you —"

But Aeriel shook her head. The yellow-haired youth grew sober suddenly.

"Sister, where are you going?" When Aeriel turned to look at him, he started, reaching to touch her cheek and shoulder. "What is this?"

Then Aeriel realized her cheek, her arm, one hand — wherever the maidens had brushed her was covered now with a fine yellow dust.

"They've left their gold on me," she murmured, brushing at it. It lit the dark.

"Who have you been trysting with?"

Aeriel looked off. "Messengers," she said.

Hadin gazed at her. "No messengers passed through the city gates."

"They did not come that way."

The Lady's son was silent. Then he said, "All of us

have known, almost from the first, that you are more than you seem, Aeriel."

She cast the mooring off, stepped down into the boat, chafing to be gone. "You speak as though I were some sorceress."

Hadin knelt upon the pier. "Will you not say where you are bound?"

"I have a task," she answered, and felt the fear in her again. She put it down. "I must begin at once." She stepped the mast, not looking at him.

"Aeriel," he said suddenly, "here. Take my robe. You may have need of it — that shift you wear would not cover a cat."

Aeriel laughed, and found the breath catching in her throat. She had not thought to feel sad at going. She took his robe of yellow silk. The feel of it was wet and cool.

"You take this, then," she said, and handed him her crumpled sari.

Hadin looked at it. "What am I to do with this?"

"Give it to Irrylath," she said softly, and turned away, pretending to be busy in the boat. Her heart felt sore within her breast, but at the same time very light. She turned back to Hadin suddenly. "But not at once. I would be clean away before Irrylath knows."

The boat bobbed on the waves of dust. Aeriel unfurled the sail. Hadin caught her hand, and for a moment she feared he meant to pull her back, but it was only to draw her near enough to kiss her on both cheeks, as was the custom at parting in Isternes.

"Come back to us."

She tried to smile. "Before the Avarclon awakes. I'll bring you a steed in exchange for your boat."

The wind was catching at the sail. Aeriel took the tiller as Hadin gave the little craft a shove. She swung the sail line into a tack, and the dustskate leapt away from shore. The stiff breeze bore her rapidly away. Looking back, she saw Hadin grown suddenly small on the distant pier. She tacked again, hard port, toward Westernesse.

Aeriel's craft sped over the Sea-of-Dust, riding the swells that rolled like water and glowed by starlight with their own internal fire. Beneath the surface, Aeriel saw the silt-fine particles constantly shifting. Wind stole a few from the crests of the waves, whirling them off in dust devils against the dark, starry sky.

So fine were the grains that Aeriel could scarcely see them, hardly felt them when she breathed, aware at first only of their faint, tangy aroma. Before many hours, though, she found her throat growing dry. Her eyes felt grainy, her fingers paper-leathery.

Tying the sail and tiller into place, she drew out from her provisions a loongrass bulb and bit through the white, parchmentlike skin. The meat inside was stiff, the juice astringent but satisfying. She needed only a few bites before the feeling of dryness eased.

The colors of the Sea were changing now. Close in to shore, the dust had been greyish, almost buff-colored. But as she sailed farther, deeper to sea, the dust grew paler, clear yellow-green, and later violet. Sometimes the waves rolled mauve.

Stars turned. Night drifted by. Oceanus peered over the rim of the world, and Aeriel's heart lifted, soared. The air was showered in its ghost-blue light. Gradually, the planet rose.

Aeriel ate of the dates, the figs, the almnut kernels in their papery shells, chewed the loongrass bulbs. Tiresome fare — more than once she found herself longing for the tiny velvet bag the duarough once had lent her. It had held, seemingly within no space at all, an endless store of delicious food.

Sometimes she stood, searching for shore, or tied the tiller and sail securely and slept. The first time she awoke to find two inches of windblown dust in the hold. Afterwards, she bailed every few hours and slept only in snatches.

The wind held mainly steady, her course needing adjustment only now and again. She steered by Oceanus and the stars. The midpoint of the fortnight loomed and passed. Twice Aeriel's craft passed close to peaks rising jagged and slender from the dust. Birds wheeled in crowded columns above those isles.

Sometimes in the distance she watched dust whales — great fish-shaped things a hundred paces long and filled with buoyant gas. They spouted and sounded, lolled sporting with their calves, or rose in towering pairs at some courting ritual.

Once, passing within sight of whales, Aeriel found floating on the Sea a lump of pale green stuff, very like beeswax, save that its odor was bittersweet, like very old perfume. She kept it, for no reason, lying in one corner of the hold. She had no idea what it was.

Once she passed through a flock of skias, sleek raucous

birds with silver bodies, long wings and black-masked eyes. They flocked and plummeted above the waves, snatching bits of something from the dust.

As Aeriel drew near, she realized it was tiny crayfish they were catching. A swarm had gathered, feeding upon algae that lay like reddish bloom upon the Sea. Aeriel leaned over the gunwale, flipped one of the little creatures into the hold.

Its segmented body was crystalline clear. It had many whiskers upon its nose, two small, black eyes on stalks, jointed legs and a broad, flat tail. In a moment it had buried itself in the dust of the hold.

A skia landed on the gunwale, cawing. It eyed the spot where the little fish had disappeared, but Aeriel drove it away. After a time, the plankton, the swarm and the flock of skias fell behind. Aeriel sifted through the dust.

At first the little creature scurried from her fingers, hiding itself again, but presently it grew tamer, sat upon her palm while she fed it bits of date. Soon the little fish hid itself in the folds of her robe rather than in the dust when Aeriel bailed — though now she never threw out so much that the dustshrimp did not have its little pocket in one corner of the hold.

The third quarter of the fortnight went by. Once they passed what seemed to be a wellspring in the middle of the Sea — but the dust that welled from it was neither green nor gold, purple nor grey, but blue, very deep: dark as blown colored glass. It ran in little rivulets among the other strands of color, seemingly heavier, for it quickly sank from sight.

Aeriel scooped up a handful as she passed, it was so

pretty, and tied it away in one sleeve of Hadin's robe.
As soon as it had dried, she had wrapped her bandolyn
in that to keep out the dust, the grey-green wax as well.
The dustshrimp carefully picked out the few grains of
blue that had fallen into the hold and devoured them.
Aeriel fed it another pinch, all it would eat, and after
that, its crystal shell was blue.

She passed a cluster of islands once, arranged in a
broad semicircle, coming within a mile of only one of
them, the farthest on one horn of the crescent. In the
distance, upon its beach she saw boats, long and slender,
turned up at the ends like Istern slippers. Against the
pale sand of the shore, she thought she saw dark figures
moving.

And then to her surprise, for she had been looking to
the island and forgetting to steer, she found herself
almost upon an outlying reef. She had to tack quickly,
very hard, to avoid being dashed. Upon those jagged
rocks knelt a boy, very black, naked but for a skirt about
his legs.

He was raising a crab net from the dust and plucking
the crabs from it, tossing them into a close-woven
basket. He had not seen her. But glancing up then as
she passed, not four paces from him, she leaning hard
against the sail lines and tiller to bank the craft, he did
see her, and started up.

They stared at one another as she swept past: the
slim, dark boy — even his eyes were black — and the
fair-skinned girl. Two crabs freed themselves from his
dangling net, dropped to the reef and scuttled across.
They buried themselves in the breaking dust.

The breeze off the island freshened then, billowed the

sail, plucked Aeriel suddenly out to sea. The dark cliffs and the crabfisher fell away behind. Not many hours and sleeps after that, Aeriel spotted the western shore — pale forested hills of Bern rising beyond the strand. The Sea had turned greenish here, closer to shore, and the fortnight was almost done.

Approaching shore, Aeriel came aware of a hollow booming. She saw spray flying ahead of her — starlit dust, finer than fine — then glimpsed through the valleys of waves, rocks jagged as dogs' teeth. The shining combers leapt over and between.

Aeriel took the tiller and sail lines in hand. She tacked for an hour along the coast, but the rocks stretched endlessly, barring the shore. Does it go on forever? she wondered at last, when her arms had grown so sore they were numb. Dawnlight touched the peaks beyond the shore, gilding them in its harsh, white glare.

Then suddenly beneath the boat, she felt motion. The craft tilted; one skate lifted from the dust. Aeriel nearly lost her balance. She luffed sail and leaned. The craft began righting itself, but the current had swept her much closer to shore. Aeriel struggled with the lines, trying to tack the little boat away.

A narrow headland jutted into the Sea not a half mile before her. A tall tower stood upon its tip, high above the waves which whipped around the headland's bend like rapids, leaping the teeth of the rocks.

Two lines of reef ran parallel there, overlapping their curves in a brief corridor. The inner line petered out just before the outer curved sharply inward, out of sight beyond the headland's bend.

Aeriel saw then, running ahead of her just under the surface of the green and shining Sea, a broad ribbon of reddish rose. Some current of different-colored dust? It undulated like an eel through the narrow passage. She followed it.

Rocks closed around her on both sides. She felt the racing red current beneath the skates, the pull upon the sail of wind whipping around the bend. The wall of rocks to shoreward ended; the right curve loomed. Aeriel leaned, tacked, luffed sail with all her strength.

She felt the right skate grate upon the stone. Its pole splintered. The craft leaned hard, hard to port, trying to turn. She felt the tiller graze the rocks, groan, split in her hand. The hold bucked, buckled underfoot.

The mast toppled. She felt the sail pulling free, beginning to drag her. She grabbed frantically, at anything. Something hard and silk-wrapped came away in her grasp. Her hand slipped on the sail line and the sail snatched away. It billowed toward shore. Aeriel found herself sinking.

She floundered, trying to wade, but nothing was solid under her feet. Incoming waves surged, shoving her. She pitched forward, closed her eyes and held her breath. The beach lay thirty paces off and she could not reach it. She was smothering in dust.

Something underneath her heaved, lifting her, carrying her toward shore. She felt air around her once again, and gasped. Blinking, she tried to see. The green of the Sea had turned vermilion.

Just for a moment, her knees and palm felt something solid, rough as overlapping shingles, warm to the touch, not cool like the fine, frictionless dust. Then she was ashore, dashed against the hard, flat stones.

Gasping, she crawled forward out of the surf. Something dragged along the ground beside her. She saw with surprise it was her bandolyn, still wrapped in Hadin's yellow robe. Aeriel's limbs gave out. About her legs, dry spume ran like water through the interstices of the rocks. She rolled onto her back, stared up into the black dawn sky.

A huge head, fringed with vermilion feathers, rose from the Sea and stared at her with serpentine, unblinking eyes.

❧❦❧

That image of the serpent's eyes remained in her dreams until Aeriel awoke. It was day. She lay on the warmth of hard, scaly shore. She brushed the dust from her eyes and raised her head from the dry shingle. Light lay upon the headland now, though the broad beach below was still in shadow. Her nightmare of the serpent's head was gone. She rolled onto her belly, pushed herself to her knees, and realized that she still held the silk-wrapped bandolyn. She fumbled with the robe, unwound it hurriedly, but the little silverwood instrument seemed undamaged.

A short distance from her lay the wreckage of her craft. She rose and went to it, but the wood was in splinters, the hempcloth sail in shreds. Her provisions had all been swept away. Aeriel sighed and champed her teeth. Her stomach shifted against itself.

"I shall never reach the sibyl in Orm, nor find the lost lons of Westernesse," she told herself, "if I starve to death on this beach." She laughed a little. "Truly, now is a time when I could make use of the duarough's velvet pouch!"

Just as she was turning away from the wreck, she caught sight of a stirring in the broken hold. In a moment, her crystal dustshrimp emerged from a pocket of dust, waving its tiny pincers. Aeriel found herself laughing again, knelt and put it in one fold of her garment.

"Well," she said, "we will see what food may be found to feed both of us."

The beach behind lay empty as far as she could see. The sheer cliff before seemed at first to be featureless white stone, but drawing near, Aeriel spotted a stair cut into the rock. The steps were only a half pace wide, and steep. Aeriel climbed slowly.

Reaching the top, she saw the headland was very narrow. Beyond, a strip of beach ran off into the distance beneath the same white cliffs. She found herself very near the round stone tower. A tree grew just at the tower's base.

Its slender trunk was crooked and many-branching, with dark reddish skin and small, pale leaves. Hanging upon the nearest bough, just at the level of her eye, Aeriel saw a fruit. It was only half the size of her doubled fist, and made in lobes so that it looked almost heart-shaped. Rose-gold in color, very dark, it shone like amber in the morning light.

The fruit was warm to her touch; Solstar had baked it. Its smooth skin was covered with fine hairs, like bees' fur. It came away easily from the stem when she pulled on it. The crystal leaves tinkled. The gnarled branches swayed. Its aroma was like honey browned in cinnamon.

Aeriel felt weak. She brushed the fuzz; it fell away like reddish dust. Beneath, the skin was gold. She bit into the fruit. Its nectar was warm and sweet, the flesh tender and tasting of spice. Aeriel swallowed, savoring. Her weariness began to fade.

A few more bites left only the hard seed. The last scrap of fruit she began feeding the dustshrimp.

"Thief!"

Aeriel turned in surprise.

"Stealer of apricoks!"

The voice came from the tower behind her. The dustshrimp hid itself in a fold of her shift. A person, very ragged and bent, appeared in a doorway to one side of the tree.

"Thief of my apricoks — thought you might simply have one and be off?"

The thin figure hobbled toward her, using a stick. Aeriel stared. Grassy weeds grew across the threshold. The tree stood unpruned. The tower within was dark.

"I did not know that anyone lived here," she began.

"Didn't know?" the old person cried. "Thought the tower built itself, I vow." It picked at and arranged its long, shabby robe. "A body cannot doze a moment but thieves come slinking. . . ."

"I am no thief," insisted Aeriel. "I did not know the tree was yours. I have just come a very long way and have had no food or drink for hours."

"Not my doing," the other snapped. "Only travelers across the Sea-of-Dust may taste my apricoks."

"I am a traveler across the Sea-of-Dust," Aeriel said.

The person blinked. "Impossible. No one has come across the Mare in years."

"I have just come," answered Aeriel. "I wrecked my craft upon the rocks."

The person peered at her with narrowed eyes, then hobbled to the cliff's edge and gazed over.

"Yes, so, I see your boat," it muttered, coming back. "Smashed into bits. Wonder you weren't, along with it. Well, you are welcome to the fruit in that case — but you must give me the seed."

Aeriel realized she still held the stone in her hand. The old body had snatched it from her before she could offer. "What will you do with it?"

The other only snorted, turning the stone over in bony hands, seemingly lost in thought.

"My name is Aeriel," Aeriel added in a moment, "and I have come from Isternes."

The other stirred. "Esternesse, do you mean?" She nodded. "Hm." The person peered at her again. "You don't dress as those that used to come from Esternesse."

"My first home was Terrain, though I have lived in Avaric since. This garment is from Pendar."

"Well-traveled," the person mused. "I take it you mean your kith come from Terrain."

Aeriel shook her head. "I have no kith. I was bought motherless, a babe."

"Bought?" the other exclaimed. "Bought?" Then it shook its head, murmuring, "Hard times that see babes bought in Terrain — elsewhere, too, I'll be bound, if in Terrain. What a long time I have been dozing." It turned back to her then. "But I see you are no longer a slave. Traveling storier — is that what puts you on the road?"

Aeriel fingered the strap of her bandolyn, slung from one shoulder. "So I hope to become." The other said nothing, seemed deep in thought once more. "What are you?" she ventured.

The person sighed. "Hm? Oh, I keep the tower. I tend the tree." It started away, back toward the doorway. "Come with me if you would see what I'll do with the seed."

5

THE
KEEPER OF THE LIGHT

Aeriel followed the keeper into the tower. A spiral stair ascended the wall. Aeriel and her guide emerged onto the top of the tower. A vaulted roof rose overhead. The wind gusting off the Sea-of-Dust was strong. At the center of the open chamber stood a dark dais, upon which lay a ring of silver metal, set with spires like a crown. From each point rose a small blue tongue of flame.

"What is it?" Aeriel asked, leaning nearer. The flame burned scentless, clean of smoke.

"What is it?" the person echoed, chafing both hands over the flame. Aeriel could feel no heat. "The beacon, of course. This is a lighthouse, wayfarer. What did you think it was?"

"Lighthouse," murmured Aeriel. The word felt strange upon her tongue. "What is a lighthouse?"

The other gave a snort and wheezed. After a moment, Aeriel realized that this was laughter. "It makes a beam to warn ships off the rocks and show the mariners the only safe landfall hereabouts — what else? How is it you have piloted all the way across the Sea-of-Dust and never heard of a lighthouse?"

Aeriel had no time to make reply. The keeper sighed.

"Ah, I remember, before they stopped coming, how the big ships used to lie off the coast. I with my raft ferried their goods in to shore. Then there was work — and never a wreck." The keeper glanced sharply at Aeriel. "You'd not have wrecked your craft, either, wayfarer, if only you'd followed the beam."

Aeriel shook her head. "I saw no beam."

The person eyed her. "No one finds the gap by chance," it said. "The Ancients made these towers, you know. To guide the pilgrims over the Sea, and then inland across the steeps. They are all connected, deep underground, so that whenever one is fed, the others flare."

The keeper stood gazing off now, shaking its head. Aeriel could not quite follow — were there other towers such as this one? The keeper sighed.

"But they do burn low now. Nothing to feed them since the pilgrimages ceased — oh, I don't know; I've been dozing so long — a hundred years ago." It nodded then. "Yes, most perilously low. Well, I've a remedy for that. Keep wide."

Aeriel fell back at the other's gesture. It cast the seed of her apricok upon the dais, within the crown of light. The flame hissed, flaring, flickered from blue to violet, and then to rose.

Aeriel stood watching. The tongues of fire grew longer, brighter, merging into a single, taller flame. Its color changed to green, to yellow, and still the fire increased until it was as tall as Aeriel.

The flame changed one last time, to white, very brilliant and pure, yet Aeriel found she could look upon it without being dazzled. It stood steady now upon its crown, and though Aeriel still felt wind gusting off the Sea, the cool radiance did not flicker.

"Ah, so much better," a voice beside her said, and turning, Aeriel saw the lighthouse keeper — but not at all as he had appeared to her before.

His robe was neither ragged anymore nor dusty drab, but blue. The color deepened, growing richer as she watched. The person himself stood straighter, seemed neither disheveled nor ancient now, and lean rather than starved. The stick he held was not a gnarled crook at all, but a tall, straight staff.

"Ah, yes, much better," he said again, holding his hands once more to the flame. "How cold one gets between travelers, and how sleepy."

Aeriel stared. "But — I feel no heat from it," she said at last, not knowing what to say.

The person looked up, as though just then remembering her. "No, of course not." He smiled. "You would not, for you have eaten of the tree, and so may see the beacon's light — as I cannot, for I have never tasted that fruit. Was it good, by the way, your apricok?"

"Very good." A little of its taste still lingered in her mouth.

The keeper nodded. "So I have heard, from the travelers. I would not know."

"But why is that," Aeriel began, "when the tree grows at your door?"

The person laughed, came away from the flame, moving with a slight haltness of step to one of the wide windows. He hardly seemed to need his staff.

"Because I am no traveler," he said. "I was not made

53

for journeying, and the tree bears only at need: one fruit for every traveler that fares across the Mare." He sighed and tilted back his head. "They used to come in droves, the travelers. But no more."

"Is that the only thing which feeds the light?" asked Aeriel. "The apricok seeds?"

The keeper nodded. "The tree feeds upon the heart of the world; the pilgrims feed upon its fruit, the flame upon the heart of the fruit, and I upon the flame."

Aeriel studied the person across from her. He had come back from the window now, stood closer to the flame. "And are you no mortal," she asked, "that eats no mortal food?"

The keeper smiled and shook his head. "Mortal, yes, but not like you. Ravenna made me. I was not born."

Aeriel caught in her breath. "Ravenna," she whispered, "that made the lons. You are the lon of Bern. . . ."

But again the keeper shook his head, laughing this time. "No lon am I," he told her gently. "Bernalon is a great she-wolf that runs along the steeps and shore, warding the land — while I have never even ventured from this headland to the wood. . . ."

But Aeriel could not keep still. A desperate urgency tugged at her. Perhaps she need not go to Orm. Perhaps she could learn of the lons here in Bern. Her eyes found the keeper's again.

"Where may I find her — Bernalon? For I must find her, soon, and the other lons."

The keeper sighed. "I do not know. I have been dozing a hundred years. Not once in all that time have I heard the great wolf crying. The last pilgrim who came here spoke of a battle in the west. Upon the border of Zambul, a winged monster defeating Bernalon and carrying her away."

"A darkangel," whispered Aeriel. Not hers of Avaric, but his "brother," another of the witch's "sons."

"What's that?" the keeper said.

Aeriel looked up. "There is a witch at desert's edge, who steals away babes to raise as her own, making them winged vampyres, the icari, who drink the souls of women. Six darkangels has she now, but her seventh in Avaric has been returned to the living before her magic on him could be made complete. Each icarus in turn overthrew a lon. One of them I have found already, the Avarclon. But there are six more I must find within the year. One of them is Bernalon."

The keeper turned away again. "Bad times," he murmured, "that see witches and their sons among us."

Aeriel drew breath. "There is a rime," she said. The wild hope that had come to her only moments before was slipping away. She seized at it. "When the Ancient Ones withdrew from us, ages ago, Ravenna foretold the coming of the witch."

The tall, steep-burning flame threw her shadow before her. The keeper stood overlooking the Sea.

"She made the rime, and sang it over the lons at the time of their making. You are not a lon, but perhaps you can tell me what it means:

55

"But first there must assemble
   those the icari would claim,
A bride in the temple
   must enter the flame,

Steeds found for the secondborn beyond
   the dust deepsea,
And new arrows reckoned, a wand
   given wings —

So that when a princess royal
   shall have tasted of the tree,
Then far from Esternesse's
   city, these things:

A gathering of gargoyles,
   a feasting on the stone,
The witch of Westernesse's
   hag overthrown."

Aeriel gazed at the keeper, but the other shook his head.

"I was made long before the Ions, wayfarer. I have never heard that riddle before. I do not know its meaning."

Aeriel cast down her eyes. Disappointment bit her heart, and dread.

"I must go on to Orm, then," she answered quietly, "and seek my answer there." She hesitated, then made herself say it. "Can you tell me the way?"

"You must follow the coast road," the keeper said, "northward until you reach Talis. Get there by nightfall, for the city gates are barred at Solset. In the morning, take the road going west into the hills. That should see you through the pass and into Zambul, which is as much of the way as I know.

"Do not stray from the road, for the woods are wild. Do not travel by night, and go with some caravan if you can, for in the time since Bernalon was taken away, the land hereabouts has grown thick with thieves."

Aeriel put on what smile she could. She gave the keeper her thanks for his warning of thieves, as he led her down the tower stair.

"But before you go," he said, "take this, will you? The last traveler before you left it, and I have no use for it."

He laid one hand upon a peg beside the door. Aeriel had not noticed it before. The garment the keeper was holding out was very small, the outside pale cream or grey—its color seemed to move and shift. The inside was some darker thread.

Aeriel threw it about her shoulders, found it, to her surprise, exactly the right size. The hem fell a little below her knees; the sleeves stopped halfway between her elbow and the wrist. The peaked hood, when she tried it, fitted, shadowing her face.

"I thank you," Aeriel began, throwing back the hood. "But I have nothing to pay you with."

The keeper shook his head. "No need. Take it as my gift — to keep the road dust off."

They emerged from the tower into the morning light, and Aeriel noticed, with a start, that the weeds were gone. What had been rocky ground was covered now with fruiting creepers. A narrow path led to the road. Aeriel spotted five more fruits hanging upon the tree.

"Keeper," she said, "what does it mean?"

The keeper halted, a frown creasing his brow. "Five more travelers upon their way across the Sea-of-Dust?"

A new feeling of unease overtook her — why she could not say. She expected no pursuit from Isternes. The keeper stood considering. At last he shook his head.

"We saw no sail from the tower. And the tree fruits only at need." He scratched his head a moment, glanced at her. "How do the fruits appear to you?"

Aeriel gazed at them, puzzled. "They look exactly the same as the first one: reddish gold and shining in the light."

"They must be yours, then. The tree never fruits the same twice. A different gift for each that comes." The keeper went to the tree, and Aeriel followed. "I have not seen such a thing before, that one wayfarer should receive so much."

He pulled the ripe fruits from the bough.

"Take them," he said. "It must be you will have need of them." Aeriel slipped them carefully into the yellow silk wrapping her bandolyn. The keeper walked with her as far as the road. "But save the seeds," he said. "There is great virtue in them."

Aeriel adjusted the cloak about her shoulders again; the hood lay flat along her back. She bowed to the keeper then, and he to her. She started away, but she had taken no more than a dozen steps when the other called, "What, a wayfarer that has no staff?"

Aeriel turned, walking backwards now, but her smile was full of rue. "I had one once, in Pendar," she said, "when I lived among the desert folk. But I lost it, returning to Avaric."

She turned again, walked along the road, shielding her eyes from low Solstar's glare. She raised the hood of her traveling cloak, glanced over one shoulder, her hand lifted to wave, but the keeper had already vanished, back into his lighted tower.

Aeriel fared steadily north. The road threaded along between the wood's edge and the brink of the cliffs overlooking the shore. She walked for a very long time with neither hunger nor fatigue.

Sometimes she unwrapped her bandolyn, reciting the tales she had learned in Isternes, how the young Lady Syllva had been courted by a stranger, a bold prince of Avaric, and gone with him for a time to be his wife in Westernesse, and other stories.

She did not venture into the woods, but from time to time caught glimpses among the slender trees of wood-deer standing no higher than her knee, treerats with their double tails, and sweet-voiced flitterwings.

Then suddenly it was noon. She had been walking with her hood thrown back, the past few hours. Aeriel halted, astonished, staring up at the black, starry heavens. Solstar, like a brilliant jewel, blazed nearly at its zenith. Raising her hood, she sat down against a tree at wood's edge. Its boughs leaned out over the road.

"Have I truly traveled half a daymonth without pause?" she murmured. Even now the taste of apricok lingered in her mouth.

She had no time to murmur more, for just at that moment, nearly directly overhead, she heard a great clapping and beating, like the slapping of a sail.

"Now where can she have vanished?" a weary voice muttered. "I was certain I spotted someone very like her faring along this road."

Aeriel scrambled to her feet, peered up through the twining branches. A long-billed bird hovered with difficulty just above. It had a long neck and strong wings, snowy white, and was clutching something unwieldy, straight, and dark.

"Could she have gone into the forest?" it panted, wingbeats becoming more labored still. It glanced the other way. "Perhaps she fell over the cliff."

As Aeriel ducked out from under the tree, her hood fell back. "Whom do you seek?" she called.

"Odds!" cried the bird, starting upward in surprise. Its toes lost their grip upon the long dark object. Aeriel threw up her arms, fell back a step — realizing too late that only brought her more directly beneath the falling shaft. She felt a blow upon her head. The world went stars, then dark.

"Duck," someone was urging her.

Her knees buckled. She pitched face-forward onto the road.

Aeriel awoke to the feel of something tugging at her garment. She brushed at it groggily, and raised herself. Her vision was blurred. A sharp ache throbbed in the back of her skull. Something stepped lightly on the small of her back. Aeriel jerked, rolled, batted at the long, sticklike legs of the heron. The white bird danced awkwardly away.

"Thank Ravenna," it exclaimed. "I thought I'd killed you."

"You came near it," Aeriel murmured, rubbing the lump on the back of her head. It was the size of a gamelizard's egg. "What fell on me?"

"I beg your pardon," the bird answered. "It slipped."

Aeriel's vision cleared. "I know you," she said, suddenly.

She remembered a heron-prowed boat the duarough had made her to escape the darkangel's keep. She had sailed as far as the little craft could take her, then had set off overland — and looking back, she had seen no boat, only a long-necked white bird winging low between the riverbanks.

"Wind-on-the-Water!" she exclaimed.

The heron lifted one wing and preened. "The same," she replied, "though my name in this form is Wing-on-the-Wind."

Aeriel remembered the lyon of Pendar telling her once how a heron of that name had come to him, bearing news of her coming.

"You are she, then," the heron was saying, "Aeriel of Terrain?"

Aeriel nodded.

"Well, you must take this," the heron sighed. Onefooted, she clutched the long, dark stave lying in the roadway, and hopped toward Ariel. "The Ancients made me for a bearer of tidings, not of heavy objects. I have searched all Westernesse for you for daymonths."

Aeriel smiled a little. "I have been in Isternes."

The heron laid the object at her knees. Aeriel drew in her breath. She recognized the dusty thing at last.

"My walking stick," Aeriel exclaimed, softly. "The one Orroto-to made me."

She ran her fingers over the straight, smooth-weathered shaft, remembering how that chieftess of the desert folk had fashioned this staff out of dark driftwood. As tall as Aeriel it stood, very slender, very strong, with a pointed heel to bite into the sand, and heavy knob upon its crown. She had killed a witch's jackal once, with this stick.

She put it from her suddenly. "I should not have it. It was my own carelessness lost it in the desert."

The heron scratched the side of her head a moment with one ungainly leg. "The lyon told me something of these staves," she said, "that are the throwing sticks and digging sticks, tent poles, and a thousand other things to the Ma'a-mbai, the people of the dunes. There is power in them, he said."

The heron cocked her head the other way.

"Perhaps you did not truly lose yours, but only laid it by awhile, its task of the moment being done and it not yet time for you to take it up again."

Aeriel lifted her walking stick from the dust. She hardly could keep her hands from the shaft. She laid it across her lap, feeling the wood, its shape growing once more familiar in her grasp. Orroto-to had taught her all its uses. It lacked only a single thing to make it a true desert walking stick.

"No figurehead," murmured Aeriel.

In the beginning, when she had first been among the

Ma'a-mbai, she had thought the heads of their walking sticks were nothing more than shapeless knobs. But gradually, as she had lived among that people longer, she had begun to see in each stick a figurehead.

Vague shapes these all were, oddly half-formed, as though their true forms lay a little deeper than the surface of the wood. But Orroto-to had given Aeriel a staff with only a blank knob on top, and when Aeriel had asked her why, the dark chieftess had drawn back a little, surprised.

"I did not know your green eyes had learned to see the shapes in our walking sticks," she had said. "It is not a thing we speak of much, even among ourselves, and our children may not be called grown until they have seen it. Only then may they be given a grown person's staff, with a figurehead."

"But Orroto-to," Aeriel had said, "am I a child, then, that my walking stick has no face? Yet, surely no child, since you have given me a longstick and would teach me to use it."

Aeriel saw the wisewoman's eyes turn away then. She said nothing for a space. At last the dark headwoman answered.

"Little pale one, I have made you no figurehead upon your stick because I have no inkling what to make. Your spirit baffles even me, the best seer-of-spirits among our band."

She turned and looked at Aeriel then.

"But something tells me, sun-fair one who is growing now so tall, that you do not yet need a figure on your staff. When the time comes, you will find one."

"How is that?"

Aeriel looked up, hearing the heron speak. The desert faded from around her, and she sat once more upon the coast road of Bern.

"My staff has no figurehead," Aeriel said.

"Easily remedied," the heron replied. Aeriel glanced at the bird, frowning, not following. She sat holding the staff across her knees. The heron took wing, alighting upon its knob. Aeriel darted to her feet in surprise, nearly dropping the shaft. The white bird settled, folding her long wings, nestling her long bill to her breast.

"I have been figurehead upon a boat," she murmured. "I can do the same upon a staff."

And as she settled, she seemed to diminish. Aeriel held the stick fully upright now, staring at it. Smaller and smaller the heron grew until she was no longer than the knob itself, seemed to have merged with it. Aeriel could not take her eyes away.

"How have you done that?" she cried. "I had thought it was the duarough's magic made you a boat, and then into a bird again."

The heron laughed, soft clucking laughter. "Oh, he merely conjured me out of storage and set me to working again. The rest I am able to manage myself."

Aeriel still studied her. "What are you?" she said.

The white bird shrugged, seemed to have grown suddenly sleepy. "A mere plaything of the Ancients that they left behind — a bringer of tidings, a messenger. I can pick locks and open doors, gain access where the way is barred, find hidden paths and things disguised. . . . But I am weary now."

The heron closed her eyes then, tucked her bill beneath one wing. Her color began to deepen, the texture of her feathers change. Before Aeriel could draw three breaths, it looked for all the world as though her staff were all dark wood from heel to crown, but that there the grain changed to a heron-shaped knot of blond.

Aeriel turned the staff in her hands, gazing on it. "But," she murmured, half to herself, "if your name changes with each new form you assume, what am I to call you now — Bird-on-a-Stick?"

The heron's eye snapped open. "You make light of me," she said, "who have headed the staves of wise-women and kings."

"No, truly," said Aeriel, instantly rueful. "I meant not."

The heron settled her wing more comfortably over her bill. Her movements were growing sluggish and stiff, her voice like green wood creaking. "No matter," she muttered. "You will not need to call me anything just now. Flying about these many daymonths, so burdened, has wearied me. Now you may bear me for a little while, and I will sleep."

Her grey eye closed and her form became suddenly even more like the wood. Her outline faded and blurred so that after only a half dozen heartbeats, Aeriel could not tell without looking very closely that the staff's crown now had the shape of a bird.

Aeriel felt lighter suddenly, renewed in strength. Her terror of Orm subsided a little. Though the road there might be long, she had a companion now — such as it was. Aeriel eyed the wooden head of her walking stick, then laughed.

I will find the lost lons of Westernesse, she told herself, before the White Witch does. She fetched her bandolyn from beneath the tree and started with a swift, sure step northward along the road toward Talis.

6

CITY OF THIEVES

Solstar slid gradually across the sky. Aeriel felt no weariness, no hunger still, nor did the little dustshrimp hidden away among her garment's folds seem to require any food. She met no one. From time to time she spoke to the figurehead upon her staff, but the heron never awoke.

The land began to fall at last. The cliffs no longer rose so high above the shore. Solstar hung due east, directly beside her. She saw the city of Talis in the distance before. It stood upon a rocky arm of land jutting out into the Sea. A steady trickle of travelers approached from the north and west.

Aeriel lifted the hood of her traveling cloak. The wind off the Sea had begun to rise. No one paid her the slightest attention as she joined the others passing between the high double gates — not the women in long tunics that fell to their shoes, nor the men in trousers and sarks. Their skin was pale, dusky blue. Aeriel had never before seen Bernean skin.

The city was smaller than Isternes, had none of the graceful arches and spires of the east. The buildings of

Talis were all squat and square, half-timbered of silvery wood and grey pearly seastone. Aeriel found herself passing through market streets and jewelers' streets. Perfumers brewed strange-scented stuff; knifemakers offered hilts set with carbuncles and pearls.

Once, in broad sunlight, Aeriel saw a jeweler draw from his sleeve a tiny glass vessel half-filled with blue fluid. Pure corundum, he whispered, offering it to the man with whom he bargained: the blood of the Sea. One sup, he said, would keep one young for a dozen years, and he was willing to part with it for only a thousand times its silverweight.

He twirled the vial then, its contents gleaming, swirling like water — but leaning closer, Aeriel saw that it was dust, and very like the stuff she had scooped from the Sea, though not so dark a blue. Neither the merchant nor his buyer even glanced at her, though moments earlier, the seller had chased two ragged boys away. Aeriel moved on.

She crossed a square and found herself before a tavern. A high wall enclosed its yard, and two tall doorkeepers stood on the threshold of the supperhall, turning would-be guests and curious onlookers away.

Aeriel approached, expecting to be told the same, but neither so much as looked at her, and she passed between them without trouble. Shrugging, puzzled, she supposed a mere player who would sing for her supper and sleep on the hearth must be beneath their notice.

The hall was large, people and tables crowding the room. The last of the dusk light streamed through the windows. A great hearth took up half the far wall. Aeriel had never before seen so much wood burned at once. In Terrain, where wood was scarce, they burned oil in lamps, but here great boughs and branches blazed, not the white or yellow flame of oil, but red.

Only two others sat upon the hearth, one a solidly built young man with fair hair and pale green skin. His companion was a girl, younger than Aeriel, lank and straight-limbed still. A circlet of twisted cloth kept her cinnamon hair from her eyes. Her skin was Bernean blue.

Aeriel knelt upon the hearth, stood her staff in one corner and threw back her hood. The blue-skinned girl, who had been gazing absently in her direction, started suddenly, staring at Aeriel. Aeriel glanced at her.

"Is anything amiss?" she asked. She unfastened her cloak and laid it down, began unwrapping her bandolyn.

The girl stared a moment more, then shook her head and seemed to recover herself. "How long have you been there? I didn't see you."

Aeriel smiled. "Only a moment. I am Aeriel." She sat, starting to tune her bandolyn.

The girl's expression abruptly brightened. "A storier? I think you must be the only storier in all Talis tonight. No wonder the doorkeeps let you in. How much did they ask?"

Aeriel looked up. "Nothing. They paid me no attention at all."

"They let you in for nothing?" the girl exclaimed, on her feet then, fists on hips, glaring sourly at the door. "We had to buy our way in."

She glanced at her companion, but the young man, though he watched both her and Aeriel closely, said nothing. In time Aeriel began to wonder if he had a tongue. The blue-skinned girl shrugged, sat down again.

"Well, no matter. We should make it back in threes tonight."

She leaned back against her companion, stretched. A server passed beside the hearth. Almost quicker than Aeriel's eye could follow, the girl had snatched six olives from his tray. The boy moved on without a glance.

Then the girl was tossing the fruits in a circle before her. The pattern became a figure eight. Just as suddenly, she had turned to her companion and the two were tossing the dark fruit between them, in intricate loops.

Abruptly, Aeriel realized the girl had passed every one to her young man, who juggled one group single-handed in a circle, while making a figure eight between his already occupied hand and the free.

Aeriel stared. She had never seen such a thing. The girl sprang up, did two handsprings upon the hearth before flipping back to her feet with a gesture first to herself, then to her companion.

"Nat and Galnor, traveling players. Feats to dazzle and delight."

Her companion caught all six olives then, seemingly at once. He tossed three to Nat, who offered Aeriel one. Aeriel accepted gratefully, bit into the dark, salty flesh. Her hunger and thirst were beginning to return. She laid her bandolyn upon the floor and glanced about to see when supper might be served.

Outside, the light of setting Solstar was growing very dim. Aeriel felt the evening chill even so near the fire. Servers began to close and bar the shutters. Torches were lit, the outer door drawn shut. Guests at table began demanding the meal.

It was brought almost at once, huge platters of brittle meal cakes and animal's flesh, baskets of violet plums. Nothing was given the players on the hearth, and now with only the taste of a single olive on her tongue, Aeriel found her mouth watering, her limbs feeling weak with hunger.

"Well," murmured Nat, after a little. "I see they mean to leave us to ourselves." She glanced at Aeriel with half a smile. "Agile fingers are good at more than juggling."

Then she rose and glided away between the tables, juggling empty mugs and plates at first for a bit of food or a sip of ale. After a while, their own hunger eased, some guests began tossing her more substantial tidbits, which she pocketed, returning to the hearth at last, well laden.

Aeriel ate gladly: new apples and fried cakes and wings of forest lizards. She fed the little dustshrimp crumbs as well, and once Galnor snatched full mugs from a passing tray so deftly the server never missed them.

As Aeriel lifted the sweet, foaming honeybeer to her lips, a strange, savage cry rose from outside the inn. Choking, she set down the mug. The talk of the supper hall became suddenly much quieter. Some had turned their eyes to the door opening on the tavern's courtyard. It stood ajar.

The cry continued. Aeriel felt her skin grow taut, a shiver take her as she listened. Then the eerie keening died away, and guests turned back to their meals and their companions at table. The hubbub gradually resumed. Aeriel glanced at the girl beside her.

"What was that?"

Nat glanced up, licking her fingers of grease. She shrugged. "Only the Beast. It has been howling like that, every now and again, since they brought it in."

"What beast is that?" said Aeriel.

The girl looked up in earnest now. "Do you not know? The Beast that has been putting the whole countryside in terror these last daymonths."

Aeriel shook her head. "What has it done?"

"They say," said Nat, "it has never done anything to any honest traveler, save stare at them and wail — though it has put thieves to flight, and more than one has felt its teeth."

The girl leaned closer.

"Merchant folk have begun to stay away for fear of meeting it, and travelers have been afraid to move along the roads, even by day, save in large, well-armed caravans — which has spoilt the thieves' trade famously. So at dawn this daymonth, the Arlish bandits set out in search of it, and they have captured it, for they brought it back to the city in a wooden cage only hours ago." She nodded. "It is they who sit there."

Aeriel followed the line of her gaze and spotted a band of roughly dressed women and men at one central table — she had taken little note of them before. Most of them wore gold in the lobes of their ears, and their captain a silver band high upon his one bare arm. All had dirks. They were eating off the finest plate in the house.

Nat was saying, "They have set their caged Beast in

the courtyard, and all the other guests are here in hopes of glimpsing it."

Again the eerie wailing rose. Again the talk grew quieter.

"What will they do with it?" asked Aeriel. The timbre of that unearthly cry set her teeth on edge.

Nat shrugged. "Sell it, I suppose. For a ruler's ransom. Sabr, the bandit queen, keeps a stable of strange beasts in the north — horses, I think they call them. Perhaps she will buy."

She began to say more, but the guests, well satisfied of food and drink, had begun demanding entertainments. Nat and Galnor rose from the hearth, tumbling and juggling: circles and arcs, then intricate patterns Aeriel could not name.

The watchers threw fruits and cakes to them at first, then spoons and cutlery. Finally, coins — which seemed to vanish unexpectedly whenever Nat juggled. The guests only laughed and tossed her more.

But at length it was Aeriel's turn. Galnor and Nat retired to the hearth. Aeriel lifted her bandolyn. She had meant to tell them some tale she had learned in Isternes, of Syllva, perhaps, and her chieftain Imrahil, but the guests — above the keening from without — roared for a tale of fantastical beasts.

So she told them the tale of the darkangel. Sometimes singing and sometimes speaking, Aeriel spoke of a Terrainean girl who followed her mistress to the dark-angel's keep, of the vampyre's withered brides, the wraiths, and of the weird gargoyles that were his watchdogs.

The quiet of the hall deepened, the click of cups, the

murmur died, the eerie yips from the courtyard ceased. Aeriel had not reached the tale's end, had come only so far as the girl's return from the desert with the horse-hoof cup, her freeing of the gargoyles from their silver chains —

A great commotion from the courtyard suddenly. Shouts, then the sound of splintering wood: cries and running footfalls. Aeriel broke off in midsentence. Two bandits burst through the courtyard door.

"Master," one of them cried, "the Beast is loose. It seemed quiet — we forgot to watch; we were intent upon the tale. It must have gnawed through the bars. . . ."

The woman broke off with a shriek. Behind the pair, the door gaped wide. No one had thought to shut or bar it. Guests nearby it scattered as a great haggard beast slunk into the room.

It snarled, doglike, and snapped. It was all over one even shade of grey: even its eyes and teeth and tongue were grey. Its shabby, matted fur stood on end. A collar of yellow metal encircled its throat.

Aeriel gazed upon it from the hearth. She felt her heart contract. Beside her, Nat shrank against Galnor. Just then the Beast caught sight of Aeriel, its grey eyes wild and wide. It padded toward her.

Those in its path shrank away from it. Some held daggers, but none dared strike. Aeriel half rose, put her bandolyn from her. She could see the creature's skeletal ribs, ridges of spine along its back. Her knees gave way.

"Greyling," she whispered. "Greyling — first gargoyle ever I tamed. What has become of you? You are all bone beneath the skin."

For a moment, the gargoyle stared at her, lips pulled

back from its broken teeth, tongue loose and lolling. It panted hoarsely. Its tattered ears lay flat against the skull. Aeriel held out her arms to it.

"I did not set you free that you should come to this."

The Beast bellied down before her on the floor. It crept forward, a strange whine gibbering from its throat. Its curved claws scattered the rushes, scathed the floorboards underfoot. The creature reached her knees. Aeriel bent to stroke it as the grey Beast laid its huge and grisly head upon her lap.

There was not a sound in the room but the soft, harsh breathing of the lookers-on and the fizzing crackle of the fire.

"A sorceress!" someone whispered then. "The storier's a witch. See how she has charmed the Beast."

Aeriel did not look up, was aware of the inn guests shifting uneasily, of Nat staring from Galnor's arms. The bandits of Arl gazed upon her in outright rage. Aeriel stroked the gargoyle's heavy, strange head, fingered its matted, thin fur.

"What has become of you?" she murmured again. "You do not look as though you have tasted food since you left me. Eat this." She reached into her pack.

"More sorceries," a woman cried. "What's that in her hand?"

"A jewel."

"A dagger —"

"It's just a plum," murmured Nat, coming away from Galnor a little.

Aeriel dusted the fine fuzz from the apricok, held it out. The gargoyle ate eagerly, almost desperately, strained to swallow against the collar about its throat.

Its grey tongue slavered, catching the runnels of blood-colored juice. When she held only the clean stone in her hand, the gargoyle set its lips to it, gnawing at it, but Aeriel drew it gently away.

"Not the seed," she told it. "I have promised to save the seeds."

She put the stone away in Hadin's robe, stroked the head of the grey beast again and again, for it yipped and trembled still.

"Witchery," she heard someone muttering. Another voice, across the room, half shouted, "She will charm us all."

Aeriel looked up then, saw people fall back as she raised her eyes. The hard faces of the Arlish bandits made her skin creep. The gargoyle stared at them, lip twitching into a snarl.

"Come, Greyling," she murmured. "I do not like our company. Let's begone."

She laid her bandolyn upon the yellow silk, knotted it deftly and reached for her staff. The gargoyle bounded away from her, gibbering. Aeriel faced about, glimpsed one of the robber band, under her captain's eye, creeping forward, her saber drawn. The gargoyle shrieked and lunged. The woman dropped her blade and scrambled back.

"A demon, a familiar!" someone was screaming.

Aeriel half turned, confused. Then she spotted the dustshrimp standing upon her shoulder, waving its tiny claws. Aeriel thrust it back into the folds of her shift, shrugged into her traveling cloak, and slung her bandolyn.

"And what of those two?" a man's voice demanded. "They were with her. They did their feats by conjuring."

Galnor and Nat stood a half step behind Aeriel. She saw the blue-skinned girl produce a dirk from nowhere. Galnor caught up a stout limb from beside the hearth.

"Take her staff," the master of the robbers shouted. "Without it, a wizard has no power."

One of the robbers darted forward and snatched the long staff leaning against the wall. The boy was away before Aeriel could stop him — but as his hand closed roughly upon the wood, the heron awoke with a startled cry. Beating her wings, she shouted, "Unhand me!"

The youth flung the staff from him with a cry. Aeriel caught it and laid her hand upon the gargoyle's collar. She approached the captain of the thieves.

"Why do you set your people against me?" she demanded. Galnor and Nat had come behind her. "I have done you no injury."

The bandit lord eyed her uneasily, tugging one tail of his moustache.

"You have stolen my Beast," he answered at last, "you with your singing and your sorceries."

"Your prisoner," said Aeriel. "I am no sorceress."

"That Beast is worth a queen's ransom," the bandit snapped.

"Will you have ransom?" Aeriel said. Anger welled in her for the first time then. She reached into the sleeve of Hadin's robe, drew out a handful of deep blue dust. "I own little the thieves of Talis would value, but perhaps you will find this worth your trouble."

She held her cupped hand over the table toward him.

"Don't touch it, lord," one of his people said. "It's witched."

But the bandit captain's eyes were fixed on Aeriel's hand. "Ah, but witches may give marvelous gifts," he murmured. "May they not?"

He drew his dirk. The gargoyle snarled, but the bandit lord, with the dull edge of his blade, only tipped Aeriel's hand so that the dust fell in a blue stream to the table top, spilled among the plates, sifted between threads of the table's cloth, and spattered like water through loose planks to the floor.

"True corundum," the robber captain murmured. "The blood of the Sea."

He scooped what remained on the table into an empty dish. One of his people dashed the drink from a cup, caught the stream of blue dribbling from the table's edge. Another crawled upon the floorboards, sweeping up what fell.

Aeriel had not yet taken back her hand. "Is it enough?"

"Enough?" the bandit captain laughed. "It is a fortune, five fortunes — and half again as much lost already through the cracks."

"It's wizard's dust," the woman who had lost her saber cried. "A dream. It will be water in the morning, or sand."

But the lord of the bandits was already pouring the blue from the dish into the wine flask on his belt. "We'll sell it for silver before the night is up," he hissed. "What's it to me if it's ashes by morning? Go, witch. Take your Beast with you." He put his dirk back in the sheath. "It is enough."

Aeriel turned toward the door. People parted to let her through, but with scarcely a glance now. All eyes had fixed upon the bloodblue dust, which the robbers still struggled to collect, their daggers now turned outward, toward the crowd.

Aeriel, reaching the tavern door, was aware of Nat and Galnor just behind. But as she made to pass through, a strong-built woman with the keyring of an innkeeper stepped suddenly in front of her.

"Here now," she said shortly. "You got in here by some devilry. Neither of my doorkeeps let you in."

"They passed me through without a word," Aeriel replied.

"None pass my door without paying the fare — and even so, you've been fed since then."

"I sang for my supper," said Aeriel.

The innkeeper pursed her lips, folding her ample arms. She eyed Aeriel's gargoyle and her staff warily, but held her ground.

"And what of the ruckus you've caused? Damage to my establishment's reputation — and no doubt a good deal of my plate's disappeared. . . ."

Aeriel felt her lips twitching into a smile. "Peace, dame," she said, "you are a thief among innkeepers, but I will give you the only other thing I have for your trouble."

She took from her pack the great waxy green lump she had found upon the Sea. The innkeeper's eyes widened.

"Ambergris," she whispered. "That's the balm that heals all sores — it's worth its goldenweight." She reached for it, then checked herself. "A physician would call it worth more than corundum."

Her fingers darted out at last, broke a small bit off.

"I'll only take so much," she said, "for I am not so great a thief as that."

But she caught Aeriel's sleeve as she made to pass.

"Go quickly out of the city, do you hear? The captain of the Arlish thieves — what's to stop him coming after you the moment he thinks of it, and having both the seablood and the Beast?"

Aeriel glanced back, but before she could speak, the woman gave a swift shake of her head, dropping her voice very low.

"You have a strange companion, mistress, and a strange staff, and strange goods in your pack, but I have seen sorcerers in my day, and you are no sorceress."

Aeriel laughed a little then, softly. She stowed the rest of the ambergris. Nat and Galnor moved over the threshold past her. Aeriel kept her eyes on the innkeeper still.

"I thank you your advice, madam," she told her. "I'll follow it."

Her companions now waited in the darkness beyond the door. Taking the gargoyle by its brass collar, Aeriel went to join them, ducking out into the night.

7

DEMON PASS

They hurried through the streets of Talis, all but deserted now, for it seemed Bern too, like Isternes, kept custom of feasting and sleeping just after Solset. The city gate was bolted fast, the gatewatch gone. The blue-skinned girl and her young man halted in dismay, but Aeriel found herself drawn forward by the Beast.

The heron spread her wings upon the staff, gave a clear, wild cry. The vast bolt barring the timber doors — too heavy, far, for them to have moved themselves — tripped suddenly, slid on its own. The portals of the city swung wide.

Aeriel had no time even to draw breath, for the gargoyle was drawing her forward again. Just outside, though, she halted, turning to the heron on her staff. "How have you managed that?"

The heron shrugged. She was pale still and feathery, not yet turned again to wood. "I am a messenger. The Ancients made me to travel unimpeded — so I can open doors."

Aeriel made to say more then, but the heron glanced at her.

"However, it is quite tiring. And by heaven, this is an excellent perch. I must sleep."

She tucked her bill, shut her eye and melted again into the hard, blond wood. Aeriel heard Nat and Galnor draw up beside her.

"You *are* a sorceress," a man's voice said.

Aeriel turned, taken by surprise, then realized it was no stranger who had spoken, but Galnor. Nat stood pressed against his side, staring at Aeriel. Aeriel shook her head.

"I thought you did not speak."

Galnor met her eyes. "I speak at need." He looked off then, up the road. The gates behind them were drawing shut. "We must not linger here."

He moved past her and the gargoyle then, his arm still about Nat. The blue-skinned girl glanced back. Aeriel heard the soft boom of the closing gates, the great bar sliding into place. Galnor and Nat were already six paces up the road. Aeriel took the gargoyle by the collar and followed them.

The road climbed steeply into the hills, crowded on either side with close-spaced trees. The gargoyle trotted before them upon its fantastically jointed limbs, its jaws agape, panting. Nat, after a little time, gained courage and came back to walk beside Aeriel.

"That girl," she ventured, "the one you told of in the inn. She was you."

Aeriel looked up, surprised. Then she nodded. "A year, a half year gone, she was me."

The blue-skinned girl looked down. "What happened in the end?" she asked. "To the darkangel."

"I overthrew him," answered Aeriel, "with the magic cup, and . . . and rescued a prince that was his prisoner." She looked away, feeling the bitterness of failure at the thought of Irrylath. "Or thought I did."

Nat said no more. They climbed on.

After a little time, Galnor spoke. "They will follow us very hard at first, I think. But the farther into the hills we go, the more reluctant they will be to pursue."

Aeriel glanced at him, but the young man was already striding on. Nat answered her.

"It will be deeper into the night," she said, "and we will be closer to the haunt woods."

"What place is that?"

"A dire place," answered Nat, "surrounding the demon's pass which leads into Zambul. Each year, they say, it encroaches a little more upon the rest of Bern, and one day will cover it all. No one will go there, even by day, for the night-haunts live there."

"Night-haunts," murmured Aeriel.

"Frights," Galnor replied, glancing over one shoulder. "Weird, ghostly things that roamed the woods long before that day-beast of yours appeared." He snorted, chafing his arms. "No one who is not desperate travels this road after dusk."

He broke off abruptly, with a glance at Nat. Aeriel saw her shivering.

"We saw them once," the girl whispered, "almost two

years ago. I turned my ankle in the woods late one daylight, not many hours from night. And no one from my village would come look for me."

She glanced up then, her eyes on Galnor's back.

"Only the woodcutter, who had scarcely ever even spoken to me but to teach me a little juggling once, took a torch and set out in search of me. They barred the village gate after him."

She glanced at Aeriel.

"We have been upon the road since then. After he found me, we kept ourselves safe with fire till morning came, though we nearly starved. But no nightfall since that time has not seen us safely within some village or inn."

"Till now," said Aeriel.

Nat looked down, fingering the dirk thrust into her sash. Aeriel was silent a little while.

"What is the demon pass?" she asked at last.

"The way into Zambul," Galnor replied. "This road leads there. A wingèd demon has settled upon the pass, a stealer of people in the night. He shuns all light save that of Oceanus and the stars."

Aeriel felt her skin grow cold. "A wingèd demon," she said, sought Galnor's eyes. "A darkangel?"

The other shook his head. "That is not a word we use in Bern."

"What does he do with those he steals?" she pressed. "Drain them of lifeblood, drink off their souls?"

The other shrugged. "No one knows. They are not seen again. Some say they become the night-haunts. There were no night-haunts before he came."

"This demon," Aeriel pressed, "he is the son of a lorelei?"

"All I know," Galnor replied, "is that he first appeared in my grandmother's time. She and her people came over from Zambul not long before his coming closed the pass. They say he overthrew the Dark Wolf that was the guardian of Bern."

"The Dark Wolf," Aeriel whispered; her breath grew quick. "Tell me of her. Do you know where she has gone?"

Galnor sighed. "I know nothing of her but what my grandmother spoke of: when she was warden of Bern, there was no demon, no haunts. No one feared the woods by night or the roads by day. There were no thieves, for Pernlyn hunted them. When travelers heard the long cry of the Wolf, they smiled and took it for a good omen."

"That is what they called her," murmured Aeriel, "Pernlyn?" The keeper had called her Bernalon.

Galnor glanced back and shrugged. "Some such. I don't recall."

Aeriel looked away and was silent for a few strides, then roused herself and found Galnor's eyes again.

"But if this road leads through the haunt woods," she said, "to the demon pass, were it not better to take another road?"

The young man laughed. "There is no other road."

"The woods, then."

"We are too near the city. The thieves know these woods. They would find us. We can only flee and hope they give up before we reach the pass."

Aeriel glanced about her at the dark and knotted
trees.

Galnor was saying, "For now, the road is safe enough.
And the woods will soon be full of haunts."

The road wound on, the sky a black ribbon overhead,
scattered with stars. The black grew deeper the farther
they climbed. They lost sight of Talis and the shining
Mare in the distance behind.

The trees grew more tangled; the night grew more
still. Greyling no longer ranged ahead, but stayed close.
They camped after a long time of walking. Aeriel could
not gauge how much of the night had passed, for there
was no horizon against which to measure the movement
of stars. Oceanus hung low; she caught only glimpses of
it through the trees.

They had no fire and nothing with which to make a
fire. Galnor cursed himself for not having thought to
bring a torch from the inn. They huddled together in a
wide place in the road and drew lots to see who would
keep first watch.

The short lot fell to Galnor. Aeriel and Nat lay
down and slept. After what seemed far too short a time,
Galnor shook her. Aeriel sat up beside the gargoyle then,
stroking its mangy fur.

The silence was utter, save for their own near-noiseless
breathing. The woods creaked, randomly. There was no
wind. Nat slept curled in Galnor's arms. Aeriel felt a
twinge of longing and of loss, even a little envy as she
eyed them. I have been a bride four daymonths, she
thought, and have never slept in anyone's arms.

Save Bomba's. She gazed off across the dark. When I was very young, a child in the syndic's house in Terrain, and lay thrashing, screaming in nightmares, then I slept in my old nurse Bomba's arms.

Aeriel put her closed eyes to Greyling's stiff fur for a moment. I have no husband and no kith, she thought, and am utterly alone in the world. She shook herself then, lifting her head, and struggled to throw off her useless feeling of despair.

She sat up until she adjudged three or four hours had passed. Then she wakened Nat, lay down and drifted into exhausted sleep. She started awake suddenly, some time after, to find Nat shaking her. "Hist — awake!"

Aeriel sat up groggily. She felt sore and tired still. Nat had shaken Galnor as well. He was already on his feet at wood's edge. The gargoyle stood near him, lip curled. Nat pointed.

"Night-haunts."

Two pale things lurked half hidden among the trees. One stood upright, almost human-shaped, the other, four-footed and hairless white, lifted its muzzle, testing the air. Bone — they were all strange bone under papery skin. Nat pulled a dagger from her sash. Galnor caught up a stone from the roadway and threw.

"Don't waste a dirk," he said.

The pair started, vanished like smoke among the trees. Aeriel caught a whiff of something then that smelled like lye. She noticed where the pair had stood, the earth was bare, the ground cover dying.

"Let's be off," Galnor said.

They lived on berries and crabapple pomes. Oceanus, the pale stars gave a little light. Galnor stripped the underbark from certain trees: it had a leathery, cheese-like taste. The gargoyle ate nothing. Galnor slashed fruiting gourds for water. They passed no streams.

The higher into the hills they went, the more pale, bony figures they saw. Some followed the travelers a little way, others merely stood staring. At first Nat and Galnor threw stones at every one they saw, but soon they grew too frequent and too many to be constantly trying to drive away. At length Aeriel all but forgot them, and wondered what travelers feared in them, for they never approached.

It was during their fifth camp that she awoke abruptly from deep sleep. The gargoyle beside her had lunged to its feet. Aeriel rolled, blinking, still half asleep, and saw Nat across from her nodding into a doze at her watch. A white ghost-shape crouching behind the girl was reaching its small, unearthly slender hand to touch Nat's cheek.

The gargoyle snarled savagely. Aeriel started up with a cry and swung her staff, but the creature ducked. Uncannily, it seemed to collapse like a heap of bone. Then it scrambled away; the trees swallowed it, and its long, thready wail wandered through the air. Greyling plunged after it. Nat shrieked, waking, holding her cheek.

"It touched me," she screamed.

Galnor knelt beside her, caught her face in his hands. Aeriel saw blood. He was shaking. His voice shook. "It might have killed you," he cried.

Nat burst into tears. "I was so tired. I didn't mean to sleep."

Galnor took her in his arms and stood, lifting her, carrying her like a child. "We'll stop more often," he said.

They broke camp. Nat's had been the last watch. They struggled off along the road again, Nat dozing in Galnor's arms. "It wanted to take something from me," she murmured. "The bleeding won't stop."

Aeriel remembered the whale's wax she carried, and what the innkeeper had called it. She broke off a little from the lump in her pack and, crumbling it, spread it over the tiny patch on Nat's cheek. The skin was grey there, seemingly unbroken, but oozing blood.

"Better," muttered Nat, drifting again. "It doesn't hurt now."

When she awoke later, the bleeding had stopped. Galnor set her on her feet. Not long after, the gargoyle rejoined them. Something like bone meal dusted its jaws, and there were scratches on its hide, but they seemed very slight and did not bleed.

Not a dozen hours after that, Aeriel spotted the first signs of pursuit.

They were now very deep into the wooded hills. They had stopped halfway up an uncommonly steep grade, exhausted. Through a break in the trees, Aeriel spotted a cluster of flares snaking along the road they had just traveled: pinpricks of red among the dark, far trees. Galnor nodded.

"As I feared. The Arlish bandits have come for their Beast."

They pressed on at once, though Aeriel's limbs were as sore as she could ever remember them. The trees around them grew stunted and shriveled; some had only a thin covering of leaves. Later, they passed many with no leaves at all. Food grew scarcer, and the night-haunts more bold. Then the trees themselves grew scarce until between their ninth and eleventh camps, the road ran mostly treeless, with only occasional stands of scrub.

The sound of their voices dwindled from whispers to muted nothing, the air so high had grown so thin. The night grew very cold. Nat and Galnor walked wrapped in a single cloak. Aeriel nestled the little dustshrimp on the inside of her garment, and tied the wide sleeves of her traveling cloak close about the arms.

Only the gargoyle seemed unaffected. Its strange, strangled voice carried the same as before. The grey beast did not shiver. The night around grew blacker still, the stars above more hoary bright. Oceanus appeared in the heavens again, pale blue and brilliant, as the haunt woods fell away. But always when they looked behind, Aeriel spotted the clutch of red torches, so that Galnor cursed.

"Are they mad? They will not give up until they have driven us into the teeth of the demon himself!"

They kept a sharp eye out ahead then, as well as to the rear, but at least the night-haunts seemed to have vanished. Aeriel wondered if they found the light of Oceanus hard to bear.

The torches of the bandits gained ground steadily, until at last their fire — low-burning and blue now with

the thinness of the air — lay barely an hour's distance
behind. Aeriel could see their pursuers very clearly in the
starlight.

Galnor paused, just for a moment, pointing upward.
"The demon's pass."

Aeriel glimpsed the gap in the peaks. She felt her skin
prickle. A darkangel waited there. Nat stood clutching
Galnor's hand. The young man himself looked grim and
desperate. The road led only in one direction, the surrounding slope now grown too steep to let them turn
aside.

Aeriel and the others climbed toward the pass. The
torches of the bandits were gaining below. Galnor and
Nat, their breathing shallow, were using their hands to
help them climb. Aeriel clutched her staff in one hand,
the collar of the gargoyle in the other. She saw a stone
building above them at the mouth of the pass. Galnor
nodded.

"Used to be . . . the garrison and taxhouse," he said.
"Only the demon . . . bides there now."

He laughed grimly, breathless. The stars above
burned like tiny suns. The atmosphere had grown so
scant Aeriel could move only slowly. The gargoyle
lifted its muzzle and snarled.

The bandits below were singing and shouting, giddy
with the altitude. They were seacoast dwellers, while
Aeriel had been raised in the steeps of Terrain. Her
chest felt tight, her heart huge and straining, but she felt
no giddiness. Galnor and Nat struggled ahead of her.

Aeriel spotted something, a flash in the starlight. Onto
the roof of the taxhouse a figure emerged. He was
clothed in pale garments, cloaked in a black cape thrown

back from his shoulders. Nat gasped and ducked behind a ledge at road's edge. Galnor followed. The gargoyle trembled, a rumble beginning in its throat.

But Aeriel could only stare. Her skin went numb. She felt as though she had been made into stone. Disbelief overwhelmed her: it was not he. It could not be he. She had overthrown him in Avaric — that darkangel. It seemed she would stand in the middle of the roadway, staring at that familiar figure till she crumbled to dust.

Only when Galnor grabbed her arm, snatching her into the shadow of the ledge, did Aeriel realize the figure upon the garrison was not the same, only similar to the one she had known. Crouching, gasping to regain her breath, she studied it now.

She saw its garments were not of Avaric. Only its black wings falling like a thick, dark cape, were the same — huge and umbrous. No starlight gleamed in them. They were deeper than the night-dark sky. The darkangel flexed its dozen wings.

It was not looking at her and her companions. Aeriel realized that suddenly. It was gazing beyond them at the torches down the slope, shielding its eyes from their dim glare. The giddy laughter and shouting of the bandits continued below. They had not seen the icarus.

Aeriel watched, holding the gargoyle, shushing it. The grey beast struggled as if it longed to lunge upslope after the demon of the pass. Nat and Galnor huddled behind the ledge, heads down. The vampyre crouched suddenly, and flew.

It gave a cry — strangely birdlike and inhuman. The sound of it rebounded from the cliffs. Below, the bandits were looking up. Their laughter ceased. Some of them cried out. Aeriel felt the wind of the darkangel's passing, its flight a fury of dark, churning wings. Downslope, the bandits were drawing their weapons.

"Don't look at its eyes!" she heard the bandit leader shout.

The vampyre swooped. Aeriel felt a hand close on her arm, dragging her. For a moment she struggled, confused — the darkangel was below her, nowhere near — before she heard Galnor hissing in her ear.

"The pass. Hurry — now!"

They stumbled from the boulder's shelter, out into the road again: Nat first, running desperately, then Galnor. Aeriel followed. The greyling still strained after the icarus, but Aeriel kept her hold. They passed the taxhouse, gained the entrance to the pass.

Below, she saw two of the bandits drop their torches and fall back. The blue flares guttered in the gusts from the vampyre's wings. The darkangel swooped, feinted, then seized one of the thieves by the wrist, disarming him. The darkangel hoisted the unarmed man aloft.

Aeriel cried out, halting. Those bandits who had fallen back rushed forward now, their blades catching the starlight in gleams. The vampyre hovered just above their reach, as if mocking them. It was their captain it had seized.

Galnor caught Aeriel's arm again. "Hist," he gasped, "come on while we may."

"But the bandit lord," cried Aeriel.

"He's lost!" shouted Galnor.

He was holding her staff. Aeriel stared at the dark wood in his hand. She must have dropped it — when? She realized it was with two hands that she restrained the gargoyle now. The hard brass collar cut her fingers till they bled. Galnor's grasp was bruising her.

Below, the bandit in the vampyre's grip pulled a short, hooked blade from his sash and drove it into the icarus' shoulder. The vampyre utterly ignored the wound — it seemed hardly to feel the blade. There was no blood. It buried its teeth in the bandit captain's throat.

Aeriel screamed, stood screaming. She stumbled forward then, dragged off-balance by the gargoyle's lunge. Its collar slipped her grasp. Galnor's hold on her kept her from falling. He hauled her with him into the rocky, narrow pass.

She cried out again, this time after the gargoyle, and saw it check, glancing over one shoulder back at her. Beyond, the bandit dangled limp in the darkangel's grasp. With a howl, the gargoyle sprang on toward the icarus and its victim downslope.

Aeriel lost sight of them. The lip of the canyon hid her view. She heard shouts, the greyling's furious gabbling, the icarus' inhuman shriek. Aeriel shuddered, turning away. She ran on blind beside Galnor, not daring now to look behind.

The way was very narrow, rocky, with high steep walls on either side. Aeriel could hardly see, the night had grown so dark, the starlight so scant despite the thinning of the air. Then the pass opened before them, and the road fell suddenly down. They plunged down its steepness breakneck, careless how they went. They ran until they could run no more.

Bushes and scrub brush grew along the road. None had the twisted look of those in Bern. These bushes had leaves, some of them fruit. Nat sank to the ground at last, gasping. Galnor knelt beside her, his legs as unsteady as hers. Aeriel herself could hardly talk for weariness.

In a little while, the gargoyle joined them again, loping down the hillside like one barely winded. Handfuls of fur had been torn from its shoulders, and from its jaws dangled a ravel of dull grey cloth. When Aeriel pulled it from its teeth, it burned her fingers — cold as ice.

They left the gargoyle to keep watch. All three of them slept. It was afterwards, after they had walked and eaten, toward the end of their second march since leaving the pass, that Solstar arose, spilling its white light over the hills. Nat pointed out a village below.

Not until they had reached it and stood among the villagers with pale green skin, like Galnor's skin, and yellow-green hair, like Galnor's hair, did Aeriel realize at last that they had crossed over from Bern into Zambul.

8

THE
PAINTED GIRL

The elders of the village kindly received them. They were given food and a place to sleep, and no questions until they wished to answer. They repaid their hosts with tumbling and juggling of dirks. Aeriel told the village children tales, forgetting all else, for a little while, in that dreamy serenity. It seemed they might linger as long as they liked.

Yet gradually, as Aeriel felt her strength returning, the peace and contentment of that Zambulean village trickled away. The maidens' rime came back to her. Time began to hang heavy. Orm beckoned. Aeriel knew she must be on her way again.

One hour she arose from where she sat. Her gargoyle lay dozing beside her staff. She gathered her things and whistled to Greyling. On the shady side of the village square, villagers stood grinding nutmegs into flour. Galnor and Nat sat nearby, juggling uncracked nuts. Aeriel went to them. She had put her traveling cloak on, slung her pack from one shoulder.

"I must go," she said. "I have stayed too long." The daymonth was already a quarter gone.

Nat looked up, stopped juggling. "Where will you go?"

"Westward, toward Terrain."

"You have kith there?"

Aeriel shook her head, refused to dwell on it. "I have no kith. Will you stay here?"

Galnor answered. "I have people to northward, my grandmother's kith. Nat and I will stay here a little, then go."

Aeriel bent and kissed him, on the cheek, as was the custom at parting in Terrain, then Nat. "Good journey, then."

But as she made to turn away, Nat pressed something into her hand. "Take this," she said.

Aeriel looked down, saw in her hand Nat's ivory-handled dirk. "I can't," she began, but the blue-skinned girl would not take it back.

"I took it off one of the Arlish bandits in Talis," she said. "He said he would give me a silver coin if I juggled a dozen spoons at once. I did, but he only laughed and gave me nothing. So I took it. But it is too large for my hand. It might fit yours."

Aeriel put it carefully away. She kissed the blue-skinned girl again, then went to find the elders of the village, to take her leave of them before she set out on the road.

She wandered westward across Zambul. Though the countryside was mountainous still, the hillcrests rose much lower than the high steeps of Bern. Sometimes she performed in exchange for food: tasteless, smooth bean-cheese, persimmons, coppery and tart, or coarse, sweet cakes of oakapple flour.

She passed rocky meadows of nibbling goats. Sometimes she saw beaters harvesting wild grain, or berry pickers, or goosegirls tending their flocks. Gleaners gathered deadwood from the holts. But nowhere did she pass any running streams.

The people seemed to draw all their water from wells. Watersellers stood at crossroads, offering dippers to travelers, for a price. Aeriel had to sing for drink as well as food.

Everywhere she stopped, Aeriel told her tales. The heron sat wooden upon her staff. The little dustshrimp ran along her arms when she played the bandolyn, to the villagers' delight. They called the gargoyle her great grey dog.

The land continued very poor and dry, but nowhere ravaged, as had been the haunt woods of Bern. Then one hour when the daymonth was nearly three-quarters gone, she came upon a blackened hillside, the twigs of the bushes brittle and curled. The whole place smelled scorched.

Aeriel stood a moment, gazing at it. The gargoyle whined, pacing restlessly. Aeriel quieted it, then continued down the road and across the narrow vale. She asked a boy tending kid-goats on the opposite hillside what had caused the damage, and he, looking up from the wooden flute he was piping, shrugged.

"Angel slept there a few daymonths past."

Aeriel felt a coldness glide along her back. "The darkangel of Bern ranges so far?"

But the boy shook his head. "Not Bern's. Our own."

Aeriel shook her head, not understanding. "There is a darkangel on Zambul?" The boy nodded, indifferently. "But your land is fair," said Aeriel. "No blight twists the trees. . . ."

The goatherd glanced across the vale. "There's blight."

"But the whole heart of Bern — near half I saw — was blighted because of their darkangel."

The boy laughed then, scornfully. "That's because theirs lies only in one spot, daymonth on daymonth, year after year. Lets his poison gather and spread. There's a stupid darkangel. Spoils his own hunting grounds."

Aeriel began to speak, but the boy was looking off.

"Hardly anyone but thieves left in Bern now because of it. The babes die, they say, and the children die. And before another sixty years, there'll be no one left in Bern at all."

"But," Aeriel started, "if you, too, have an icarus, how is it Zambul remains . . . ?"

"Whole?" the boy asked her. "Hale? Not half so whole or hale as it was before *he* came. Fifty years he's been here. But he never lies in the same place twice — do you see? The taint can't take hold."

The boy sat fingering his flute, not looking at her.

• "And if the spot where he settles is blighted? In a year or two years, it begins to come back. Meantime we keep our kine away; none of us go there. So we don't die, as they do in Bern, or miscarry."

Aeriel felt lost, too astonished to speak. She had thought Zambul was clean of the witch's sons. The gargoyle howled suddenly, and the boy's kids upon the hill started and bunched.

"Odds, hold your dog!" the goatherd cried.

Aeriel quieted the gargoyle, turned back to the boy. He had settled into his place again. The kids nibbled at their scrub.

"But a darkangel must hunt," she said at last. "None of the people I have met here seem to move in fear or speak with loathing of the night. No walls surround the villages; no bolts are on the doors — how can your people feel safe?"

"Ah," the boy smiled, blowing a few sweet, shrill notes on his pipe. "It is because we treat with our darkangel."

Aeriel knelt below him on the rough hillside. "How do you mean?"

"Wherever he has settled to wait out the day, the people thereabouts know it from the shriveling of the trees — and the stink of rot. So they cast lots, by household, and whatever house draws the bad lot must give one of its own to the vampyre by nightshade. Simple."

Aeriel felt her throat closing. A little breeze traced against her cheek, but her chest was too tight to take any in. Greyling against her began to growl. She shook it to be still.

"The people of Zambul give up those of their households so willingly?" she asked.

The boy shrugged. "Some willingly, some not. What matter, as long as the angel leaves? He has his fill and flies away, doesn't trouble the same place again for years."

Aeriel shook her head. She felt hollow, and realized she had not eaten in a half-dozen hours. "Who goes to the darkangel?" she asked the boy.

"Daughters," the goatherd told her, "sons. New-born babes or criminals, strangers. No sick or moribund. No old people unless they are vigorous. But mostly the ones that fall to the icarus are slaves."

Aeriel shook her head again, trying to quell the panic which rose within her. "Slaves? I have seen no slaves in Zambul."

The boy looked up from his flute. "Haven't you? In all the towns you've played in? Half us common folk are debt-bound to the high ones. Have to buy water, don't we? And the rich ones own the wells. They're the ones with money to buy real slaves, too — rose-skinned ones out of Rani, or goldenskins of Avaric, or blue ones out of Bern. Whites ones, too, I suppose," he said suddenly, eyeing Aeriel again. "Where is it you are from?"

"Terrain," she said.

He laughed, tossing the hair out of his eyes. It lay yellow against his light green skin. "Terrain," he said. "Then you know of slaves."

Aeriel stood up. "Go on," she said. "You were telling me about the high ones and their slaves."

"And the lots," the boy answered, smiling. "The bad ones seem to fall mostly to the rich, don't they? — I don't say how. What's it to them? They grumble, true, but they don't give up their daughters or sons, or even their good servants, do they? Just tie the surliest young oddskin to a tree near the blight where the angel lies, and go home again, leave that one to the dark."

The light, dry wind brought the stench of the blasted hillside back for a moment then. Aeriel felt dizzy. Her stomach clenched. She raised the hood of her traveling cloak against the sun.

The goatherd gave a sudden cry, started to his feet, staring at her. Aeriel glanced at herself, then back at the boy, who now cast his gaze back and forth over the hillside as if searching for something. He seemed to be looking straight through her.

Aeriel turned away and started down the slope. She did not understand what he was doing, and did not care. The gargoyle trotted after her. She heard the goatherd behind her cry out, "Sorceress!" and glancing back, she saw him hurriedly shooing his kid-goats uphill and away.

She found rosepears growing wild along the roadside farther on and filled the inner pocket of her robe with them, but their taste cloyed, noisome in her mouth. She ate them anyway. The dustshrimp took tidbits. Nothing was wrong with the fruit.

Aeriel sang for her supper in the next village she came to and had enough coin left to buy a small water flask, but she did not stay.

"If they do not scruple to give up their slaves to the dark," she thought, "how much easier simply to hand over some passing stranger?"

She traveled on, often raising the hood of her cloak. She played at bandolyn for her food and drink, but never again slept in any village. She passed more blighted hillsides. They seemed to come more closely together after a time, so that when Solstar hung low, perhaps three hours from setting, she found herself murmuring,

"I thought the boy said this darkangel never roosts long in one place — but that blasted heath we just skirted makes the third such we have passed in two hours' walking."

She stroked the gargoyle's mangy fur, gazed off into the trees. They were walking along a wooded stretch.

"Well perhaps it does not like the fare it has received hereabouts, and so stays to extort better —"

Before she had even finished her words, she heard a creaking of laughter like a rusted hinge. Looking up, surprised, she saw an old woman standing just off the road, bent nearly double beneath a load of sticks.

"Well, maid," she called, "you have murmured truer than perhaps you know. All these lands belong to the majis. The bad lot fell to him three daymonths gone."

Aeriel halted. "Did he refuse?"

"Refuse?" the old woman cried. "Pah. Never. Tried and tried, three times now going on four, to feed the wingèd fiend — only the angel is not satisfied."

"Why is that?"

The bent woman heaved the bundle of sticks from her back and straightened a bit. "Have you any water about you, maid? Ah, how the gathering does make one dry."

Aeriel handed her her flask, and the other drank greedily, then wiped her mouth upon her sleeve and handed the empty vessel back to Aeriel. She tugged peevishly at her bundle, as though it had suddenly become too heavy to lift.

• "Don't trouble yourself," said Aeriel, balancing the load upon her hip. "Will you give me the tale?"

The gatherer's lined face cracked once more into a smile. "My cottage lies this way," she said. "I might as well talk upon the way as not. Come along."

She hobbled off, and Aeriel followed. The gargoyle roamed through the trees ahead.

"It is almost four daymonths now since the birdman last took a soul — but that is not because the majis has failed. Three dawns running his people, returning to the spot, have found the silk cords cut and the offering gone.

"The birdman will not fly. Each daybreak, he settles in a new quarter of the majis' lands. The majis is in a rage. It has never been heard of before, for the angel to spurn offerings that were healthy and young. The bird-priests say their god is displeased. The majis must offer someone nearer his heart — a different sort of sacrifice."

"Priests," whispered Aeriel. "They have made a god of this icarus?"

The old woman shrugged. "When I was a young, we prayed to the Old Ones, but they never come into the world anymore. Shut away in their cities, while the world winds down. Pity they did not build it to last." The gatherer sighed. "I think they must all be dead by now."

Aeriel protested. "Ravenna is not dead. She lives — she must live. She promised to return."

The other clicked her tongue against her teeth. "Our air bleeds off into the void. Rains do not fall; trade dwindles. News hardly moves between the kingdoms anymore. The majises rule and the rest of us slave to the waterdebt." She clicked her tongue again. "I think Ravenna is overdue."

Aeriel said nothing. The old gatherer sighed and shook her head.

"Even the spotted panther, Samalon. The last good god we had."

"Samalon," said Aeriel. "Do you speak of Zambulon, the warden of this land?"

The old woman shook her head again. "I know nothing of that. I was just a girl. She is gone. A new god is on Zambul now, and his priests." She began to laugh again suddenly, like a cartwheel squeaking. "Ah, the birdpriests say they know their god, but they are guessing. They know less in this matter of the majis than even I."

"How so?" Aeriel shifted the bundle upon her hip. The twigs pricked her.

"Well," the old woman said, "there was a girl. I came upon her in the woods not two daymonths past, when my gathering kept me late abroad past Solset. She seemed quite breathless with running and with weeping, her wrists all bruised as though they had been bound. My hut was not far. I took her there, but she would not stay, she was in such fear.

"She told me she was a slave in the majis' house, had been intended for the darkangel, but a great monster had come out of the woods, chewed through her bindings and set her free. I thought her mad. She ran away then, and would not come back to my calling.

"I went into my hut after, and barred the door. And sitting alone all fortnight, I remembered me how I had heard of the majis' offering the daymonth before, but the angel spurned the gift. And I began to wonder then if perhaps it was this grey wingèd creature the girl had spoken of that had freed both offerings, not the angel's scorn."

The old woman walked on a little while in silence then, but presently she resumed.

"Next daymonth, at my gathering, I came upon strange tracks in the woods — great pawprints like none I had ever seen before, and two huge feathers, all grey and mitey: far bigger than any bird's should be. And once I heard strange wauling, but it put me in such dread I left my bundle on the ground and went the other way as quickly as I might.

"In the late afternoon of the same daymonth, I ran into a traveler, who told me the majis' offering had again been scorned, the vampyre's angry screams heard. He still roosted near, so the majis would have to offer yet a third time by evening if he did not wish to lose more land to blight.

"That fortnight, to be sure, I was home long before Solset, and barred my door. The next morning, just at daybreak, I went to a neighbor of mine to get the news, and she told me the strangest thing.

"She said a boy had run past her daughter's house not two hours into the night and, falling, had entangled himself in the vines making her fence. She went out with a torch to see what was the matter, but the boy only wailed and thrashed.

"She saw about one of his wrists a length of thick blue cord that had been chewed at — not cut, but damp and chewed. And the boy's clothes were not common flox, but tram, that silkier stuff they wear in great houses, even the servants.

"She went back into the house to get a hack to cut him loose, for she feared in his thrashing he would break an arm. But when she came out again, he had gotten free somehow and gone.

"So I told my neighbor what had befallen me two fortnights ago, and what I thought. Then I went back to my gathering, for I was late about my task that day, and slow as well, for I was deep in thought. Just put those down on the doorstep, my girl. I will put them where I want them in a bit."

They had reached the old gatherer's cottage. Aeriel dropped the bundle where the other had bade, but though the woman offered food and a place to sleep, Aeriel would not stay. She was desperate to be out of Zambul now, and she had no idea how far off lay the border of Terrain.

At length the old dame refilled her water flask and gave her a bran cake in thanks. Aeriel whistled the greyling to her side as she stepped from the trees onto the path once more. The dustshrimp nibbled its crumb of bran.

The road wound on through a long, broad valley, and presently the woods on either side fell away. The road forked, and Aeriel took the path that began to rise. Below her she caught glimpses of a town.

She had no time to study it, for from around a bend ahead, she caught sound of voices and the tramp of feet. The air was very still, without a hint of wind. Aeriel had raised the hood of her traveling cloak to shield her eyes from the low sun's glare.

Around the bend came a small party of officials and

soldiers. Aeriel stood off to let them pass. Not one
them so much as glanced at her. Dust rose behind th
in a choking cloud. The foremost official was mutterii
seemingly more to himself than to the woman and man
white robes who flanked him.

"My best orchard — ruined, along with two fiel
and a meadow in four daymonths. I cannot afford i
and the people up in arms. If the fiend does not tak
that to his heart" — the man gave a slight jerk of hi
head over one shoulder, back up the road — "I canno
answer for what may come."

"The angel," one of the white-robed people correctec
gently. "The *angel*, majis."

Aeriel caught no more of what they said, but she had
noticed two things as the party passed by: that the
priests wore collars of black feathers, and that the
majis toyed nervously with something in both hands as
he walked. She caught only a glimpse of it, a small
metal key.

Aeriel stood gazing after the retreating figures, but
the gargoyle pulled free of her suddenly and bounded up
the road. Aeriel whistled, but the grey beast would not
come back. With an effort, she started after it. The road
began to climb rapidly.

Rounding a turn, she came upon an orchard suddenly,
all blighted and spoiled, the leaves lying crisp upon the
ground, the fruit shriveled, black upon the boughs.
Solstar, very low in the east, cast long black shade. Aeriel
heard screaming, then sobs.

The gargoyle dashed away through the bars of darkness and light. Aeriel began to follow, and nearly

stumbled over a girl. She was dressed in fine garments; bangles upon her ankles gleamed. Her head and face were veiled but for the eyes. All her skin had been painted black, save little dots and swirls where the pale showed through.

It was she that had screamed. She was panting now, straining hard against a chain that held her to a tree. The metal of the shackles gashed her wrists. The bark of the trunk flaked away where the chain chafed it.

Aeriel threw back the hood of her traveling cloak and went toward her. The girl started, staring, shrank from her with a cry, then lost her footing in the leaves. She fell heavily, then struggled awkwardly to one knee.

"Spirit," the painted girl gasped at last, sinking again. Behind the tree, the chain had slipped: she could not rise. "Spirit, for the love of the old gods, help me. I must get free before Solstar sets."

She began to struggle again. Aeriel cast off her pack, set down her staff and knelt. She took the chain between her hands and stared at it.

"I am no spirit," she said. "Only a traveler. I passed your father upon the road."

The painted girl twisted her arms, trying to make her hands small enough to pass through the bands. "He is not my father," she spat. "I am a slave in his house. Can you free me?" Her voice grew desperate again. "Oh, the Beast, Savingbeast — someone must have told him, or he would not have used a chain!"

Aeriel tugged with all her strength, then rested a moment and tugged again. "What do you know of a beast?"

"Someone told me the village talk, that a monster had come into Zambul to spoil the Bird's hunting. It would set me free, they said — but what beast can bite through chain?"

Aeriel pulled the ivory dirk from her robe. She pried at one of the links, then sawed at it. The blade's tip snapped. Aeriel threw the dirk aside. "The links are welded shut," she said.

"Gods help me; gods help me," the painted girl sobbed. She cried out suddenly. "Even now — he wakes!"

Aeriel whirled, and abruptly, she saw. In the heart of the grove, thirty paces distant, stood a massive tree. Upon one branch crouched something dark.

It looked like a bundle of black velvet, as tall as Aeriel and nearly as great around. The blighted tree looked almost grey in comparison, for this thing threw back none of white Solstar's light. It was itself completely shadow. Not even heaven was so dark.

It was the black of a darkangel's wings. Aeriel felt the blood shrinking beneath her skin. The painted girl tore at her chains. The folded wings upon the low tree limb were stirring.

"He wakes! He wakes!" the painted girl cried. Solstar behind them was half set away.

The bundle shuddered, paused, then stirred again. Layers of darkness unfolded from it like the petals of a huge night-blooming flower. The painted girl thrust her wrist into Aeriel's grasp.

"Break my hand," she cried. "Force it through."

Aeriel found herself powerless to move. The unfolding of those wings fascinated her. Two of the wings now were fully extended. Another pair poised half unfurled.

The darkangel was turned away — Aeriel realized that with a start. It was its back she watched, its face still hidden from the light. She came aware of someone's hands upon her. The painted girl had said something.

Aeriel shook her head dully, half turned to her. "Even broken, your hand would not pass through."

"Cut it off, then!" screamed the girl.

Half the darkangel's wings were open now, and the others beginning to unfold. The girl was groping desperately for something among the leaves. Aeriel realized suddenly, like the lifting of a spell, in only a few minutes more Solstar would be set.

She turned, saw the painted girl snatching the dagger up, laying her wrist upon the ground and putting the broken blade to it. Aeriel stooped and caught her hand. "Hold," she told her. "I have thought of a way."

"Heron," she hissed, catching her staff. "Bird-on-a-Stick. Awake!"

The heron shivered, let out an outraged squawk, became flesh. "What is the matter?" she cried. "Why are you addressing me by ridiculous names?"

The white bird clutched the head of the staff in her toes, flapping for balance. Aeriel thrust her closer to the shackle about the painted girl's wrist.

"Can you pick a lock?" said Aeriel. "You unbarred the gate for us in Talis. Can you open that lock?"

The painted girl stared at the heron, her sobs choked into breathless gasps. The heron eyed the shackle's keyhole, began to tap it with her bill. The girl shrieked suddenly.

"He stands!"

Aeriel started, turned.

"Hold me steady," the heron snapped.

The vampyre stood upon the black branch now, its back still to the vanishing sun. The heron put her eye to the keyhole. The stink of rotten matter grew smothering. The icarus fanned and flexed its pinions. Aeriel wondered wildly where her gargoyle had gone, and where was the strange beast the old gatherer had spoken of?

Solstar sank lower, barely a fingernail above the hills. Oceanus peered, pale blue through the curled, black trees. She heard a scratching sound. The staff tipped in her hands. She saw the heron giving her neck an odd, lunging twist. The tip of her beak in the keyhole turned. The painted girl tore the shackle from her wrist.

Solstar set. The sky above turned black as nothing. The orchard around them was drenched in shade. The vampyre upon the far tree turned, lit now with the ghostlight of Oceanus and the stars. Aeriel had only one glimpse of pale garments on a young man's form, a face savage with hunger, and blank, colorless eyes.

The painted girl screamed, bolted from Aeriel. Aeriel wheeled to follow, but the vampyre was already flying. The wind of its wings flattened her garments against her, billowed her hair. Aeriel threw herself flat to the ground, hoping it must miss her, wheel around for another try.

Even as she did so, the rhythm of its wings changed, steadied. It hovered now, above her in the air. Aeriel scrambled to her knees, caught up her staff. The icarus stooped. Aeriel swung — her staff struck nothing, for the witch's son had drawn back suddenly.

A form, two forms had leapt out of the grove. They sprang over Aeriel, Greyling clamping the darkangel's forearm in its teeth. The other beast, grey like the first, seized the vampyre's leg in its taloned paws. Two pairs of skinny wings thrashed upon its shoulders. A collar of brass encircled its throat.

"Catwing," gasped Aeriel. "Gargoyle, Catwing!"

The wingèd beast sank stump teeth into the vampyre's leg. The icarus screamed, inhumanly shrill, and shook its attackers off as though they were nothing. Greyling fell, but the wingèd beast recovered in the air, gaunt pinions straining. It seized one of the darkangel's wings.

Aeriel held to her side, gasping for breath. Her fall had knocked the wind from her. Nearby, the greyling rolled, gibbering, gathered its fantastically bony limbs and sprang. Someone was pulling at her. Aeriel staggered to her feet.

"Fly, fly!" the painted girl shouted.

Aeriel sprinted away with her into the trees. Cat snarls, yelping and birdlike screams rose in the distance behind them. The girl dragged her till Aeriel regained her stride, but then it was the girl who clung to Aeriel, gasping and stumbling.

They left the orchard suddenly, burst onto open ground. Earthlight washed around them, pale, pale blue. The stench of blight faded. Aeriel gulped the clean air. Her staff felt lighter suddenly. She stared at it, realized she had been carrying it, her pack as well. The heron launched off into the air, skimming ahead of them downslope, toward another vale.

"Follow," she cried. "I can find the best path," and sailed low, whiter than woodsmoke in the pale earth-shine.

9

THE
SUZERAIN

The heron led them through close woods, down dry ravines and along shadowed paths. Aeriel heard. still the vampyre's screams, the yelping of two gargoyles in the distance behind, and bit her lip in fear for them — the icarus seemed able to bat them aside at a blow.

All at once, after they had been running what seemed a very long time, a great angry shriek rose behind them. The vampyre burst into the air above the hills, circling. His white garments blazed amid the nothing-darkness of his wings. Aeriel listened hard, straining her ears, but she heard no sound of the gargoyles now.

Above the trees, the icarus scanned, eyes sweeping the hills. Aeriel and the girl shrank deeper into the crack along which they fled. Presently, with a chirrup of rage, the witch's son swooped away — toward town, and the majis' house.

They followed the heron till the veiled girl was staggering. Aeriel came to a halt in a thick brake of trees. "Heron," she cried. "We must rest."

The white bird curved around in a low arc, alighted. "Mortal creatures," she murmured. "I had forgot."

Aeriel leaned wearily against a tree. The painted girl crumpled at her feet, trembling, her breaths shallow and pained. Aeriel sipped from her water flask, then offered it to the girl, but she turned her head away. The blood on her wrists was dark and dry. Aeriel used a bit of water from the flask to wash them. The girl clenched her teeth, made strangled little cries.

"I am sorry this hurts," said Aeriel, "but I have a balm that will help."

The painted girl dried her wrists upon her veil, shaking her head. "My feet," she managed after a moment.

She shifted gingerly. Aeriel did not at first know what she meant. She took one of the girl's dark-painted feet upon her lap and brushed the dust from it. She saw gashes and blood upon the sole.

"How did this happen?" she cried. "I felt nothing sharp underfoot."

The girl shook her head. "Before you came. The majis cut my feet so that even if I escaped his chain, I could not run."

Aeriel started, stared. As gently as she might, she washed the feet of the painted girl, using the hem of her desert shift for a cloth. The veiled girl's breath grew ragged suddenly. Aeriel was not sure whether with laughter or sobs.

" 'I love your dark beauty,' " she spat. " 'I love your dark love.' "

She was weeping, the swirls across her cheeks growing muddy with tears. Aeriel did not understand what she had said. The other unfastened the veil from her face, and Aeriel realized then, with a start, it was not paint that made the girl's skin dark. The dots and whorls upon her cheeks were not pale, unpainted places, but white paint daubed upon dark skin.

"It was what he used to say to me," the girl went on. " 'My dark beauty, my dark love, I'll give my own child to the Bird before you.' "

She turned her head away again. Aeriel said nothing for a little. Irrylath, Irrylath — she could not get the thought of him out of her mind suddenly, and did not know why. She gazed at the painted girl's skin, black as the boy she had seen upon the Sea.

"I did not realize you were so dark," she murmured at last. "I thought the paint..."

The girl put one hand to her cheek. "This?" The stuff came away on her fingertips. "Bride paint — they thought he must want something other than a meal this time."

She scrubbed at it, suddenly fierce, and at the backs of her white-daubed hands. It smeared. Aeriel caught her breath in then. The thought welled up all at once, without her bidding. I, too, have been a darkangel's bride. False lover. False love.

Aeriel washed the painted girl's cheeks, her hands. She took ambergris from her pack and crumbled it, rubbed the waxy green granules into the soles of her feet, her wrists. Very carefully she bound them up, using the dark girl's veil. Aeriel touched her feet again.

"Do they pain you still?" The other shook her head. Her hair was parted in little squares, braided close to the skull. "Then why do you weep?"

The dark girl sat limply against the tree, her breathing quieted. She spoke dully.

"When I was in the majis' house, the rose-skinned ones used to say, 'When I am free, I will go to Rani,' and the blue-skinned ones, 'To Bern. When I am free. Where my kith are. Where I was born.' But where are my kith? Where was I born?"

She shrugged, shivering, chafing her arms.

"My first mistress bought me from a Bernean trader who would not say where he had got me. I have never heard of any land where the people are like me."

She looked at Aeriel.

"The majis used to let me leave the house and walk abroad when I would. He knew I could not run away. 'You will never leave me, my black chick,' he said. 'You have nowhere to go.' "

Aeriel knelt, putting her hand on the dark girl's hand, and strangely, for the first time since the heron had brought her her staff, she was not afraid of Orm.

"Come with me awhile," she said. "I was once a slave, bought as a babe. I have no kith and no home — I go where I like. But I do know where you are from. I passed it, crossing the Sea-of-Dust: a boy stood fishing on a reef, his skin like shadow. I am going to Terrain, but after, I must cross the Mare again. I'll take you, if you'll come."

The dark girl looked at her.

"What is your name?"

"Erin," the other said. Her tears had stopped.

"I am Aeriel." She offered the girl their last water, and this time Erin drank. "Why did you call me 'spirit' in the grove?"

The other handed back the flask. "I did not see you come. You seemed to appear out of the air. Your skin was so white, the sun shone clear through you. I took you for the orchard sprite."

Aeriel laughed. The girl stood up, leaning against the tree. Aeriel made to help her, but the other shook her off.

"I can walk. The cuts are not deep. He is too much a coward to cut me deep. But he rubbed salt in the cuts to make them burn. What you put on them . . ."

"Ambergris."

"It has taken the burning away."

They continued on through Zambul, following no road, only the heron's flight. The hills had grown more wooded here. Not long into their second march, the two gargoyles overtook them. Aeriel embraced them, laughing with relief. Tongues lolling from running, they fawned on her.

They looked battered and disarrayed, but otherwise unharmed. Aeriel stroked the winged one. It rubbed its head against her hand, made in its throat a thrumming sound like beetles' wings. She fed it the second of the apricoks from her pack, saving the seed, and watched some of its gauntness leave it.

"Catwing," she murmured, stroking its scabby chin.

The air grew cooler as the fortnight rolled on. When Erin and she slept, Aeriel put the traveling cloak over them both. They had no water now, and access to none, for they kept wide of cottages and towns, but Erin showed Aeriel where to find succulent nightfruit, or winesheath in flower, and how to cook the fresh-laid eggs of lizards and birds on red ovenrock, that held the heat of Solstar long into the night. Aeriel sang Erin tales when they camped.

The ground they traveled seemed to be rising, the vegetation growing lusher. Fruit on the trees became more plentiful; the hollow reedgrasses they sucked for moisture were fatter now with juice. The fortnight was nearly done when Aeriel heard a gentle, lapping sound.

"What is that?" she said softly, halting.

Erin, playing with the dustshrimp, looked up. "I hear nothing."

Aeriel took a few steps through the trees. The noise was faint, familiar — she could not think what it was. Erin put the dustshrimp back on Aeriel's sleeve. The white heron was nowhere to be seen. Both gargoyles had lifted their muzzles, testing the air. Aeriel, too, now could smell it:

"Water," she murmured. "Running water."

The gargoyles bounded away through the underbrush. Aeriel pushed forward through the foliage. She heard splashing ahead, stumbled into a clearing. A tiny pool lay before them, feeding a stream that spilled away among the trees. The gargoyles had flung themselves into the water. The heron alighted beside the channel.

The gargoyles wrestled and nipped each other. Aeriel and Erin had to duck their spray. The dustshrimp hid from the wet in a fold of her garment. Aeriel laid her things at wood's edge, slipped from her traveling cloak and shift. She waded into the pool.

The water was warm, steaming in the cool night air. The gargoyles subsided. The heron speared a fish. Erin pulled off her travel-stained garb, knelt at the pool's edge and cupped her hands.

Aeriel leaned back, let the water support her. Its taste was very slightly sweet. Earthshine fell blue, the starlight pale grey, but their light in the pool wavered yellow and white.

Erin came into the pool, and Aeriel noticed for the first time that though she was very slender, her breast was not quite so flat as a boy's, her hips not quite so lean. They bathed in the still, bright, steaming water, and drank.

Aeriel looked up suddenly. The gargoyles had long since clambered back onto the bank, shaken off and now lay sprawled there, one dozing, the other nibbling its matted fur. Above the lapping and soft plashing, Aeriel heard a sound.

Erin, lying back upon the water, opened her eyes. "What is it?"

The noise had been so faint — distant, dying. It did not come again. Aeriel shook her head. "Nothing. It must have been wind among the trees."

There was no wind. The night was still. Erin closed her eyes again, but Aeriel stood a few moments, listening. Nothing stirred. She came out of the pool, letting the cool air dry her. Then she dressed and sat toying with her bandolyn.

Presently there came another sound, louder, nearer than the first: a belling and bawling like wounded kine. Then, nothing. And suddenly, much nearer, the breaking of brush. Greyling and Catwing bolted to their feet. The heron looked up. Even Erin lying upon the water had heard it. She stood.

A grey beast came out of the trees across the pool. Its ribcage heaved; its snorted breath curled, white upon the air. Its body had the shape of a skeletal calf, its knobby limbs hoofed. A nest of horns tangled its brow.

It did not seem to see them at first. Staggering, it pitched to its knees beside the pool and sucked at the water, straining against the brass collar encircling its throat. Aeriel recognized it then.

"Mooncalf," she cried: the last of the six gargoyles she had tamed, the one that, even tame, had been so skittish. It was starving now, gaunt as bone. "Mooncalf," she whispered.

The grey beast started up, snorting, staring. Erin in the pool shrank back from it. It stood at wood's edge, head up, seemed on the verge of bolting. The greyling yipped. Catwing gave a throaty cry, and the grey beast's glazed eyes seemed to clear.

Aeriel reached into her pack, held out an apricok. The rich, pungent scent hung in the air. The mooncalf's nostrils flared. It forded the pool, swam past Erin without a sideward glance, folded its limbs before Aeriel and lay down, let her take its thorny-crownèd head in her arms.

It ate the apricok, and seemed to sleep. Its grey eyes closed; its panting eased. The gauntness of its sides grew less. Aeriel put up the seed and stroked the mooncalf's nose. Erin came out of the water, staring at the new beast, and at Aeriel — but the dark girl said nothing as she dried and dressed.

Then of a sudden came another sound: a questing cry like the calling of horns. The mooncalf sprang to its feet, and fled away through the trees. Without a sound, Greyling and Catwing followed.

A party of horsemen came out of the trees. Their skin was pale amber; their horses were black. Footmen held leashes of lithe, dappled hounds. Aeriel stared. She had never seen horses that had no wings.

One rider, the foremost, rode forward a few paces, raising one hand to keep the others back, made the footmen still the yelping and baying of their dogs. He wore a turban upon his head like the women of Isternes.

"Ho, what's this?" he said, gazing at Aeriel. "We have been hunting the Grey Neat this long fortnight, but it is other quarry we have found. Maid, you are a brave one to be abroad in these parts all alone."

His words puzzled her. "Why do you call me alone?" she asked.

Erin knelt in the grass half behind Aeriel. The horseman glanced at her. He smiled. "One unarmed boy would do you little good against brigands, maid."

Erin said nothing. Aeriel said, "Is Zambul a country of brigands, like Bern? If so, you are the first that I have met."

The horsemen behind him glanced at one another, but their leader merely threw back his head with a laugh. "Zambul?" he said. "Do you take this for Zambul — that waterless bone?"

"Have we come into Terrain, then?" said Aeriel, startled — though the woods were like nothing she had ever seen in Terrain.

The rider smiled. "Terrain lies west of here. You have come too far north if you meant to cross over from Zambul. This is Pirs." The horseman reined his champing horse. Again he was laughing at her. "And as for brigands, maid, I spoke in jest. There are none such on my land."

Aeriel rose. "Can you point me the road to Terrain, then? And we will trouble you no more."

The huntsman did not answer her at first, leaned forward in the saddle, eyeing her. "My villa lies upon that road," he said. "It is not far. Surely you must be weary of travel, maid. Stop a little and honor my house."

Aeriel fingered her staff. Sometime between the coming of the mooncalf and the huntsmen's arrival, the heron had settled again, faded back into the wood. Erin stood beside her, utterly silent, refusing to speak. Aeriel studied the man on horseback before her, but could not read him.

"We will go with you," she said carefully, "if you will show us the road to Terrain. I must go on to Orm as soon as may be." She lifted her pack. "I am Aeriel."

"Welcome, Aeriel," the horseman cried, offering her his hand. "You will ride with me. Nightwalker can easily bear double."

Before she could speak, he had pulled her up beside him on the horse's back, sideways, as though it were a couch. The horse moved a step, and Aeriel gripped the saddle's back to keep from falling.

"Put your arms about me," the huntsman said.

Instead, Aeriel doubled one leg across the horse's back till she was astraddle and could grip with her knees. The rider glanced over his shoulder at her, then laughed.

"As you will." He motioned his riders, clucked to his horse, but Aeriel touched his arm, looking at Erin. The huntsman reined, shrugged impatiently. "Your boy can come after, with the dogs."

Aeriel made to get down from the steed. "Erin will come with me."

The horseman caught her about the waist, his tone hurriedly gentler. "Hold, maid. No need." He called sharply to one of his riders, who caught Erin's arm and hauled her up behind.

"I have told you our names," Aeriel said, glad when the rider released her to gather the reins. "Will you not give us yours?"

"Mine?" the huntsman said, spurring. The other riders fell in behind. Aeriel clung to her staff and the saddle's back. The turbaned man laughed. "I am suzerain here," he answered her. "The suzerain of Pirs."

❧

Aeriel endured the journey, clamped her teeth at the sudden jolts and drops through the constantly down-sloping land. At last they came in sight of the suzerain's palace. It was fashioned all of cream-colored stone that glowed in the cool Oceanuslight. Aeriel saw gardens. Among the greenery, fountains played.

They passed under the arch of a gate into a yard. As soon as the suzerain had made his mount stand still,

Aeriel sprang down and stood off. Only then did she see that he had turned in the saddle to offer her his hand.

The suzerain dismounted then, and though he smiled still, Aeriel could see a hard edge had come into his smile. So be it then, she thought, for she did not much like being handed up and down the backs of horses as though she were a pack.

Erin, too, had slipped down from behind the guard. The suzerain nodded his companions away across the yard. He was tall, Aeriel realized now that she saw him standing. Erin, who had come up silently beside her, stood eyeing the turbaned man as well.

Servants appeared, bearing cups and trays. Aeriel realized how famished she was. A warm, steaming flask was pressed into her hand. The suzerain tossed his off in a draught; Aeriel sipped. The sweet, salt broth warmed her wonderfully. She took a tidbit from a tray, but noticed when servants offered Erin cup and tray, the dark girl turned away.

After only a moment, the suzerain clapped his hands and the servants departed. Aeriel's hunger had only been whetted, and she gazed longingly after the disappearing trays. Her finished cup was taken gently by the boy who had given it to her. The suzerain said:

"Come, my guest. I know you are weary, but let us walk awhile in the garden, and when we are done, I promise you a feast worthy of your welcome."

The suzerain strolled through the grounds of his palace. After a time, Aeriel realized with unease she had become separated from Erin. But however slowly she paced her step, a bevy of courtiers seemed always to intervene.

Nor did the suzerain allow her to fall back or wait. He led her along winding footpaths, told her what land this frond was from, what suzeranee had constructed that aquifer until Aeriel's head was fairly spinning and she wondered if they would ever pause.

Then the suzerain was leading her out of the garden, up steps onto a broad, stone-railed terrace. Cushions and white groundcloths lay spread before them. Braziers and lampstands blazed. Servants were kneeling, just setting the last dishes in place.

There were platters piled high with roasted game-chicks, bowls of nutmeats, tureens of thick broth. There were loaves of bread no bigger than a fist, candied fruits stuffed with nuts, and baked fish bedded on cress.

Aeriel caught a whiff of it all, and felt giddy with hunger. Her knees nearly gave. She scarcely noticed when the suzerain laid his hand upon her arm. She knelt and reached for whatever came closest to hand.

Erin was not among the others, she noticed suddenly, and her uneasiness returned. Glancing back toward the steps, she caught a glimpse of a figure slipping into shadow, moving quietly away among the trees. Aeriel frowned. Was that Erin — what was she up to? No one else seemed to have noticed the dark girl's departure.

They feasted in silence for a little time. Only when Aeriel began to feel satisfied did she realize she had not had anything to drink since their arrival. Looking up from her plate, she saw all the courtiers had cups. She glanced at the suzerain. He, too, had a goblet from which he drank. Aeriel's throat felt thick and dry.

The suzerain noticed her glance and seemed to start. "Wine," he called, then muttered, "dawdling servants." Louder, "Where is the wine I ordered for my guest?"

A steward came forward, bent to murmur in his sovereign's ear.

"Well, see to it, can't you?" the suzerain said. The steward hurried away. The lord of the villa turned back to Aeriel, all smiles. "Some delay in the kitchen, I suppose."

Aeriel said nothing, wondering why the suzerain did not simply take one of the empty cups and fill it from any of the wine pitchers before them. But the wait was brief. The steward returned, half dragging, half shoving another servant before him.

"Have a care with that," the suzerain snapped as the steward nearly caused the serving man to spill the pitcher he carried.

Aeriel loosened the laces at the throat of her traveling cloak. She had fastened them against the chill night wind during the ride and had kept them fastened since. But she was warm now, with food and the heat from the braziers. She turned her head a little, to avoid the suzerain's eyes. They seemed ever to be searching her.

"Utmost apologies, my lord," the steward was mumbling, signing the servant to fill the cup he held in his other hand. "The herbalists said they had difficulty . . ." He stopped himself suddenly, at the suzerain's glare, then stammered on. "With . . . with the proper spices, my lord."

The servant poured from the pitcher into the cup. "How is that?" Aeriel inquired. "Is my wine different somehow from the rest?"

The suzerain shrugged, irritably. "Oh, how should I know," he muttered, "everything my servants do? Perhaps they sought to honor you with some special wine. Give her the cup, can't you?"

A gleam of sweat had formed on the suzerain's brow. She wondered at it, for the night around them was pleasantly cool. The suzerain was suddenly staring at her.

"Your eyes," he said.

She looked at him.

"They are green."

Aeriel nodded, shifting uneasily beneath the directness of his gaze. "Yes," she said.

The serving man held out the cup.

"I had not realized before the color of your eyes."

"I cannot help their color," she answered. It was a strange color for eyes, she knew. "They have always been so."

Aeriel reached for the cup. The suzerain's hand caught the serving man's suddenly, twisted the goblet from him. A sup spilled across Aeriel's outstretched fingers.

"Fool," the suzerain growled. "That is not the wine I bade you bring."

"My lord, it is exactly . . . ," the steward cried.

"Then I have changed my mind," said his lord with a savage glance. "I will not have such young trash served at my board. Never dare bring it before me again."

He dashed the contents of the cup across the far tiles of the terrace. The pitcher followed with a clang. Dark liquid ran from the vessel's neck into the squares of earth where fronds and lilies grew along the balcony's stone rail. With a brusque gesture, the suzerain sent his steward and the servant away. He wiped his brow with a linen lapscarf.

"Here, you must have wine," he said, a little breathless, and poured from his own pitcher into her cup. Aeriel made to protest, but he would not have it. She saw his hand tremble ever so slightly as he set the pitcher down. "Take mine; take mine. I am done and they will be all fortnight fetching something fit."

He lifted the cup.

"You see? This is old wine, excellent." He took a sip, and Aeriel was not sure whether he drank to steady himself, or to show her that the wine was good. "Here, take it."

He pressed the cup to her hands, nearly forced it to her lips. Aeriel did drink then, and deeply, though she had never drunk wine before, save half a year ago, when she had shared a wedding cup with Irrylath.

The suzerain's wine was hot and sweet. It brought back her weariness to her. She noticed Erin then, just coming up the terrace steps, slipping silently into place upon an empty cushion. Aeriel felt relief at her companion's return, hardly noticing the dark girl's face was strangely drawn. She stared at the suzerain, then at Aeriel.

Shortly thereafter, the suzerain ended the meal and had them escorted to their rooms. Aeriel noticed Erin stayed beside her the whole way. She would not be parted from her when they reached the chamber that was to be Aeriel's.

"But my lord has ordered other quarters for your boy," the chamberlain said.

"We will share this one," Aeriel replied.

The old man seemed perturbed. "But lady, there is but one couch."

"I am not a lady," said Aeriel, "and it makes no matter. Erin will stay with me."

The chamberlain looked at Aeriel, and she back at him. Erin beside her glanced beyond him down the hall. In a moment, the wizened man cast down his eyes and muttered, "As you wish."

When the suzerain's chamberlain had departed, Erin rose quietly from where she sat and drew the door shut. The cool draft of air from the windows ceased. Aeriel stood her walking stick in one corner. "Why did you do that?"

Erin came back and sat down near the broad, high window that opened onto the balcony. "So that I may speak with you," she said.

"We may speak with the door open, surely?" Aeriel said, fanning herself with her hand. "There is no one about."

"The suzerain has posted four guards on you. Did you not see?" Aeriel shook her head; it felt heavy. "They are just down the hall."

Aeriel started toward the door, then thought better of it. "When did he do that?"

"After the feast."

Aeriel sat down, took off her traveling cloak. The wine had made her flushed and hot. "Why did you eat nothing?" she asked. "Why did you slip away?"

Erin looked off. "I do not like him."

"We will not be here long," Aeriel said. "Your feet..."

"My feet are well," Erin snapped.

Aeriel rubbed her neck. "You have eaten nothing," she began.

"I found fruit in the garden," the dark girl answered, "and clear water. I found another thing in the garden, too."

Aeriel looked up. "Go on," she said. Her eyelids felt heavy. Erin was watching her.

"A boy, a youth about your age, very finely garbed. Some courtier. He was knocking down plums from a tree with a stick. He gave me some."

Aeriel sighed. She felt stifled. Her limbs seemed loose.

"He said I would do well to watch my fare at the suzerain's board," the dark girl said.

Aeriel shook her head. Her senses were swimming. "Why was that?"

"When I pressed him, he drew from his breast a little withered wort he had seen one of the herbalists gathering among the kitchen herbs."

"It was a spice, then," sighed Aeriel, leaning heavily upon one hand.

Erin shook her head. "He said the leaves were used to make blue dye, but that the root held a juice to kill you in two breaths."

Aeriel lay down upon the couch, for she was weary. The suzerain's wine was making her head ache. Erin was speaking, but Aeriel could hardly follow.

"When he said that, I ran back toward the feast — though the young man cried out in surprise, 'Boy, what do you care if your master drinks my uncle's draught? It will set you free.'

"He thought you a youth, I think, from that distance, and me a boy. He did not follow me. When I reached the terrace steps, too out of breath to cry warning, I saw your cup still dry, the suzerain's servant pouring wine — when suddenly his lord dashed the cup from your hand."

"He said the vintage was bad," muttered Aeriel. She could not keep her eyes open. She was not used to wine — it made her thoughts sluggish. She did not understand what Erin was trying to say, nor did she care.

"He said he had changed his mind!" Erin cried angrily, but Aeriel scarcely heard. The suzerain's wine was numbing her limbs. Already she was drifting into sleep.

10

HUNGERSPICE

When Aeriel awoke,
Solstar was already two hours into the sky, floating a
half degree above the western horizon. She felt vaguely
sore. Her head ached. Erin sat by the window still, looking as though she had not slept. She remembered the
dark girl speaking of something hours before — of finding plums in the suzerain's garden.

"I do not think I will drink wine again," said Aeriel,
rising. "It makes me stupid with sleep."

Erin said nothing. Aeriel frowned, trying to think.
There was something else she was forgetting, it seemed.
Some task, some purpose had put her on the road —
companions waiting for her in the woods?

Odd. The memory would not come. Even now, she
was not very clear-headed — she remembered only
hazily how they had arrived at the suzerain's villa. She
sighed and shook her head, resolving to think about it
later.

The hours of the daymonth passed. Whenever the
suzerain lent Aeriel his company, he questioned her in-

cessantly about herself, her kith and whence she came. She had no kith, she told him, was an orphan for all she knew. She came from Terrain.

But the thought of Terrain made her uneasy somehow. She turned away from it. After a time she remembered Isternes, what the maidens had told her, and their rime. But it all seemed very distant somehow, far behind her, long ago.

"I must go soon," she told the suzerain once, in the beginning, not quite sure why, but he put his hand on her arm.

"Not yet. Stay awhile. Pirs is a small, rarely traveled land, and I get so few visitors."

The suzerain showed her more of his gardens, his fountains that spouted from pools of red and golden fish. Aeriel laughed and tossed them tidbits — sometimes forgetting her dustshrimp completely until the little creature tugged at her garments and pricked her through the cloth.

And the suzerain showed her all the rooms of his palace, the great library with its many scrolls and books. These the suzerain unrolled or opened for her, that she might see the pictures, for she could not read.

Often, as by accident, while wandering the garden paths or palace halls, they happened upon the makings of a feast, ready laid, but no servant near. Then the suzerain was her servitor, pouring her cup and holding the tray. Never again did she take wine from him, though, so that after a time, he too drank only clear water in her presence.

The thought of Irrylath came to her once — he who

had never walked with her, dined with her, conversed with her pleasantly on nothing at all. In all things now the suzerain was at pains to adjust his manner to her mood. Aeriel shoved memory away.

Yet, somehow, always in the suzerain's company she felt an odd distress. Something waited for her beyond the villa walls. And Erin did not like their host, which troubled Aeriel, for she could not find in him anything to dislike.

Nor could she truly enjoy the feasts he laid continually before her, for though the food was always deliciously spiced, her thoughts seemed to wander when they dined, and she found herself hungry again after only a little time. She plucked fruit in the garden then, when she was alone, only to feel oddly guilty eating anything he had not given her.

The fortnight came. All daymonth and now into the night she heard horns and the yelp of hounds in the woods. Sometimes she saw the suzerain's young men riding out on their black horses.

"What do they hunt," she asked the suzerain, "that they ride so, night and day?"

The suzerain shrugged. "Nothing in fine. They are huntsmen. They must hunt."

But another time, he said to her, "Last daymonth there was only one Grey Neat in my woods. Now my riders tell me there are three: all different of foot and shape, but all stone grey with brass collars."

Some memory twinged in Aeriel, but she lost it again before she could catch it. She heard the suzerain saying to himself, "What might they be, I wonder?"

And she found herself answering, "Gargoyles," without knowing why. The word meant nothing to her. The suzerain only laughed.

Once he offered to take her riding with him beyond the villa grounds, but she declined, saying she had had enough of horses. It was only afterwards, when she was alone, that she realized she had refused because she would have had to lay aside her walking stick.

It came to her then that ever since she had come to the suzerain's villa, she had clung to her staff as to a weapon. She had not set it from her for a moment. Walking, she carried it with her, and when they sat, she laid it across her lap.

Once he had offered to take her in a little boat to an island in the largest of the fish pools, but she refused, saying she could not swim. Only now she realized it was more because she would not have been able to take her walking stick.

Through a kind of haze, she began to notice he was forever asking her to do what would cause her to lay the stick aside. He led her up narrow, precarious steps to walk the parapet along the wall, down tangled paths in the garden, through great, echoing chambers of the palace where her staff's heel made a thunderous click.

He only did so when Erin was not with her, though that was often now. He had begun to stand closer to her when they were alone, speak more warmly and familiarly then. At first the dark girl had kept close beside Aeriel almost all the time. Now more and more, she slipped away.

Aeriel was never aware just when she went, her going

was so soft. She only realized her absence afterwards, when returning to her chamber, she found the dark girl sitting, very quietly. Erin would not say where she had been.

The fortnight was only a dozen hours from daylight, Aeriel realized with a start. She sat with the suzerain in one of his great halls. They had just finished a feast in which the food had been more hotly spiced than ever. Aeriel had drunk half a pitcher of water to cool the burning in her throat. She felt dizzy and strangely hungry still.

A servant had brought his lord a bandolyn. The wood was ebony, the strings silver, the neck inlaid with ivory and shell. The suzerain sat tuning it.

"Why do you always turn away?" he asked her suddenly. "Whenever we sit or speak, you will not look at me."

The tone was still a hair's breadth off.

"In Terrain, where I am from," said Aeriel, "it is not the custom to stare."

"Do I stare at you?" the suzerain asked.

"Yes," she answered, searching for her cup. Her throat still burned.

"You had a bandolyn with you when you came," he said. "Why have I never heard you play?"

"I play to pay my way." The clear, cold water did not slake her thirst. "Am I not your guest?"

The suzerain laughed. "I will play for you, then," he replied, touching the strings. Aeriel shuddered. The

pitch of the drone strand was still too high. The other
stopped, adjusting it. Aeriel already knew the words.

> *"The world wends weary on its way;*
> *The haze hangs heavy on the Sea.*
> *If only there would come a day*
> *When you would not turn from me. . . ."*

The cup in Aeriel's fingers slipped and overturned.
She had risen to her feet before she realized. The
suzerain stopped.

"What is it?" he said.

Aeriel blinked and shook her head. She did not know
what had come over her. Her limbs felt oddly hollow,
light. "I beg you, do not play that song."

The suzerain laid his bandolyn aside. "Forgive me.
I thought to please you. . . ."

"No. No, it is not that," she heard herself saying.
Such things would please me, she thought, if only — if
only this were Isternes. If you were Irrylath. She glanced
at the suzerain and felt herself shudder. A strange, fierce
longing for Irrylath overcame her. The suzerain had
risen.

"Are you ill? Sit down. I will call my herbalists —"
He had taken her arm. Aeriel pulled away from him
awkwardly, steadied herself. She schooled her voice to
stop shaking.

"No need. I am only overtired. I must go to my
chamber, and rest."

She left him hurriedly, almost running. He began to
follow her; then seemed to think better of it. She heard

him halt. Relief swept over her as she fled into the hall. He was not following.

***

She found Erin sitting beside the window, toying with something in her hands. Aeriel sank down heavily upon the couch.

"Where have you been?" Erin asked.

"With the suzerain," Aeriel replied. She felt breathless still.

"Feasting?" the dark girl said. Aeriel nodded. Erin looked up at last, and Aeriel realized what it was she held in her hand: a disc of polished silver. The dark girl said, "What is he feeding you that you are growing so thin?"

Aeriel looked at her, confused. Erin rose and stood before her, holding the mirror that she might see herself. Aeriel started, sucked in her breath. The face before her was hollow-cheeked. She felt the bones of her ribs beneath the skin.

"But," she stammered, "I have eaten well...."

"And how do you feel?" Erin asked, laying the silver disc aside.

"Dizzy," muttered Aeriel.

"Starved," Erin said.

"Yes," murmured Aeriel. "I am hungry. Strange."

The dark girl fetched a bowl of bread and fruit. "Eat this."

But Aeriel turned her face away. The fragrance of the plums sickened her. "I cannot eat that."

"Why not?" Erin said, kneeling, refusing to take the bowl away. "It is good plain fare such as you and I both ate before we came here. Now you will eat nothing but what the suzerain serves."

"I cannot," Aeriel said, shoving the bowl away. "It has no bite to it, no savor...."

"That's hungerspice he has been feeding you," cried Erin. "Roshka has told me of it. It will muddle your thoughts, make you forget yourself — cause you to hunger always and will not satisfy."

Aeriel stared at her. "What are you talking of?"

"Do you think I do not know you are some magical person?" The dark girl said, "You have told me not one whit of what errand puts you on the road or calls you in such haste, but I know it has nothing to do with that man or this place. We have been here a whole day-month!"

Aeriel glared at her, but realized with a start that she had not even thought of leaving since nightfall. What had the suzerain, what had his feasts and his palace of fountains and gardens done to her? How had she stayed so long?

"Magical?" she muttered, finding herself angry now, for no reason. "Magical — what do you mean?"

"Did you think I had not noticed?" Erin answered. "Do you think *he* will not?" She touched her wrists. "No mortal carries a salve to heal all sores."

"It was ambergris," snapped Aeriel. "I have told you of that salve."

"You appeared out of the air to me in the orchard."

"I never appeared out of the air," Aeriel screamed, standing up. She had never in her life felt such a sudden rush of rage. Her voice was a shriek. "You were frightened and you did not see me."

"Aeriel," said Erin, her own voice grown suddenly quiet again. Her black eyes gazed at her. "You have no shadow. You had no shadow in the orchard. That is why I took you for a sprite."

Aeriel stopped, panting. She swayed a little where she stood. Her knees were weak. She tried to quiet her voice, speak steadily. "What do you mean?"

"Look. Look," Erin cried then, seizing a lamp and holding it near.

Aeriel looked down. No shadow lay beneath her feet. She jumped, looked behind her, all around. Every object in the room had its own shade, flickering and darting in the white lamplight — everything but she. Aeriel felt her knees begin to give. She put her hands to her face. Her whole frame shook in a passion of uncontrollable tears.

"Where is my shadow?" she gasped. "Why don't I have one? I had one when I crossed the Sea-of-Dust. Where has it gone?"

Erin set the lamp upon the floor, fetched back the bowl of fruit and bread. "Here," she said. "Eat this. Eat this before you swoon."

At last, to please her, Aeriel ate. The meat of the plums tasted at first immeasurably bitter in her mouth. But gradually, strangely, it washed the spice from her tongue. She began to be able to taste the fruit again, and then the bread. Her throat ceased to burn, and she was ravenous. Her whole body ached. Soon she had eaten all there was in the dark girl's bowl.

Erin said, "You must talk to Roshka. He has told me something of the suzerain, but he says he must see you."

"Who is this Roshka?" Aeriel muttered, wiping her red eyes now and glancing about furtively for her shadow.

"The youth I met," Erin replied. "The one by the plum tree. He is the suzerain's nephew. I have told him I am not a boy, but he has warned me to let no one else discover it. It was he who suspected his uncle must be feeding you hungerspice — but I will let him tell you himself."

Erin turned then, toward the wide window overlooking the grounds. Aeriel followed the line of her gaze. The foliage beyond the balcony wall had begun to tremble, as though someone below were scaling it.

A pair of hands, then a young man's head and shoulders appeared. The youth pulled himself easily over the balustrade. His skin was mauve, the color Aeriel's had been before the desert sun had burned it fair.

He wore trousers and toed boots, a turban as his uncle did. Erin went to help him through the window and into the room. He knelt. His lashes were pale gold with a green cast to them. His voice seemed oddly familiar to her.

"Crown Prince Roshka to serve you, lady."

Aeriel began, "I am Aeriel, and no lady," but before she had finished, the young man drew breath. He leaned back a little in surprise.

"You have green eyes."

"So have you," said Aeriel.

"Do you come from Esternesse? Erin says . . ."

"I have lately come from there."

The other paused. "I have never seen anyone else before that had green eyes," he said at last. "Though they say my mother had. She was a lady of Esternesse."

Aeriel frowned. "There is no lady but the Lady in Isternes. Her name is Syllva, and her eyes are violet." The young man had fallen silent again. Aeriel watched him. "Erin said you would speak to me."

He looked up and seemed to come back from his thoughts. "I know that you are in danger here. My uncle has given you hungerspice." Aeriel turned her face away. The dark girl sat quietly, watching them both.

"Why has he done this to me?" whispered Aeriel.

"To keep you," said Roshka. "That you might hunger for his fare alone, and not depart."

"Why?" Aeriel said.

But the young man shook his head. "Tell me, have you noticed nothing odd about this villa in all the daymonth you have been here?"

Aeriel frowned a little, thinking. Her head had cleared somewhat now that the hungerspice had been washed from her mouth. "Nothing," she murmured, "save . . ."

"Yes?"

"I have seen no women."

"There are no women," Roshka said.

Aeriel looked up. "None in the villa at all?"

"None save the two old, old herbalists — past bearing, both. A long time past. Lady . . ."

Aeriel raised one hand. She could not follow him. "I am not a lady," she began.

"What is my uncle's name?"

Aeriel stopped short. "I . . . I do not know," she said, surprised. "He has not said. But why ask me — do you not know your own uncle's name?"

Roshka shook his head. "I do not. Nor does anyone in this villa, or in all of Pirs."

"He has no name?" said Aeriel. "How may a person have no name?"

"He had one once," the prince replied. "He was given one, as others are — but it is not his anymore. Not his to use, not his to tell. He has sold it. It has been taken."

Aeriel felt suddenly cold. "What do you mean?" she said.

Roshka looked down. "I will try to tell you," he said, "as clearly as I can. My uncle is not the rightful lord in Pirs. By rights he should only be regent. My father was the suzerain, but his brother seized power after his death and my mother's death. My sister and I were only a year old and some."

"Birthsiblings?" said Aeriel. "You have a sister born with you?"

The crown prince nodded. "She was the elder by a few minutes' space, heir to my father's lands. . . ."

"Green eyes," murmured Aeriel suddenly. "The lady Syllva told me once how her sister had green eyes. She was Lady in the city for a dozen years while Syllva was in Avaric. Later, she went away on a trading voyage, and never returned. Her name was Eryka."

Roshka looked at her. "That was my mother's name. And my sister's, though we called her Erryl, which is to say, 'little Eryka.' "

Aeriel studied him again, wondering if it was the Lady

of Isternes he reminded her of. All his movements, even his way of speech seemed eerily similar to someone she knew.

"You are Syllva's nephew," she said slowly, "and so are cousin to m—" She had almost said, "To my husband," but stopped herself. Any memory of Irrylath was painful to her.

"You are some kith to this Lady of Esternesse?" Roshka asked.

Aeriel shook her head. "Only slight kith."

"I must call you cousin, then," the crown prince said.

Aeriel looked away. "But you were telling me of your uncle, who has no name."

"Oh, yes," said Roshka. "He had a name, a name used by everyone, until my father died. A hunting mishap, they said. But I will tell you what my father's footman told me once.

"He said a fortnight before my father rode out to hunt, a black bird alighted in the far watchtower. No one knew what manner of bird it could be, all black, and at first the guards tried to drive it away. But it would not go, and bothered no one, so soon everyone ignored it.

"All but my uncle, who gazed at the tower. Then at a quiet hour, my footman said he caught a glimpse of my uncle going along the wall. A while later, the black bird flew, north and west toward Pendar and beyond. My uncle came down from the tower then and was very silent. Not even my father could draw him out.

"About the middle of the fortnight, the black bird came again, or another like it, and my uncle went again to send it off. Then my uncle was even more silent and brooding than before, but he would tell no one what had passed between him and the bird.

"And only a half dozen hours before dawn, as my father's servants prepared for the hunt, the rhuk came once more to the tower. My uncle seemed to know it was there before he was told, and went up to it without a word.

"This time the bird flew almost at once, but my uncle did not descend for some time. When he did, looking very spent and drawn, he told my father he was ill and would not be coming with the hunt. It was after that no one could recall his name. They called him 'lord' or 'the suzerain's brother.' "

The young prince paused and glanced about the room. He drew breath. The lamp Erin had placed between him and Aeriel burned high. The dark girl sat in shadow, listening.

"My father rode off into the hills at daybreak," Roshka said. "The hunting was very good. Nightwalker, my father's mount, ran far ahead of the other steeds. But something bursting from the brush startled him and made him shy. My father was thrown and killed. No one saw what had flown in Nightwalker's face, only heard it beating away through the trees.

"My uncle made himself suzerain then, and black birds have come to the tower since. My uncle goes to treat with them. Each time he returns looking worn and spent, for which the herbalists give him draughts. A rhuk came only a few hours before he rode out and found you, though none have come yet since."

Aeriel looked up. She felt cold as dust. The lamp

flame could not give her warmth. "I do not like the sound of those birds," she said, "or the quarter toward which they fly. Has your uncle ever spoken of the Witch of the Mere, of a lorelei?"

"Witch?" said Roshka. "No witch that I know of. Though I have heard servants say that after the bird comes and goes, he cannot sleep, only dozes, muttering of a white lady in his dreams."

Aeriel flinched and turned away. She started to speak, and then stopped herself. In how many others' dreams did the lorelei speak? What would become of the world if she recaptured the lost lons of Westernesse before Aeriel could find them?

She closed her eyes and could have groaned. What am I doing here? she thought. I might have been in Orm by now. She opened her eyes and glanced back at Roshka.

"But what has become of your sister?" she said. "You said she was the elder. Should it not be she, then, who is crown princess?"

The young man nodded. "I was coming to that. When my uncle seized the throne, he said if the Lady Eryka would marry him, he would forgo children of his own and make her children his only heirs. But my father's footman had shown her a great black feather he had found at the spot where my father died, and she refused.

"He set her in a tower then, that tower where he had met the bird, and said he would never let her out but she would wed him. He fed her hungerspice to make her forget her former love and long for her captor alone — and she ate, pretending to suspect nothing, until at last she had made herself thin enough to pass through the narrow window of the room.

"Her maid had brought her bits of silk to fashion a rope, but the stone sill wore through the cord before she reached the ground. She fell — not far, but because she had made herself so thin and frail, she did not live."

Roshka eyed the lamp burning between himself and Aeriel. His lips had grown thin, his green eyes dark and hard.

"My mother's maid says they searched the tower, but could not find the princess royal. I had already been taken away from my mother, but her maid claims my uncle was unable to get the little girl from my mother's arms without violence, and so left her, meaning to return and take her while Eryka slept.

"My mother's maid swears she saw a great white bird alight at her lady's window just before she fell and carry away the child. But I think she must have been mad with grief, and that my uncle murdered the crown princess."

Aeriel stirred upon the couch. Her shoulders were stiff from sitting so long. "What has any of this to do with me?" she asked. "And how, if your uncle would be lord in Pirs, has he let you live?"

Roshka smiled a little, thinly. "I am in no danger yet. My uncle has no wife."

"Wife?" said Aeriel.

"To bring him an heir," the crown prince said. "I am his only heir until then. All the women of this villa fled long ago. The daughters of the noble families hide underground — the peasant women, too.

"They live as the underfolk once did, before the underfolk went away. No one tends the land anymore. It will not bear. The Torch has grown dark. The light-bearers have no beacon to follow inland. . . ."

"Lightbearers?" said Aeriel. She had lost his thread. The young man still knelt, now staring off. His voice had fallen to a murmur. He glanced at Aeriel.

"The pearlmakers," he said. "They bring the blue salt from the Sea. They once made Pirs so lush it was called the jewel of the West. Now everywhere save the suzerain's own private gardens and hunting wood has grown barren."

"Because the suzerain has no wife?"

"No woman will have him, a nameless man. My uncle sends his huntsmen out daily to search for them. In all the years he has been hunting, he has captured five women, but all have found ways either to escape him or die. He has another means to hunt them by night."

"Another means," murmured Aeriel.

"A wingèd seraph," Roshka replied. "A gift from the mistress of his dreams. They say its wings are darker than the dark. . . ."

"But," Aeriel said, "he was hunting the Grey Neat, by night, when he found us." She glanced at Erin. The dark girl watched.

"Ah." Roshka nodded. "I should have said. He has been hunting the Grey Neat these last daymonths, and no other, for the white lady's seraph has been hunting it, too."

"She wants it, the White Witch?" said Aeriel. "Why?"

"Who knows? He does not. But she values it, that much is sure. Perhaps if he can capture it before she does, he might use it to buy back his name."

Aeriel said nothing. She could not think, felt herself growing silent as Erin, as a shadow. None of what the prince said made sense to her but this: the suzerain had been hunting her gargoyles all this daymonth, and she had known it, and somehow it had meant nothing to her. *Hungerspice*. She shivered hard.

"There is a prophecy," the young man was saying. "The last woman his huntsmen took, four daymonths gone, shouted it at him just before she killed herself with a bit of bone. She cried it was written on the rocks, carved below ages past by the underfolk, that the Torch would blaze again, and Pirsalon return, and the rightful heir come once more in the land."

Aeriel started. "Pirsalon."

"The great stag," said Roshka, "warden of Pirs. The seraph bore him away when it came."

Aeriel felt heat coming back into her blood. "I am looking for Pirsalon," she said. "I must find him."

Roshka hardly seemed to be listening. "I will come of age in a year," he said. "And my uncle fears to be overturned. The high families want no more of him. They know there is some curse on him. Only by getting a wife, an heir, can he prove them wrong. . . ."

"But what am I in all of this?" Aeriel demanded, again. Her head fairly ached from so much listening.

The green-eyed boy knelt, looking at her. "He means to wed you, Aeriel."

11

A
NAMELESS MAN

Aeriel found herself coming out of her thoughts. How long she had been sitting, lost in contemplation, she did not know. The lamp Erin had set upon the floor was burning very low. She looked up then, and realized it was not the flame that had dimmed, but the room that had grown more light. Dawn lit the highest spires of the villa. By the window, Erin awoke and seeing the dawnlight, gave a cry.

Aeriel stood up. "We must flee this place, at once, while darkness holds. I dare not stay another hour."

Erin was also on her feet. "We cannot pass the gate. I tried to once. The guards refused to let me by."

Roshka shook himself, arose. "There is a door in the wall I picked the lock of years ago, that I might steal in and out again unseen. If we can make our way . . ."

His words were interrupted by a rapping at the door. Erin jumped. Roshka bit his whisper into silence. Aeriel turned.

"Who knocks?" she called.

"My lord's chamberlain," came the reply. "The suzerain requests you to come to him upon the terrace."

"Do not go," the dark girl hissed. "Say you are ill."

"He would only send his herbalists."

"Lady?" the chamberlain called.

"Tell your lord," Aeriel said, "that I will join him shortly. I am only just awake."

She listened carefully. Slippered feet beyond the door padded away. Erin plucked at Aeriel's sleeve.

"Quickly. While we have the chance."

Roshka was already on the balcony. "Come. We can flee west. The high families will take us in."

But Aeriel hung back. "If we go now," she said, "we are sure to be taken, for the suzerain will soon grow impatient and send to see why I have not come. You two go on and I will follow."

"No," said Erin, coming back from the window. "I will not be parted from you."

"I will eat nothing he gives me," said Aeriel, kissing her cheek. "You knew his game from the moment you saw him, and I should have listened to you at the start. Wait for me by the plum tree. I will come when I can."

Then she turned and caught up her walking stick, went from the room too quickly for Erin to even cry after her.

Aeriel went out upon the terrace overlooking the garden. He stood at the balustrade, gazing westward toward the dawn. As Aeriel approached, he turned, smiling.

"Forgive me if I woke you," he said. "But dawn over my garden is too beautiful for you to miss a second time."

Aeriel joined him.

"You look weary," he ventured.

"I . . . slept badly," she murmured.

Solstar arose, slowly, taking an hour to pass from where its rim first edged above the near, tall hills until the last of it broke free. The suzerain held up his hand, shielding his eyes from the light.

"Aeriel," he said, "all Pirs, all I hold could be yours." His gaze took in the gardens, his estates beyond. "These things I would give you if . . ."

Aeriel felt weary and distracted. She smiled a little, thinly, and spoke before she thought. "If I were your brother's heir, they would be mine. They are not yours to give."

The suzerain's gaze snapped around to stare at her. "Roshka," he whispered. "You have spoken to Roshka."

Aeriel's head felt suddenly clearer. She had not meant to say what she had, but now it was done. With an effort, the suzerain regained his calm.

"My nephew is mad. He can never take the throne. He caught a fever shortly after my brother died — his mother and sister, too. It killed them. He alone lived, but he has been mad since, telling everyone I caused their deaths."

Aeriel did not answer him. The suzerain seemed more composed now, his smile no longer forced.

"He has deceived you well, I see. Do you doubt me still? Come, I will take you to meet someone. Then, I think, you will no longer doubt."

He held out his hand, as if expecting her to take it. Aeriel gripped her walking stick. The suzerain shrugged. He turned and started away. Aeriel watched him a moment or two, but he did not pause or look behind. She followed.

He led her along the wall that bordered his villa grounds. The parapet was only wide enough for one. The suzerain went quickly, not looking back. They reached a tower at the corner of the walls. The suzerain disappeared into the arched doorway. Aeriel hung back, then followed again.

They ascended a flight of curving steps to the small room at the top of the tower. He unlocked the door and held it wide for her, but Aeriel would not enter until he had first gone through. She stood with her back to the wall, just inside the door. The room was small, plain, scarcely furnished. It was empty save for the two of them.

"Where is this person you would have me meet?"

The suzerain stood at the narrow window, gazing out. "He is not here yet," he said. "But he will come."

Aeriel listened, but could hear no footsteps on the stair. The suzerain turned and went to a grey wooden chest with panels carved in the Istern style. He knelt, lifting the lid.

"I loved a woman once, that had green eyes."

Aeriel said, "Her name was Eryka of Isternes."

The suzerain started, looking up. "Ah, Roshka. I forgot." His teeth had clenched behind his lips. "He would have told you her name."

The lord of Pirs reached into the chest, brought out a garment of pale green. The cloth was the same fine stuff they wore in Isternes. He held it bunched at his breast as he spoke.

"She was of your height," the suzerain said. "Fine-boned, your build. Her skin was mauve, her hair pale yellow with a green sheen to it. . . ."

"Like Roshka," said Aeriel.

"Like you."

Aeriel said nothing, taken by surprise.

The suzerain nodded. "You have been in the desert. But I can see your complexion was mauve once. Your hair had green in it before it grew so fair. And your eyes are green."

Upon his knees beside the chest, he shook the pale green garment out. Aeriel saw it was a robe such as the lady Syllva had worn.

"If I gave you this gown," said the lord of Pirs, "would you wear it for me?"

Aeriel shook her head. She would have drawn away if the wall had not been at her back. "That is another woman's garb."

The suzerain let the gown fall, rummaged in the chest. He drew out a little wand of ivory. Aeriel had once seen Irrylath's brothers in Isternes using such a thing to turn the pages of a book.

"If I gave you this wand, Aeriel," the suzerain said, "and taught you to read, would you give up that accursèd staff you cling to so?"

Aeriel shook her head again. "It is my walking stick."

The suzerain let the little rod fall. He reached out.

"Aeriel," he whispered. "Take my hand."

Aeriel stared at him, said nothing, feared to move.

The suzerain rose. "I would marry you." He moved toward her and Aeriel edged closer to the door. "I love you," he cried.

"You have known me all of one daymonth."

"I admire you."

"You need an heir."

The quietness of her tone stopped him. His eyes grew narrower, his lips harder.

"Roshka," the suzerain muttered. "Is that what he told you, that I need an heir?"

"He will come of age in a year. He says the high families suspect you."

The suzerain shook his head. "You mistake me. Not even Roshka knows all. It is not an heir I need — I can deal with the high families. It is a wife. I must wed, Aeriel. I must wed."

Aeriel gazed at him steadily. "I will wed you," she answered him at last, "when you have told me your name."

The suzerain began to laugh. The sound was hard and desperate. He wiped his eyes.

"Even that?" he said. "Has my nephew guessed that, too? Well, I will tell you all, and perhaps in the end you will pity me."

Aeriel stood ready to run if she must. She wanted only to be gone from him.

"When Eryka of Esternesse first came to Pirs," he said, "my brother and I both courted her, but she chose him in the end. She bore him children, and I was sick with jealousy. Then the black bird came and told me I might have my heart's desire for only a little payment, a small nothing. It served a white lady, it said, who wished me well.

"But I did not like the look of it. Twice — twice I sent it off. But always it returned, and in between, I dreamed of Eryka. Its mistress whispered in my dreams. At last I went to it and told it yes, take anything, only give me my heart's desire.

"Then it told me, 'Lie down,' and I did so. It said, 'Turn your face to one side,' and I did. Then I felt its claw standing upon my throat and the other upon my cheek — cold, cold as night. It drove its beak into my temple. I felt a burning, and another sensation, as of something thin and thready spinning away from me. Then nothing for a while. When I awoke, the bird was sitting on the window again, watching me.

" 'What have you done?' I said. My temple bled into my hand and my ears rang faintly.

" 'I have taken my lady's payment,' the black bird croaked. 'A little thing. Only your name. You never use it yourself. No one will ever use it again — save my lady, to call you in your dreams. Now you shall have your heart's desire — but do not go riding with your brother on the morn.'

"Then it flew, and I went down. The blood had stopped, but I felt very ill. I did not ride with my brother that day, and that was the day his horse threw him. 'My heart's desire' !"

The suzerain laughed.

"She would not wed me, Eryka. I thought the witch

meant Eryka: my heart's desire. But she meant Pirs. My love killed herself and I got Pirs instead. I did not want it, nor my brother dead. I only wanted Eryka. . . ."

"Then why are you still suzerain in Pirs?" spat Aeriel. "The lorelei of the Mere is a marvelous reader of hearts. Perhaps she read yours better than you knew."

The suzerain stared at her. "I did not need to sell my name to some sorceress to be told if my brother died I should get his lands!" He turned away, pacing vehemently. In a moment his voice grew quieter again.

"For years after, I could not bear the sight of women. I sent them from me or they fled. But then I began to see I must have a wife, to break the witch's hold on me — any woman would do. It did not matter who. But by then, there was not a woman in all Pirs to be found.

"Oh, there were women — somewhere. Underground. I sent my horsemen out hunting them, but the Stag thwarted my huntsmen at every turn. And the women killed themselves rather than be taken. They had all heard of me by then, a nameless man.

"So the lady sent me her seraph, her wingèd son, to help me. She told me she sympathized, would be delighted to fulfill the terms of our agreement. I must have a wife. Oh, yes. Her seraph captured Pirsalon and carried him away. But since then he has been no help. I am less his master than his slave. He makes me send him young boys to feed on.

"I want a wife!" the suzerain cried. "I must have a wife, for the curse holds only until my wedding day."

His skin was drawn, his eyes upon her desperate. His tone grew soft, almost entreating. "The witch promised to free me on my wedding day."

Aeriel let out her breath. All she felt now was dismay. "And you believed her? The lorelei is a maker of empty promises."

She heard hunting horns sounding faintly in the woods beyond the wall. The eyes of the man across from her grew fierce.

"I will give her the Grey Neat, then," he replied. "Her seraph has been hunting it by night, and I by day since I learned of its coming. She wants it for some reason. I will give it to her instead of you—"

He stopped himself abruptly, as though he had bitten his tongue. Aeriel looked at him.

"Did you mean to sell me to the White Witch, then, when first I came here," she asked him, "in trade for your name?"

But her words were cut short by a flapping of wings. She and the suzerain turned. A black bird had alighted on the sill. It stood as tall as Aeriel's forearm, its wings dark as nothing in the white sunlight.

"So," the black bird said, bobbing. "So. This is she? The one my lady sent word of?"

"It is she," the suzerain said. His face had gone ashen beneath the coppery cast of his skin.

"Cht," the black bird clucked, eyeing Aeriel. "Cht. Alive. Why?" Its eye was so black she could find it only by its gleam among the sheenless feathers.

"Tell your lady—" the suzerain began.

"Our lady," the bird clucked, looking at him.

"Our lady," the suzerain snapped, "that I have the

one she told me to look for, but she is mine now, to do with as I choose. She will stay with me under my protection. She will not leave this villa or trouble your mistress. . . ."

"Our mistress."

"She will trouble her no more," the suzerain half shouted. He drew a deep breath, regaining himself. "But she is mine."

The black rhuk coughed, ruffled, hopped down from the window into the room. It was darker than its own shadow. The suzerain fell back.

"That is not what our lady required of you," the bird said, "if you should come upon the one she sought." It reached the robe of pale green silk, hopped onto it, picking at it, toyed with the rod of ivory.

The suzerain stared at it. "Are you a messenger, or the lady herself?" he whispered. "Do you presume to speak for her? Go — take my message to our mistress and be done with you."

He started toward the bird, shaking. Aeriel was not sure whether with terror or rage.

"And tell your lady to give me back my name!"

The rhuk hopped from the crumpled silk. "Nameless man," it muttered, taunting, almost laughing at him.

Then it gave two strong hops and flew, skimming toward the window, toward the light. Aeriel was running forward before she was aware. She gripped her walking stick, brought the great blond knot of the crown down upon the bird, batting it out of the air. It flopped with a squawk to the ground, one limb broken.

"Fool," the suzerain was crying. "Do you think I have not tried to kill them?"

Aeriel brought her staff down upon the bird again. It screeched, floundered away from her. "Do you not know what I am?" it cawed. "Girl, do you not know?"

Aeriel followed. "I can guess." The bird was on the silk. "The White Witch makes her sons' wings from the feathers of your kind."

"Let me alone," the black bird shrieked. "My lady does not wish to harm you, only to speak with you . . . !"

Aeriel swung the walking stick a final time, felt bone beneath the pinions crunch. The bird lay in a heap upon the green silk gown. A trickle of blood came from it, not pale like mortal blood, but dark.

The garment, the stone of the floor smoked a little where the blood touched them, gave off a bitter stench. The suzerain stared at the bird.

"That is some magic staff," he murmured. "I could not kill it with a mace the time I tried." He was silent a moment. "But what does it matter?" he said bitterly. "The lady will send another when her first does not return."

"I shall be a long time gone by then," Aeriel replied, then darted past him and was out the door.

❧❦❧

Aeriel fled down the winding steps, along the narrow parapet. She saw the plum tree across the garden. The suzerain was coming after her, swiftly, but he did not run. He seemed to have no fear of losing her. She found a stair and descended. The suzerain called after her. She dodged into the thick of the trees.

The vegetation of the garden closed around her, and

suddenly she was lost. Panting, out of breath, she found herself at the foot of another stair. She climbed and came onto the terrace where she and the suzerain had watched the dawn. White cloths now lay spread upon the tiles, but no cushions or platters of food.

She spotted the plum tree again from the balustrade suddenly. Turning, she started back toward the steps to descend and sprint for it — when abruptly she halted. Two paces from her lay one corner of the terrace. Long dry, a dark stain marked the flags where the suzerain had cast the wine from her cup a daymonth ago.

The lilies in the square of earth where some of the wine had run stood brittle now, withered and stiff. Two dead butterflies lay beside the sweet juice, and the bones of a lizard now moldering. Aeriel knelt and touched the dust.

"Aeriel," the suzerain said, and she realized he had come onto the terrace. She did not turn, only stared at the lilies, at the flies.

"The rhuk," he said. "What I said in the tower — I meant only to show you what peril you are in. If you leave this place . . ."

He stopped himself, began again.

"The White Witch is hunting you. She calls you a sorceress. She wants you dead. One of her birds came to me that fortnight before I found you, saying I must look for you and take you if I could. Her darkangels are hunting you."

"Erin was right," said Aeriel, running her fingers over the dark-stained stones. "My wine was different, that first feast you gave. You meant to poison me." She touched the lizard's bones again, then raised her eyes to meet the suzerain's.

"I had not seen your eyes," he whispered. "Stay with me. Be my wife. I will ransom the Grey Neat and its fellows for your life. . . ."

Aeriel gazed at him, and hated him. "Leave my gargoyles alone."

The suzerain frowned. "Gargoyles?" he said.

"Greyling and Mooncalf and Catwing," she said. Half her rage was at herself — to have left them to the suzerain's huntsmen all this time. "I freed them from a darkangel in Avaric."

The suzerain shook his head. "What are you talking of? They are wild beasts."

"They are my beasts," said Aeriel fiercely, rising. "They are my beasts."

"You *are* a sorceress," the suzerain whispered. Then his tone grew suddenly fierce as well. "But you *will* wed me."

"You will never have me willing," whispered Aeriel, "and wedding is no wedding but that I say yes."

"You will say yes," the suzerain said, stepping forward. Aeriel raised her staff between them and the suzerain seized it. "You will."

He pulled at it roughly, as though expecting her to yield. Almost without thinking, Aeriel locked her fingers about the dark wood and made her body limp. She let herself fall, rolling backwards as in the desert Orroto-to had taught her. Losing his balance, the suzerain fell.

Aeriel braced her arms, brought her knees to her chest and snapped her legs. The suzerain landed behind her, on his back, his startled cry choked off as the breath was knocked from him. His hands slipped from the staff.

Aeriel sprang to her feet, saw the suzerain rolling painfully to hands and knees, one arm cradling his ribs. He could not seem to catch his breath. Then all at once, he had started to his feet and was lunging at her.

Aeriel fell back, sidestepped and brought the crown of her walking stick around in a low arc, catching him behind the knees. She hauled back on it, hard, yanking his legs from under him.

The suzerain sprawled backwards upon the smooth stone flags. She heard a crack as his head struck the tiles. He lay still then, and Aeriel knew she should run, that instant, but all she could do was stare. She wondered if she had killed him.

She drew a little closer, knelt. He barely breathed. She heard a sudden clanging crash, felt something strike the back of her head. She turned, dazed, saw one of the palace serving boys with a tray in his hands, raising it to land another blow.

She felt movement beside her, saw the suzerain springing up and realized his swoon had been feigned. His one hand closed over the wrist of her hand that held the staff, his other over the staff itself.

Aeriel twisted, tried to get free of him. He was pulling the staff from her. She grabbed at it wildly with her other hand. She felt another crash on the side of her head. The terrace tipped. Solstar went dark.

Dimly, she heard the suzerain shouting, "Stop it, boy. I don't want her dead."

She felt her fingers still about the staff, the suzerain

tugging at it angrily. She opened her eyes and dragged in a breath. All her movements were sluggish. Her mouth tasted of copper.

"Bird," she panted. "Heron, awake."

She kicked at the suzerain, felt his ribs beneath her feet. His hand on her wrist lost its hold, but not his hand that held the staff. She shook the staff with both hands, against his grip.

"Wing," she cried out. "Fly!"

The walking stick shuddered in her grasp. The blond wood of its figurehead shimmered, paled, opened its wings. Aeriel heard the suzerain cry out, heard a shriek, then a crash as the servant boy dropped his tray. The heron launched into the air.

"What is it?" she cried out, hovering awkwardly. "Why can you not call me by my proper name?"

"Erin and Roshka," Aeriel gasped. "Tell them to fly."

She tried to get to her feet, but her bones were all loose inside her skin. She could not balance; the sky lolled and swayed. The suzerain had her by both wrists now. The heron lunged at him. He seized her by one fragile leg. The white bird squawked, stabbed at his fingers.

"Fly!" Aeriel said. All her muscles had lost their strength. "Fly," she muttered, putting her hand to her head.

One leg buckled. She fell sideways. Her elbow struck the stone, then her temple and chin. She heard shouting, a number of feet upon the stone steps now — shod feet. Not servants. Soldiers. Short, whipping sounds, whizzing: bowcords, she realized, arrows flying. The heron must have gotten free.

The stone of the terrace had lost its hardness. It was cold suddenly, and very still. Her cheek seemed to be sinking, slowly, the surface under her gently giving way. Her skin felt no more cohesive than water, or dust. It felt as though her whole body were falling into the stone.

12

PRISONER

Aeriel was aware
of a coldness against her back. Opening her eyes, she
found herself huddled in a tiny space. Through the
barred window in the stone wall behind, morning light
streamed. A wall of masonry rose just in front of her,
with no door, only a tiny chink partway up where no
brick had been placed. To her right, the other wall was
sloping, earth and stone: a hillside, mostly in shadow.

Her arm had been chained to the window wall. She
tried to rise, feeling very stiff. Her legs below the knee
prickled. She flexed and chafed them, then her arm. She
felt dizzy and a little sick. Peering out the window, she
judged it must be a dozen hours since dawn, and she had
not eaten for hours before that. She rubbed her temple
and the back of her head. They were sore.

Two eyes appeared in the chink across from her. "So,
little witch," the suzerain said, "awake at last. How
deep you slept — right through the walling up of this
dead-end passage."

Aeriel realized what the faint odor she detected was:

fresh mortar. "What do you intend to do with me?" she said.

The other laughéd. "I intend to take great good care of you."

"Why have you walled me in?"

"Locks can be picked," the suzerain replied. "But this cell has no door to be unbarred. Little sorceress, I am not completely a fool."

"I am not a sorceress," said Aeriel.

The suzerain smiled. She saw the skin beneath his eyes creasing. "And I suppose your staff did not become a bird? Oh, you were careful to conceal your magic from me. But now, without your staff, I think you can have little power."

Aeriel felt herself shivering — with anger, not with cold. "Oh, it is well you are a nameless man. I can think of nothing to call you that could be fouler than your name."

"Impertinent girl," the man beyond the wall replied. His eyes vanished. He shoved a breadcrust through the chink. "Fill your mouth with that. Perhaps when I have caught my nephew and that boy of yours you will not be so insolent."

Aeriel felt the blood come to her face. "Roshka and Erin are long gone by now."

The suzerain did not seem to hear her. "You will say yes to me in time," he said. "If I leave you alone long enough, you will come to hunger for my company. You *will* say yes."

"Eryka," said Aeriel, "did not say yes."

She heard a cry beyond the wall. The masonry shuddered when he struck it. "Witch," he shouted. "Cursed witch!"

She glimpsed him going, heard his footfalls down the hall. They faded. The cell grew still. Aeriel felt herself continuing to tremble. I could never be your bride, she thought — and then, almost against her will — for I am another's bride.

Irrylath. The memory of him was suddenly all she had to cling to against the suzerain. Her legs felt weak. She sat down abruptly, and felt the shackle yank her wrist. The eyespace gaped vacantly. She was alone.

Aeriel let the crust lie a long time before she touched it. She dusted the dirt from it at last, tasting carefully, but she could detect no taint, no hungerspice. She ate hungrily then. A movement along her shoulder startled her. She turned to see her dustshrimp standing there. Had it been hidden in the folds of her garment all this time?

She offered it a crumb from the crust, but it would not take it, wandered restlessly along her arm. After a little, it crept down to the floor, began exploring the tiny cell, investigating every niche. Finally it found a crack in the earthen wall and there it stayed, refusing all crumbs. It never moved, but seemed perfectly content. Its little eyes on stalks watched her.

Aeriel paced her tiny cell, as much as the chain on her wrist would allow, for she began to grow so weary from lack of movement she felt like sleeping all the time. She practiced stories, without her bandolyn, and watched what she could through the close-barred window. Sometimes the tramp of soldiers' feet and the rattle of horses' hooves came to her, or the groan of the great gates being drawn.

The suzerain came to her cell at odd hours. He informed her how the search proceeded, soldiers combing the garden and grounds, huntsmen riding in the woods. He spoke at her for hours through the crack, pleading with her, sometimes threatening. Aeriel said nothing, refused to look at him. More than once he merely flung her a crust and stalked away.

The daymonth had worn itself half away when she heard a scrabbling behind her, whirled and saw the heron at the window, white against the black noon sky.

"Wing," she cried, then caught herself. "Why are you not with Roshka and Erin?"

The white bird bobbed, clinging awkwardly to the window bars. "Oh, they have not gone. Roshka poled Erin to a little island in the middle of the garden pool. So far, no soldiers have thought to search there."

"But," cried Aeriel, "they will be taken if they remain here. Why did they not fly at once, as I bade?"

"Erin would not go without you."

Aeriel fell silent. "What have they been living on?" she asked at last.

The heron shrugged. "What I can bring them: fruit of the garden, fish. What have you?"

Aeriel sighed. "What the suzerain brings me. Moldy bread. I get what water I can from a trickle down the wall."

The white bird cocked her head. "Only water and bread? No wonder you are so pasty grey. You cannot live on that. Wait here," she said, without thinking, so

Aeriel nearly laughed. The heron flew away in a slow stroking of wings.

Almost at once she had returned, grasping a peach-melon in each foot and a sprig of fat currants in her bill. Aeriel took them and ate. The yellow fruits were deliciously sweet, the currants tender-skinned and tart.

"Your arm is chained," the heron said. Aeriel looked up. She had grown so used to the shackle, she had almost forgotten it. "Hold your wrist over here."

Aeriel did so, bringing it as close to the white bird as she could. Inclining her head, the heron inserted her bill into the keyspace and turned. Aeriel felt a click, and the shackle fell free.

"I could not come before," the heron was saying, "because there was a guard beneath your window, but he and a serving boy stole off into the garden a little while ago."

Aeriel rubbed her wrist. "Is that how you knew where to find me, by the guard?"

"Roshka made a guess. Hist, I must go," the bird said suddenly. "Your guard returns. I will come again when next he goes."

"Tell Erin," cried Aeriel, "tell Erin she must go now, without me. She and Roshka must flee."

The white bird shrugged. "I will tell her. She will not listen. They dare not move now, in broad day, in any case. The suzerain is combing the woods too well."

The heron flew.

Next time the suzerain came with a crust, Aeriel flung it back at him through the niche. He gazed at her through the crack, surprised. "Where is the chain," he cried, "the chain I bound you with?"

"I grew weary of wearing it."

"Someone has given you the key," he cried. Aeriel watched him. He vanished from the niche; she could hear him pacing. "Someone has brought you food and a key," he muttered. "Do my own people betray me? Henceforward, you will have guards posted here as well."

His eyes reappeared, bloodshot, dark-circled.

"How well have you slept these past hours," Aeriel inquired, "with the black bird pecking at your dreams?"

"Guards!" the suzerain shouted. She heard his footsteps down the hall. She felt a moment of panic then, suddenly, realizing that if the suzerain's guards watched her through the crack, the heron could not come to her again.

The fear swiftly faded, though, for though Aeriel had soldiers outside her cell from then on, after the first hour of their gazing in on her uneasily every now and again, she heard them move off down the hall. Their murmured talk drifted in to her, and the rattle of counters as they played at dice.

The suzerain returned no more. Her food was brought her by the guards. Whenever the heron came, bringing fruit, she and Aeriel kept their voices low. Aeriel ate the fruit, and felt her strength beginning to return.

The daymonth rolled on. Aeriel exchanged messages with Erin and the prince by means of the white bird. Roshka sent word that he had found a hollow upon the isle, all overgrown with bower brush. Investigating, he had discovered a tunnel, running deep, beneath the pool. He and Erin had begun to explore it, wanting to find where it led.

Shadows grew longer. Solstar hung five dozen hours from setting. The white bird came to Aeriel then, saying Roshka and Erin had gone down into the hollow again but had not yet emerged. Aeriel felt a twinge of fear. They had never been gone so long before.

The twinge became a tremor when the heron came again, perhaps a dozen hours later, and said Erin and the prince were still below. Aeriel felt a gathering despair when, just before Solset, the white bird appeared a third time with no word. She began to give them up for lost.

Not long after, the suzerain came. She heard him roaring at his soldiers for playing dice in the crosshall instead of keeping watch outside her cell. His eyes appeared in the niche.

"I have come, little witch, to bid you farewell."

Aeriel looked up, left off gnawing the last crust the guards had brought her. Her stomach clenched. The suzerain smiled.

"I have decided you are more pain to me than you are worth. The white lady has told me she will give me back my name when I capture your gargoyles. . . ."

Aeriel felt a cold sweat cover her. "She is a liar. She will never give you back your name."

"You are a witch," the suzerain cried. "I'll have no witches for my wife. I saw your birdshape at the window. Last time it came to you, I watched. Well," he laughed fiercely, "it will find you no more."

Aeriel wheeled. Outside her window, one of the villa guards sat suspended from a rope. He reached into a sack that hung from his belt and drew out a brick. Aeriel stared as he slapped a trowel of mortar into place, fitted the brick, and reached for another.

"You will kill me," she gasped. "Brick up that vent and I will have no air."

"I do not care," the suzerain said. "I have no more need of you."

"Then let me go," she cried.

The suzerain laughed. "I cannot. The mistress will not allow it."

"Kill me yourself, then, coward," Aeriel shouted.

"Ah, little witch," the suzerain replied, "you would like that, wouldn't you — to have me tear down this wall and come at you? But I have tasted enough of your magical strength. I'll not grapple with you again."

Outside, the guard laid the last brick in the window. All light in the room was suddenly gone, save that crack of brightness around the suzerain's eyes. She saw him hold something to the niche, begin to shove. The light was no more than a knifeblade now. Aeriel cried out, rushed at him. She heard his laughter beyond the niche.

"Farewell, little witch," the suzerain said, and fitted the wedge into place.

❧

Aeriel stood in darkness. The cry died in her throat. The wall was sealed. She felt along it, frantically, and found the wedge closing the chink. She pushed at it, tried to lever it, but it was stuck fast.

She groped her way to where the window had been. Already the air was growing stale. She felt the bars, the new bricks beyond. The mortar between the blocks was soft. She scratched it with her fingernails and shoved at the bricks between the bars, but they must have been braced from without, for they would not give.

Panting, gasping for breath, Aeriel sank down against the wall. She could not stand. Her limbs trembled. How much time had passed? Her head was whirling; her chest felt tight. She pressed her cheek against the cool stone wall, staring into the airless dark.

A very long time later, she saw a light. It was small, very far away — though strangely, it shone plainly in front of the wall of the tiny cell, illuminating it. Pale yellow, like a flame — it was moving nearer, slowly growing. Then at last it stood before her, tall and flickering, and Aeriel realized it had a human shape.

"Eoduin," she gasped. "Eoduin."

The other smiled. "You have not forgotten me in all these daymonths."

"Eoduin," cried Aeriel. "I can't get out."

"I cannot stay," the maiden said. "I only came to waken you."

"Waken me?" Aeriel shook her head. "I have not slept."

"You have," the other said, "for hours now. The last crust the guard brought you was drugged."

Aeriel gasped for breath. "He has shut me in. . . ."

"List," said Eoduin. "You are not trapped. The

176

suzerain does not mean to let you die. He only means to frighten you."

"The air is bad," choked Aeriel.

The maiden shook her head. "It is not. That is fear making your chest so tight. The drug has worn off. Breathe deep."

Aeriel drew breath slowly, deeply — and strangely felt no tight band about her ribs, no more trembling in her limbs. She could breathe, and the air in the cell was cooler now, more damp.

"The mortar," said Aeriel. "It has cracked and is letting in the air."

The other shook her head again. "The window is sealed, as is the chink. The drug in that crust was meant to make you sleep so deep you could lie sealed in this room a dozen hours and not suffocate. But you ate only a little of the crust. If this tiny room were truly sealed, you would be dead long before the suzerain came to dig you out.

"But there is a source of air to this chamber that the suzerain does not know about. This new air you feel comes from that source. You must find it. Awake; awake. Make haste, or you will lose the light."

"Awake?" said Aeriel. "I am awake. . . ."

Eoduin was receding from her, growing smaller and more pale. "Then open your eyes."

Aeriel blinked. Eoduin was gone, but the little cell was light still, with a dim glow — but it was white light not yellow. Even that faint illumination made her squint. Just above her, before the cell's blocked window fluttered a tiny creature no bigger than her hand.

Its body was fingerlike and soft-looking. It had no legs. Two pairs of gauzy wings, tear-shaped, gave off a clear, cool light. Each soft wingbeat intensified the glow briefly. It fluttered about the bricked window, as if searching for something.

After a time, it seemed to give up on the window, fluttered about the far corner of the cell, following cracks. It examined the blocked chink thoroughly. Aeriel tried the window and the eyespace again; neither gave. The creature had no fear of her, fluttered slowly, ceaselessly about. Then it went to the earthen wall, exploring the crevices one by one.

Aeriel drew near the wall. The air in that corner seemed cooler, fresher. Standing very still, she felt a slight current against her cheek. Aeriel scrabbled up the earthen wall. There was a vent there, somewhere.

She remembered her dustshrimp suddenly. The lampwing hovered above its niche. Aeriel gave a dismayed cry, catching sight of it, then checked herself. It was not her dustshrimp she saw, but only its shell — split down the back and empty now, as though it had simply been housing some other creature that had only now gotten free.

The lampwing circled Aeriel's head. She saw that it had many whiskers. Its eyes were set on tiny stalks. "Are you my dustshrimp?" she said softly.

The gauzy-winged thing fluttered away, back to the wall. Aeriel saw, just where ceiling and wall met, a crevice. It was only two handspans long and half of one high, but the air flowing through it was clean. Aeriel shoved at the dirt, scooping it toward her. The lampwing fluttered about the enlarging hole.

Aeriel dug. The lampwing flitted through. Aeriel scrambled, forcing her shoulders against the give of the earth. A hard stone ceiling formed the top of the passage. Aeriel wriggled. Echoes of sliding earth told her the space beyond was large.

The loose soil gave unexpectedly. She found herself sliding down a soft incline. She came to rest on a cool stone floor. The lampwing fluttered in the space above. Aeriel straightened, dusted the dirt from her. It took her a moment to catch her breath. Blinking, she stood up and peered around.

She stood in a natural chamber of stone. The gauzewing's light was very dim, illuminating only a small sphere of air around it. Aeriel caught glimpses of walls twenty paces distant. They looked smooth, as if water-carved, but the floor beneath her feet was dry.

The lampwing fluttered off across the chamber. Aeriel followed it. It disappeared through a slender opening in the far end of the room. Aeriel saw similar openings on either side, but the current of fresh air seemed strongest from this one. Aeriel turned herself sideways and slipped through.

A tunnel lay on the other side, narrow and dark, the walls jutting. The lampwing flitted on ahead. Aeriel followed. In time, the tunnel opened into a larger chamber. The lampwing hovered a moment, then chose an exit.

This passage was wider, but very low. Aeriel had to walk slowly, half-bent. Her back grew painful, her legs cramped. The lampwing pulled farther and farther ahead of her. Aeriel had to trot, bent double, to catch it again.

Again the tunnel opened out, into a chamber much bigger than before. Aeriel stood upright, stretching, until her back creaked. She bent to rub her ankles and calves. The lampwing hovered overhead. She sank to her knees a moment to rest. She had not eaten since that last, drugged crust hours ago. It must be night by now, she thought. Solstar must have been long set.

The lampwing began to flutter on. It seemed to fly more urgently now. Reluctantly, Aeriel stumbled after it. Gazing at the height of the ceiling above, she had a sense of being deep underground. They would have to climb again to reach the air.

Halfway across the broad hall, she stumbled. Looking down, she saw a tiny pick, all made of pale metal, heavy enough when she picked it up, but short and squat, as if made for a hand smaller, squarer than hers.

She thrust it into the pocket of her robe and followed the lampwing through a fold in the rock. Here the tunnels changed. They seemed for the most part natural, irregular, but they ran straighter, as though widened in places. The floor seemed flatter and more smooth.

And the corridor was wide. Aeriel could stretch her arms and still not touch both walls at once. The ceiling was not high, though. She could touch it without un-crooking her arm. The lampwing fluttered on ahead.

The floor began to slant downward. Aeriel walked with one hand trailing the wall beside her. Cross passages appeared at intervals. They, too, ran straight — like hallways in a house, or village streets. She fingered the small, heavy pick in the hem pocket of her robe, and wondered what manner of people could have lived here. What had Roshka called them? The underfolk.

With a start, she realized the feel of the stone beneath her hand had changed. Glancing at the wall, she saw carvings running in a broad band. They were all of eels: some smooth, some scaled, rilled or gilled, and some with fins. Now and again, the lampwing's light gleamed on a glass-smooth jewel forming an eye.

The band rose in arcs over the doorways she passed. After a while, the eels turned to fishes, then dainty ledge-swallows with forking tails. Later, lizards, then scarabs and crayfishes, salamanders and skinks. Tiny bats seemed to skim along the stone, their wings so delicately carved, Aeriel was afraid they would tear if she touched them.

They were all creatures that lived underground, as the underdwellers had done. But where were the underdwellers now? Gone away, the prince had said.

Not long afterwards, the carvings upon the walls grew rougher and finally ceased. The tunnel slanted more sharply down, growing tortuous. Aeriel had to slow her pace. Hunger exhausted her. Fatigue weighted her limbs. Her eyes began slipping shut as she walked. Her throat was very dry.

The lampwing, unencumbered, drew ahead. The hall curved sharply right, then left again. Aeriel stumbled into the narrow bend, finding herself in darkness suddenly. The lampwing's light was visible only dimly beyond the bend. Aeriel heard movement ahead of her, low down in the dark. A voice, slow at first as from exhaustion, muttered,

"What's that?" Then harshly, whispered: "A light — a light!"

Another voice answered, muffled, no more than a noise in the throat.

The first voice croaked, "Get up. I saw a light."

"No light," the other muttered. "You're dozing, a dream."

"There, there," the first voice hissed. "Around the bend. You are the one who's dozing. Get up!"

A surprised intake of breath, the sound of something scrabbling to its feet. Aeriel was so startled, so weary, so used to moving and the slant of the floor so steep that she did not stop. She collided with something, heard a cry of alarm. She cried out herself. Something struck at her. She grabbed at it.

"What is it?" The first voice, speaking now for the first time above a whisper.

"Run, Erin! It has me by the arm — I can't get free."

Aeriel recognized the voices then, finally. Giddiness and exhaustion welled in her. She started to laugh. Bent double, leaning upon the arm she held, she could not stop.

"No, I won't leave you," cried Erin, beginning to flail at her. "What is it — a cavern sprite?"

The three of them stumbled around the tunnel's bend into the light of the lampwing again. The prince was dragging her, struggling to break free while the dark girl, grimacing, dazzled by the light, scratched and tore at her.

"Leave off," gasped Aeriel, breathless, releasing Roshka to catch Erin's wrists. "Leave off," she said again. "It's only me. It's Aeriel."

The dark girl peered, then stared, stopped struggling. Roshka shielded his eyes from the light. The lampwing was paces ahead of them now.

"Aeriel," Erin whispered. "Aeriel, how?" Now it was she who clung to the fair girl's arm.

"I dug my way out of the suzerain's cell — but hurry, or we shall lose the light."

The lampwing's glow had grown very distant and dim. They hurried down the corridor, not speaking at first. Erin kept one hand on Aeriel's sleeve, as though afraid she might abruptly vanish.

The corridor had become completely natural now. It was narrow, full of twists. The ceiling sometimes rose in cavernous cracks. Soon they caught up with the light-bearer, and Aeriel could see her companions better. Roshka kept staring at her.

"We were trying to come to you," he stammered. "I found a tunnel once, when I was young, in one of the cellars near the kitchen. I thought the passage under the isle might lead to it. But the way kept turning, and there were so many branches. We lost all sense of the way; then our torches gave out."

He fell silent a moment. Aeriel glanced at Erin. The dark girl walked beside her, saying nothing. She was weeping. Aeriel put one arm around her, kissed her and drew her close.

"I don't know how long we've been below," the prince said.

"Six dozen hours," said Aeriel. "Solstar is long set by now. You must be famished."

Erin shook her head, wiping her eyes. "We have not starved. Roshka brought provisions."

"You have food?" Aeriel cried. She felt suddenly weak. Her stomach was a knotted lump. "The last I ate was a drugged breadcrust before Solset."

The prince lifted something he had been carrying, began to rummage in it. Aeriel had paid no attention before, but she recognized it now: the yellow silk wrapping her bandolyn. Roshka drew out two green greatfruit and a handful of leatherstalk.

"All we have left."

Aeriel took them gratefully. The green flesh of the greatfruit was slippery and full of juice, the leatherstalk tough and sweet. Aeriel nearly choked suddenly. All that was left, Roshka had said? She snatched her pack back from him and sorted through it desperately.

She felt her bandolyn, the lump of ambergris, the three apricok seeds. . . . Her panic subsided as she felt the two remaining apricoks. Roshka and Erin had not found them, or had left them alone. Aeriel sighed with relief. She had promised the keeper to save that fruit.

The path began to slant upward now. The way grew rough. They followed the lampwing through the rising corridors. The ceiling rose seemingly endlessly, lost in darkness overhead. Aeriel had the feeling they were higher now than at any point since entering the caves.

Their path made a sudden rise, then a sharp, close turn. The lampwing fluttered around the bend, and its light seemed suddenly to disappear. Aeriel scrambled after it, rounding the turn, and saw an archway into another corridor.

She stopped, staring. Two lights flickered in the dark ahead. She felt a rush of cool air along her cheek, heavy with the scent of forests and the night. One light held fixed, twinkling. A star.

The archway was an opening. Aeriel found herself upon a steep hillside. Forests lay below. The second light, the lampwing, fluttered on, but Erin and Roshka halted beside her. They stood a moment, gazing about them, breathing in the deliciously redolent and heady air.

13

THE
LIGHTBEARERS

The hillside was high, rising above the other slopes. Oceanus hung like a great, cloudy eye in the heavens before them. Far below, beyond the trees, Aeriel spotted the suzerain's villa, its white stone gleaming in the pale earthshine.

Something stirred near the mouth of the cave. Erin started and shrank back against Aeriel. Roshka's hand went to his sash, though he wore no weapon. But Aeriel recognized the snowy form. The long neck lifted, untucking the bill from beneath one wing. She flexed her wings.

"Heron," Aeriel cried.

"At last," the heron sighed, rising. "I expected you hours since. Here is your staff."

Aeriel spotted a dark length of wood beneath the white bird's feet. She snatched it up with an astonished cry — so swiftly the other danced, getting out of the way.

"Where . . . ?" Aeriel began.

The heron shrugged. "Your suzerain very carelessly left it unguarded. I thought you might have need of it."

Aeriel ran her fingers over the dark, knotted wood. "How did you know where to wait for us?"

The white bird fluffed her feathers, preened. "I am a messenger," she said, "and can follow any path that is. I can also find the beginning and end of any path. This is the nearest exit to the ways beneath the suzerain's villa. I knew you must emerge here, if ever you emerged."

Aeriel saw Erin's expression sour. "How delightful to know you were so sure of our welfare." The heron turned and looked at her. "Well, you might have come in search of us," cried Erin. "You might . . ."

"Underground?" the white bird exclaimed. "I am a heron, not a bat."

The dark girl began to say something more, but Roshka moved between them.

"Look."

Aeriel followed the line of his arm. There was a commotion on the grounds of the villa below. Aeriel saw guardsmen, figures running, and in the stillness of the night air, caught faintly shouts and cries. The heron tested her wings.

"They seem to have discovered your escape," she said. "We had best be gone. He will be sending his huntsmen, I imagine, soon."

Aeriel heard a dull booming. It drowned out the last of the white bird's words. She heard Roshka catch in his breath.

"The gong," he whispered. "The gong of Pirs."

"What is that?"

The prince did not turn. His voice was tight. "In bygone times it was used to summon the people to arms, or the suzerain home from the hunt if some pressing message had arrived. But my uncle has for it another use — it is all he uses it for now."

Aeriel glanced at him.

"To summon the darkangel."

The heron launched into the air. "Come," she said. "We must away. I can show you paths hidden from huntsmen, but not from icari, I fear."

Erin was tugging at Aeriel's arm. "Come," she bade her. "Aeriel, come."

Aeriel stood only a moment more, watching the soldiers swarming the grounds below. They seemed so distant now, so small. She turned with the others then as they followed the heron down the opposite hillside.

They ran through starlight, through earthshine, through shadows of the trees. The white bird glided ahead of them, low over the hills. Sometimes, far in the distance, Aeriel thought she saw the lampwing fluttering.

The heron guided them through hollows between hills, behind rises and along riverbeds where no water flowed. But always behind, they heard followers — sometimes nearer, sometimes less near: horse hooves, the riders' shouts, horns calling one another through the trees.

Once they crouched in a dry ravine while a dozen riders thundered past. Once, far behind them, they saw two parties meet, one led by the suzerain upon his tall black steed. The heron was just leading them over a saddle between two hills.

"There is no other path here," she said. "Hist, quickly — do not stand against the sky."

Then turning, looking back, Aeriel heard one of the riders cry out, saw him point toward them. The suzerain gave a shout, spurring his mount. The horsemen surged forward. Aeriel bolted with the others. She could hear the horses plunging through the thick undergrowth after them. Her breath grew very short.

But before long, they seemed to have lost their pursuers. Aeriel thought she heard wauling, strange yelping and belling in the distance behind, but that noise, too, faded hastily away. She and the others ran on then, in silence, for as long as they could. Then they slept.

Erin kept watch, then Roshka. When Aeriel awoke a few hours later and they pressed on, she realized groggily that they had let her sleep. They stumbled on. The night rolled by. Sometimes the noise of huntsmen sounded again in the distance behind. They ran, and slept only when they could run no more.

They had no food or water now, but Roshka showed them certain stones in the dry riverbeds that were not stones at all, but plants with smooth, waxy rinds that could be breached with rocks. They lived on those and what fruit they found.

Abruptly, the land over which they traveled began to grow barren. Roshka explained that they had left the suzerain's private estates. "This is what the rest of Pirs looks like," the crown prince muttered, "since my uncle came to power." After that, they heard no further noise of pursuit, and Aeriel prayed they had lost the huntsmen for good.

Nightshade was three-quarters past when she glimpsed behind them, low in the sky, some of the stars winking out. Little patches vanished, reappeared: a blot of darkness moving against the dark.

Aeriel's blood stopped in her veins. She remembered another time she had seen a darkangel. Standing upon the high steeps of Terrain, she had watched him, far in the distance over the white plain of Avaric, blotting the stars as he moved across them, coming to bear her way.

Aeriel turned to Roshka, the breath catching in her throat. She reached to take his arm, struggled to speak — but then Erin took hold of Aeriel's arm suddenly, murmured, "Look."

She said it so softly, with such absence of fear that Aeriel was startled, did not at first understand. Then she saw that the dark girl was gazing ahead, not behind. Before them, the heron was alighting.

They had just crested a hill. A broad, steep-sided valley opened before them, winding away into the distance ahead. Filling all the valley from side to side, flowing away from them, lay a river of moving stars.

A star floated past her, drifting down toward its fellows. They were lampwings, Aeriel realized, a few fluttering from the hills here and there to join the flood. There were thousands of them, a thousand thousand, more — all flying, all alight in a vast, airborne stream.

Far in the distance, a great blaze was burning. Aeriel could not see it, only its glare against the sky. It was toward this that the river of wingèd things was streaming, following the valley's curves.

"The lightbearers," cried Roshka, halting. "They

have returned. There have been none in Pirs since the seraph came."

His words jarred Aeriel. She too had halted. She started now, remembering.

"So many," Erin was murmuring. "So bright."

Aeriel cut her off. "The darkangel . . . ," she started, but even as she spoke, its cry tore the air. Erin and Roshka wheeled. The heron took wing, sailing down into the stream of lampwings. She floated among them, white in their glow.

"Quickly," Aeriel cried. "We must do the same."

She shoved Erin ahead of her down the hillside, heard Roshka following. Lampwings surrounded them as they reached the valley floor. Aeriel looked back, but the wingèd stars obscured her view. She could not see where the darkangel was.

She heard it scream suddenly, nearly upon them. Erin cried out, flung herself flat to the ground. Aeriel felt the wind of the darkangel's wings. The lampwings wheeled and darted, then flowed on, unperturbed. She had seen it, swooping high overhead, its face turned, one arm shielding its eyes from the lampwings' light.

"It didn't . . . ," Erin began, picking herself up. The fall had knocked the breath from her. "It went by."

Aeriel helped her. "It didn't see us," she said. "Darkangels have keen eyes for the dark, but they cannot bear the light." She stopped and pulled Roshka to his feet. "But come, hurry," she said. "We are safe only so long as we stay with the stream."

They hurried on.

"It did not see us," the prince murmured, "but somehow it must have known we are nearabouts."

"Does it hear us?" whispered Erin.

Aeriel shook her head. "Perhaps. Smell us, perhaps. Or senses us by some means we cannot know."

They plodded on, for hours — Aeriel could not keep track. They dared not sleep. The heron skimmed ghostlike ahead of them. The lightbearers floated and darted all around. The darkangel's scream severed the stillness occasionally — before them, behind them, savage and shrill.

Aeriel passed her hand over her eyes. She had been half dozing as she trudged. "Look," she whispered, shaking Erin, "ahead of us. What is it?"

The others roused themselves. Far ahead, the hills parted. Upon a steep, jutting rise in the valley stood a great tower, its crown all ablaze with firelight. It was that blaze which threw the glow upon the sky toward which the lampwings headed.

"The Torch," whispered Roshka. "The Torch is lit."

As they drew near, Aeriel saw the tower was made of black stone. Its blaze would have rivaled Solstar. All the valley was awash with its light. They came to the outcropping and climbed the brief, steep slope to the tower's base.

All round the tower the lampwings swirled, circling one another in triplets and pairs. The heron alighted a little way off. Aeriel and her companions sank down, exhausted, at the tower's foot.

"But she said," Roshka was murmuring, "the peasant woman said it was not to be until the rightful heir . . ."

He passed his hand over his eyes suddenly, as if realizing how weary he was.

They watched the dancing of the lampwings. They had not heard the vampyre's scream since coming into the tower's light. Aeriel guessed it could not bear such brightness, and sighed, relieved they had lost it. Glancing at Erin and Roshka, she saw they had dozed against the stone.

Aeriel took off her traveling cloak and laid it over Erin, who shivered. She watched the dance, hardly aware how many hours passed. The lampwings began to drift apart. One by one, they ceased to spiral about the tower, fluttered aimlessly — and much more slowly, as though exhausted. The light in their wings began to dim.

Aeriel cried out then, for the lampwings were falling, floating slowly to the ground. A few settled on her shoulders, many others at her feet. The heron watched her from its perch upon the rocks. Aeriel knelt, peering closer at the lampwings.

They crept about the ground now, like worms, for they had no legs. Their wings bobbed uselessly. Those that had landed on Aeriel's shoulders cast themselves off again, fluttering to earth.

Each dug a depression in the dirt, and there it lay, struggling slowly until it had laid a pearl the size of a chickseed on the ground. And then each gradually ceased to move. The light in their wings went out.

Aeriel felt upon her shoulder a stirring, saw a lampwing there, moving feebly. She made to brush it off so that it might flutter to the ground as the others had done, but it clung to her, without legs, by some means she could not fathom.

She took it gently into her hands. Its body was yielding, like the supplest glove. Its wings were velvety and slightly warm, rubbing off a silver dust upon her fingers. The lampwing undulated, turning over and over in her upturned hands. She saw a pearl upon her palm.

"Are you my dustshrimp?" she asked it softly.

The tiny creature was hardly moving. Its wings darkened, began to cool. Aeriel cupped her hands, breathing upon it, tried to warm it, but its body stiffened and at last grew still. One brittle wing broke off in her hand. Aeriel's vision blurred. She had to blink.

She set the little thing upon the ground. The pearl upon her palm glistened, while all around her the lightbearers drifted to earth. She put the pearl away in her breast. Her head was singing. Her limbs trembled from lack of sleep.

Roshka and Erin were awake. She saw that presently, turning back to the tower. They blinked and stared, as if puzzled they had slept. Erin threw off Aeriel's traveling cloak, stood, stretching like a cat. Roshka yawned. Aeriel turned away from the tower, and started violently.

"I have a shadow," she whispered, staring. It lay like a black swatch upon the ground. "I have a shadow in this light." She turned back to Erin and to Roshka. The prince was stretching now. "I have a shadow," she cried.

Erin looked up, began to speak. Then she gasped suddenly. She cried out, gazing past Aeriel, down the slope. Her one hand clutched at Roshka's arm; the other pointed.

"Aeriel, Aeriel," she cried.

Aeriel turned, looked, and felt her heart constrict to a pinprick within her breast. A stone obstructed her throat. Blood cold as wellwater trickled through her. She gazed, not even breathing. A figure stood in the darkness of her shadow at the bottom of the slope.

꒰ᵔᵕᵔ꒱

She heard Roshka behind her cry out and scramble to his feet. She threw out a hand to keep him back. He and Erin were both behind her, higher on the slope. Their shadows did not fall as far. The tower, looming above them, cast no shadow on the rise. The lampwings all had fallen now.

Aeriel's shadow stretched before her like a road. The figure at the end of it stepped forward, slowly, keeping to her shade. It wore rags of what had once been finery. Its skin was grey as deadwood, colorless. It held one arm across its eyes, hiding them from the light.

With the other hand, it groped ahead of it, seeming to sense Aeriel's shadow by feel. Whenever its fingers neared the light, they drew back. The black wings draping its shoulders stirred. It took another step.

Roshka threw himself flat to the ground, pulling Erin with him. She saw their shadows shrink. "Aeriel," he cried, "get back; get down — it follows your shade."

"I know that, Roshka." The steadiness of her own voice surprised her.

"It's the seraph," Erin screamed. "We must fly!"

"Where to?" asked Aeriel. She did not turn; she could not take her eyes from the creature groping toward her. "A quarter of the night remains. It is three dozen hours till Solstarrise. We stand in the brightest light there is, and still it comes."

She felt very cold, and strangely immobile — too exhausted to flee another step. Her limbs felt as though they were turning to dust.

"It has found me by my shadow, and there is nowhere left to run."

"No," whispered Roshka. "Come away."

"You two must flee," said Aeriel. "It has not come for you."

She saw Erin's shadow on the ground lengthen suddenly, heard the dark girl scrambling up.

"I will not let it take you," she panted. "Let it have me instead of you."

Her shadow darted, caught something from the ground. Aeriel heard a stone whistle past — she saw it gash the darkangel's arm. The creature did not flinch, did not react in any way. Its grey-white flesh refused to bleed.

"Erin, no!" Aeriel heard Roshka cry.

She could not take her eyes from the grey thing before her. The shade of Roshka's hand caught Erin's wrist. Their shadows struggled. The dark girl seemed to be trying to rush forward.

The darkangel came on. Oddly familiar: it was so like that other darkangel she had known, who had carried her away from the steeps of Terrain. That icarus had been beautiful — strangely vibrant, otherworldly fair. Erin was screaming now, Roshka shouting above her screams,

"Don't look at its eyes — Aeriel! They say it can kill you with its eyes. . . ."

One arm was still flung across its face. Aeriel saw it grimacing, as though even the little light that reached it in her shade was painful to it. The other arm groped for her, its black wings poised.

She remembered vividly that other darkangel, spreading his wings to her upon the steeps of Terrain to reveal a face so beautiful she had lost all nerve, all will, and would have fallen before him, begging only to serve him or die.

The seraph of Pirs stood within reach of her now, still in shadow. She clutched her walking stick, her heart sick with pounding, and wondered if the seraph's stare would kill her before she could land a blow.

The creature took its arm from its eyes. For a moment, the lids remained closed, and Aeriel saw with a start that its face was grey, more skull than flesh, the muscle all fallen away under transparent skin.

Slowly, the icarus opened its eyes: colorless, strangely flattened, like a fish's, or buttons of glass. Only the pupils were black, deep, seemed to go down forever into darkness. For an instant, she almost felt she could grow lost in them, floating in their emptiness until she, too, became nothing.

But the moment passed. After, Aeriel found herself strangely unmoved. No tug of power now, no surge of weakness in her limbs. Not even fear moved in her anymore, only revulsion. For unlike that young, unfinished icarus that she had saved in Avaric, this was a true darkangel — an empty thing standing before her now. It had no soul.

The creature fixed its gaze on her. Aeriel jerked her staff up, holding it heel first like a throwing stick. The creature's expression changed suddenly, from snarl to frown, then blank surprise. It grimaced then, staring at her. Its lips parted. It opened its mouth — and then it screamed.

The darkangel threw its arms up in front of its face, ducking, as though the sight of her eyes was too hideous to bear. It shrieked and wheeled away from her, choking, as if the air about her were somehow poison to it.

Aeriel stood frozen, her walking stick half raised, motionless in surprise. The witch's son stumbled away from her, down her shadow's path, its black wings beating erratically. When it reached the end of her shade, it leapt from the slope, pinions thrashing.

They caught their rhythm now at last, carrying it aloft. It sped away above the hills, its screams filling the night. At last they faded. The air settled again, dark, fluid and cool. The valley grew once more still.

❧❦❧

When Aeriel found that she could move again, she put down her arm. It seemed to dangle from her shoulder. Her walking stick hung loosely in her hand. The prince came up behind her.

"You said you were no sorceress."

She shook her head, still gazing after the icarus, though he was long gone now. "I am not."

"You banished the seraph," cried Roshka. "What did you do?"

Again she shook her head. "Nothing. I looked at it."

She turned away and went past him, past Erin. The dark girl gazed after her. Aeriel sank down beside the tower, pulled on her traveling cloak, for she was cold, very cold.

"I have no shadow," she whispered suddenly. She searched the ground for it, but could find it nowhere. Her head throbbed dully. She could not understand. "I have no shadow anymore."

Erin had gotten to her feet. "What is this place? she demanded. "This tower?"

She spoke to Aeriel, but it was Roshka who answered. "We call it the Torch, and it marks the road into Terrain. Once it blazed, they say, with a light like Solstar. But it grew dim over the years, because people no longer traveled the roads on pilgrimage." He broke off a moment, gazed upward. "Now it is lit again."

A thought stirred in Aeriel. "When I came across the Sea-of-Dust," she said, "I landed at a tower like this. Its keeper told me there were many such, all connected somehow, so that what fed one flame fed all." She remembered the apricok seed he had cast into the light, making it blaze.

Roshka was speaking. "But the seeing woman said — said all Pirs was in darkness, because of my uncle and his seraph. The light would never return, she said, till the right heir returned — I thought she meant returned to power. I am the right heir, for my sister is dead. . . ."

He looked at Aeriel all at once, very hard, his green eyes wide and searching. She gazed at him, and he snatched his gaze back suddenly. She knew what had come into his mind just then, as surely as if she had thought it herself.

The silence around them was cool and still. Then the

night wind rose, stirring the air, sweeping the dead lampwings away. They lifted and swirled like transparent leaves. Only the pearls remained.

Weariness crept over Aeriel. She leaned against the tower. "I must sleep."

She closed her eyes, lay down, rested her forehead against one arm. She heard the prince exclaiming suddenly. "Pearls! Erin, look —" as though he had only just then noticed them.

Erin came, kneeling by Aeriel. The dark girl touched her and said something, but Aeriel was already drifting into sleep.

When she awoke, it was to see Roshka gathering pearls. He had taken the turban from his head and tied the corners up. His hair was short and fair. Erin was helping him.

"Why are you doing that?" Aeriel asked, sitting up.

"These are seed pearls," Roshka said.

"They are lampwings' eggs."

The prince shook his head. "The lightbearers spring from the Sea-of-Dust. There are no young within these pearls, only mineral salt. . . ."

"Corundum," Aeriel said.

"We must gather them," said Roshka, "and take them to the high families. Where these pearls are sown, the land will grow fertile again."

Erin left off gathering and brought Aeriel something to eat. Aeriel sat munching the dry, bitter lichen without interest, when abruptly she stopped, shielding her eyes.

Grey figures had appeared upon the valleyside — not human: they were four-footed.

"My gargoyles," she cried.

Greyling and Catwing bounded toward her down the slope, their strangely jointed limbs flexing and buckling, their skeletal bodies moving with an eerie grace. The other figure held off, mincing skittishly, a nest of horns upon its head.

"Mooncalf," Aeriel called to it. "Mooncalf."

Then Greyling and Catwing were upon her, panting and rolling and nipping each other. Aeriel knelt, ran her hands along their bony hides. They yipped and whined. Dry blood was on the greyling's lip, on one of the catwing's paws. Aeriel halted suddenly.

"What have you done?" she whispered, taking the greyling's head into her hands, and then the catwing's paw. "What have you done?"

The blood was old and not their own.

"They have brought us a mount," cried Roshka. He whistled.

Aeriel looked up and saw the mooncalf descending the slope, herding before it a tall black horse, saddled and bridled, but riderless. It whinnied at the prince's cry.

"Nightwalker!" The mooncalf skittered away, but the suzerain's mount came on, nuzzled the prince. He stroked the long crest of its neck. "Nightwalker. My father's steed."

"Mooncalf," said Aeriel again, softly.

Erin stroked the other two, picked the blood from their fur. The mooncalf came nearer, approaching at last. It touched its grey nose to Aeriel. Roshka took the bit and bridle from the horse's mouth, the saddle from its back.

"Nightwalker will carry us when we go," he said. "The high families lie north of us now, and a little east."

Aeriel did not reply. She let the hours of the fortnight pass in silence. She tuned her bandolyn, thinking of the maidens' rime, and wondered how far it was to Orm. The heron disappeared into her staff, saying she was weary and would rest.

Roshka gathered his pearls to fill Nightwalker's saddlebags. Erin foraged for stonelike waterworts. Aeriel collected seeds and lichens for their food, while the black horse and the mooncalf grazed the barren valleyside. Disappearing from time to time, the other gargoyles seemed to do their own hunting.

The fortnight passed. At last dawn broke in a white glare down the valley's length. The light of the tower grew dimmer in comparison. Roshka saddled and bridled Nightwalker.

"Why do you stare at me?" Aeriel asked him at last. She sat, turned a little away from him, sipping from a stonewort. "You have been gazing at me ever since we came to this place."

The prince quickly cast down his eyes. He tightened Nightwalker's girth. "I did not mean to stare."

"You think I am she, don't you?" said Aeriel. "Because the Torch is lit. Because I have green eyes." She looked at him. "The suzerain thought I resembled your mother."

The young man gave up his pretense of adjusting the girth. "Your hair," he said softly, "and your skin are very like mine, though greatly more pale. Your voice is like mine, your build." He came around the black horse then. "Even your name —"

"My name is Aeriel."

"Some slaver's name for you," Roshka exclaimed. "Your own name is Erryl, my sister's name."

"Bomba gave me my name," Aeriel answered, more forcefully than she had meant. "My old nurse in the syndic's house. I loved her well." She fell silent a moment. "Your sister is dead."

The prince knelt down across from her. "Eryka's maid said she saw my sister carried away. . . ."

"By a white bird?" cried Aeriel. "I come from Terrain. I was born there — I must have been. I have no memory of any kith. I have no kith, and my name is Aeriel."

Roshka turned away. "When we go before the high families," he said, "we will let their seeing women decide."

Aeriel fingered her staff moodily. "When first I started upon this trek, many daymonths past," she told him, "I came following a rime:

> "But first there must assemble
> > those the icari would claim,
> A bride in the temple
> > must enter the flame,
>
> Steeds found for the secondborn beyond
> > the dust deepsea,
> And new arrows reckoned, a wand
> > given wings —

So that when a princess royal
             shall have tasted of the tree,
Then far from Esternesse's
             city, these things:

A gathering of gargoyles,
             a feasting on the stone,
The witch of Westernesse's
             hag overthrown."

Aeriel sighed. "I had almost forgotten it." She glanced at Roshka. "Does it mean anything to you?"

He shook his head. Her eyes went to Erin. The dark girl had drawn close, listening. She, too, shook her head. Aeriel looked down, resigning herself.

"Then I must ask the sibyl in Orm what it means." She looked up, finding their eyes again. "Go to the high families and wait for me."

Erin started across from her. "No," she whispered. "I'll not be parted from you."

"Sister," cried Roshka. "Pirs needs its suzerain."

"You are its suzerain," said Aeriel. Then softer, "I am not your sister."

Erin took hold of her sleeve. "Do not leave me," she said.

Aeriel turned. "And you, Erin," she said. "Do you think me the princess of Pirs, as well?"

"I do not care," the dark girl cried. "You are Aeriel. Take me with you. I want to go with you wherever you go."

Aeriel touched her cheek. "Terrain is a country of

slavers," she said. "I will not be safe there, nor would you. And the White Witch is hunting me. I know that now. Go with Roshka."

The dark girl drew back from her, let go her sleeve, but her eyes were fierce and her voice very still. "I will not go with him," she said. "I will follow you."

"You must not," Aeriel exclaimed. "How will I find you again if you are not with Roshka?"

"You promised to take me," said Erin, "across the Sea, to those isles where the dark people dwell."

"I shall, I shall," said Aeriel. "I will return for you."

"Don't leave me," Erin cried. Her cheeks were wet.

Aeriel bent and kissed her eyes. "I will return for you." The dark girl clung to her and would not let go. "Roshka," she gasped, struggling to pull Erin's arms from her, "don't let her follow me."

The prince's arms closed around the dark girl, holding her. Erin fought him. He gazed at Aeriel.

"You are my sister," Roshka said. "I know you are. I cannot hold you, too, but you must promise you will come back."

"I will not be long," said Aeriel, and hoped that were the truth.

"No, don't leave me," Erin gasped. "Aeriel, don't go."

The dark girl strained in the prince's arms. Aeriel drew back from her. She felt a tight band winding about her throat. Her vision blurred and ran.

"I cannot take you with me," she whispered. "I dare not."

She turned then, wrenching herself away. She whistled

her gargoyles and they sprang up, came loping to her. Aeriel shouldered her pack and picked up her staff. She raised her hood against the white sun's glare.

Behind her, she heard Erin and Roshka both cry out suddenly. Turning, she saw them standing startled, amazed. They stared after her, into the sun, but they were gazing past her, through her, in such astonishment Aeriel was puzzled.

It was as if they could not see her, as if she had vanished suddenly from their sight. Erin gave a low moan, slipped through Roshka's arms to the ground. She covered her face with her hands.

"I will return to you," Aeriel cried, walking backwards, away from them, and Erin screamed, weeping into her hands. Roshka knelt, trembling violently, held her against him. With his other hand, he caught Nightwalker's bridle. The horse was sidling; its eyes rolled.

Aeriel turned blindly and followed the gargoyles. Catwing and Greyling walked beside her on either hand, the mooncalf ranging on ahead. Aeriel fared shadowless between Solstar's and the tower's light, down the road toward Terrain.

14

MAGE

By the time Solstar had climbed a third of its way toward zenith, Aeriel knew she had crossed into Terrain. The rocks had grown cream-colored, no longer grey. Here and there slides had scarred the brittle surface of the steeps.

The road led very nearly north. She met no one, avoided towns. Below her, in the valleys where the denser air gathered, leaf fir and hardy fingergrass clustered, higher up, white starblaze and brittlescrub. She walked with her hood raised against the sun, went quickly and steadily, took little rest.

She found herself growing very hungry and weary. She felt chilled from having walked the last hour in the shadow of a steep. Halting where the road curved around a boulder, she sat down in the sunlight. Two of her gargoyles lay panting in the boulder's shade. The third browsed along the road's edge ahead. Aeriel felt ravenous.

And she had no food, she realized, searching her pack. She must have finished off what little she had brought out of Pirs the last time she camped. She eyed the last two apricoks a moment, fingered them — but no.

She put them up again and turned to gaze up the barren road ahead, wondering what root or seed she might gather there. Again, as she had on the beach in Bern, she found herself longing for Talb the duarough and his little velvet bag of delicacies.

Aeriel started from her thoughts. A figure rounded the bend ahead. The mooncalf shied, but the traveler brushed by without seeming to see it. The figure was swathed in a long dark robe, a deep hood hiding the face from view. Sleeves covered even the fingertips. The hem of the garment dragged on the ground.

The traveler was very short, Aeriel realized as it neared, stood little more than half her height. It nearly wandered off the cliff's edge before righting its course. The fair girl sat staring. The gargoyles beside her had begun to growl.

The figure tripped on the hem of its robe, sprawling flat in the middle of the road. After a moment, it picked itself up and progressed diagonally across the path. It came up against the hillside presently, halting with a muffled curse.

"A plague upon this garment! I vow, let the witch take it — I hate it so. *Oof.*"

It collided with the hillside across from her again. Aeriel's mouth had fallen open.

"You," she said, getting to her feet. "What are you about? Throw back your hood or you will come to harm."

The figure started violently and whirled, feeling the air with its sleeve-hidden hands.

"What's that — who's there?" came a voice much smothered in cloth. Greyling had begun to gibber and Catwing to yowl. "I warn you," the figure cried, "I am a wizard, and you had best be one yourself if you mean to harm me."

Aeriel took the greyling by the scruff of the neck and shook it to be still. Catwing slunk around behind her.

"I am no wizard," she answered, "and I mean you no harm. I only meant you will harm yourself if you do not watch your way. I am Aeriel."

"Aeriel?" the figure exclaimed, struggling with its hood. "Did you say Aeriel? I cannot hear properly in this sack. Where's a shadow?"

Its arms groped for a moment, until they touched the boulder's shade. The figure ducked into the shadow of the rock and threw back its hood. Aeriel gave a little cry, for she recognized the wizened face, the stone-grey eyes and long twining beard. The duarough stood blinking.

"Talb," she cried. "Little mage of Downwending."

The duarough cast about him. "Aeriel?" he said. "Where are you, child?"

"Here," said Aeriel, directly before him now.

The little mage frowned, peered straight through her, then away. He caught sight of the gargoyles suddenly. Greyling yipped and Catwing snarled. The mooncalf on the slope above sent a shower of tiny stones raining down.

"Stop that!" the little mage exclaimed. "Cease, you monstrosities. Aeriel, come out and call off your beasts. Where are you? This is a fine greeting."

Aeriel stilled the gargoyles with a word. "I am right

here," she answered, kneeling before the little man. "Can you not see me?" She put back her hood to be able to see him better.

The duarough's eyes found her suddenly, at last. He stared a moment, then began to laugh. "Of course I can see you, daughter — now. Where ever did you get a daycloak? I could well have used one, these last day-months, in place of this wretched garb."

He gestured to his own ill-fitting garment, then fingered the material of her cloak.

"It is a simple traveler's cloak," she told him, puzzled. "I got it in Bern four daymonths past. What is so re-markable in it?"

"Do you mean," exclaimed the duarough, "you have traveled all the way from Bern in a daycloak and did not know it?"

Aeriel gazed at her robe, feeling the material now herself. It seemed as it had always seemed to her, very soft, pale without, darker within.

"My people make such cloaks," the little man said. "We cannot bear the light of Solstar, for the Ancients made us to dwell underground. We may travel by night, of course, without difficulty, but when we must go over-land by day, we must wear a daycloak. That, or swaddle ourselves completely in other stuff."

"But how is my cloak different from yours?" asked Aeriel.

The little mage took off his own dusty overcloak, careful to stand still completely in the boulder's shadow. He wore, underneath, the garment she remembered, a loose grey robe with many folds.

"Hand me your cloak," he said. Aeriel did so. The duarough shook it out. "The fiber is such, and the weave is such — an ancient art, and one I regret I never learned — as to make the wearer unseen by day, for it is invisible to the light of Solstar."

"Unseen?" said Aeriel, and began to laugh. "I never vanished."

"Not from your own sight," the little man replied. "Those who wear daycloaks can always see themselves." He put the daycloak on.

"And I can see you now," Aeriel said.

"Naturally," the mage replied. "My hood is down. But lift it —" He did so. Nothing happened. Aeriel saw him still, as plain as plain in the shadow of the rock. "And step from the shade —" He stepped into the light of Solstar then, and vanished.

Aeriel started. The gargoyles whined. She heard the duarough's chuckle, and a scuffing as of someone walking. Little puffs of dust rose from the road. She saw footprints there, but no shadow, no form. The little mage reappeared, stepping back into the boulder's shade.

"Of course, I don't dare put back the hood in sunlight," he said. "I'd be visible then, as were you — but being a duarough, I'd turn to stone."

But Aeriel was hardly listening now. "The hood," she murmured. "It only works by sunlight, you say? *That* is why Erin said I appeared out of the air," she cried, "why she and Roshka looked suddenly so frightened when I left them — why Nat jumped so when she first saw me. The goatboy called me a sorceress. . . ."

She turned back to the duarough, lost for words.

"It fits you," she found herself saying in a moment, for the garment did, fitting his much shorter, stockier frame exactly as it had fit her tall, slender one.

The duarough nodded. "It is a virtue of daycloaks always to be exactly the proper size."

Aeriel said, "Is that why I have had no shadow? Even by night, by lamplight, I have no shadow." But gazing down at her feet, she saw with a rush of relief she was casting a shade again, for she was not wearing the daycloak now.

The duarough nodded again. "Who wears a daycloak has no shadow by any light." He sat down, leaning against the rock. "Have you been wearing it hood-up by daylight, daughter?" And when Aeriel nodded, again the little man laughed. "Then no wonder the White Witch has not managed to find you yet."

Aeriel looked at him.

"Oh, yes. She has been hunting you, and me, these many daymonths. Prince Irrylath, too, I suppose, though he is safe in Esternesse."

The mention of her husband's name brought a painful sensation to Aeriel's breast. She turned that the little mage might not see her face. "What do you know of the White Witch's hunting?" she asked him softly.

The other shifted where he sat, stretching as one very weary of travel. He began rummaging through the many pockets of his robe. Aeriel remembered suddenly how ravenous she was.

"I mean to tell you, daughter," he answered then. "But I am hungry. Let us eat first."

So they ate. The duarough produced tiny melons the size of fists, plump rosy appleberries, yellow rumroot wrapped in husks, shelled halver nuts and the great white mushrooms of which he was so fond, along with a sprig of withered, aromatic leaves.

Aeriel gathered sticks, and the little mage conjured fire. The melons they roasted until they split, crackling and fizzing over the low, licking flames. The rumroots they baked, basting them with the juice of appleberries, and the mushrooms they ate between handfuls of halver nuts.

Then, to Aeriel's surprise, the duarough drew from his robe a tiny kettle, which he filled with water from a flask, then steeped the leaves to a dark green tea which smelled of ginger and tasted of lime. They sipped it from the halves of the split melon rinds.

He told her of all that had befallen him since they had parted a half year ago in Avaric. How he had journeyed to the witch's palace of cold, white stone, pretending to be some servant of her "son" so that Aeriel and her prince might have time to weave their sail of darkangel's feathers and escape to Isternes.

He told Aeriel of the witch's scream when she had learned at last that Irrylath was lost to her, how he himself had fled then, avoiding her hunters ever since. At last his tale was done; they could eat no more. The little man eyed Aeriel a moment, sipping his tea.

"Were you very unhappy in Esternesse?"

Aeriel sighed. Was it so obvious? "Irrylath loathes the sight of me," she said.

"Does he?" the little mage asked, gently. "The only loathing I saw in him was self-loathing, when last we parted."

Aeriel hugged Greyling, shivering slightly. She did not want to think of Irrylath. "Maidens came to me," she said, "that had been the vampyre's brides in Avaric. They told me the second part of Ravenna's rime." She looked at the duarough then. "That is why I came away."

The mage's brows went up. "Did they?" he murmured. "Recite it for me."

Aeriel said:

> "But first there must assemble
> those the icari would claim,
> A bride in the temple
> must enter the flame,
>
> Steeds found for the secondborn beyond
> the dust deepsea,
> And new arrows reckoned, a wand
> given wings —
>
> So that when a princess royal
> shall have tasted of the tree,
> Then far from Esternesse's
> city, these things:
>
> A gathering of gargoyles,
> a feasting on the stone,
> The witch of Westernesse's
> hag overthrown."

The little man nodded. "You have learned it perfectly," he said. "I could not have taught you better myself."

Aeriel laughed, resting her head against Greyling. "That part of the steeds," she said, "is all I understand. Do you understand it?"

But the duarough shook his head. "I hardly understood the first part, daughter."

Aeriel looked off. Would she never find the answer? Was there no one who might help her but the sibyl in Orm? Her blood chilled. She shivered. She was so weary of journeying, and the task hardly even begun.

"I am going to Orm," she told him, "to ask the sibyl what it means."

"I will go with you," the little mage replied, and Aeriel felt her heart lift, just a little. She smiled her gratitude at him. The duarough said, "But tell me what has befallen to bring you this far."

Aeriel spoke then, of crossing the Sea-of-Dust, of the keeper of the light and the city of thieves. She told him of blighted Zambul, of Erin and Roshka, of the suzerain in Pirs and the caves of the underdwellers there. So saying, she showed him the little pick she had found. The duarough ran his fingers over it, testing the heft. It fit his smaller hand.

"A miner's pick, or a smith's hammer," he murmured. "I cannot tell." He put it away in the daycloak's pocket. "But it is strange. In all my journeying since Avaric, I have seen no other of my kind. Their halls stand empty, long unused, and the only answer I have gotten from those overlanders who even remember us is 'The underfolk have gone away.' "

He gazed off, fingering his long grey beard.

"It is strange, very strange. And it troubles me."

Lastly, Aeriel spoke of the lightbearers, and the blazing Torch, and of the darkangel that had gazed into her eyes, and screamed, and fled.

"Why was that?" she asked him. She shook her head. "I do not understand."

"Do you not?" the mage replied. "You are a slayer of darkangels, child. You have stolen the witch's last 'son' away and restored him to mortality. You wear his hallowed heart within your breast. Do you think a seraph cannot see that when it looks into your eyes?"

The duarough shook his head.

"The lorelei has been a fool to try to frighten you with darkangels, and she has called them all home to her now. As I crossed out of Elver, I saw the darkangel of that land, flying northeast toward Pendar, joined by the icarus of Terrain. Two blots of darkness against the stars — I wondered at it.

"But if she has called those two together to her, then she has called them all home. Be sure, she is still hunting us, but I do not believe she will use darkangels against you again."

Aeriel closed her eyes. She could not fathom any of this. It was all beyond her understanding. "Talb," she said, "the witch is hunting my gargoyles. Why?"

The little man across from her shrugged. "I do not know. They are a mystery to me. Where they come from or what they are, I do not know. One thing is certain, though. Whatever the witch's purpose for them, it can be no pleasant one. It is well they are mostly in our hands now, not hers."

"Mostly?" said Aeriel. "I had six gargoyles in Avaric. I have come upon only three. . . ."

The other had gotten to his feet, brushing the crumbs from his robe. He had begun to pack up the little kettle, but stopped himself now. "Oh, did I not tell you? How absentminded I have become." He began searching his robe. "Where did I put them? Here it is."

He drew from one sleeve a little drawstring bag of black velvet no bigger than his hand. Aeriel knew it at once. When she had journeyed in search of the Avarclon, that little bag had contained all the food she had needed for daymonths. She stared at it now, puzzled.

"When I learned the witch was hunting your gargoyles," the duarough was saying, "I set out to gather them. It has taken me daymonths, and I have caught only two, but added to your three . . ."

Aeriel was on her feet before she was aware. "My gargoyles," she cried. "You have them — where?"

She cast about her, at the roadway, at the rocks. The little mage looked up.

"Why, in here," he answered, holding up the bag. "For safekeeping. And of course, they really are not tame. . . ."

Aeriel looked at him. "They are tame," she said.

"For you, daughter." The duarough tugged at the knotted drawstrings, then turned the little bag over and shook it. "Come out," he said, "the pair of you."

Aeriel saw the fabric twitch. Something very small fell from the bag. One moment it was as tiny as two fingers — then in the next it had grown as large as two people. Aeriel scrambled back.

It looked something like a long-necked hen with

neither feet nor tailfeathers, its body merging into a great eel's tail that coiled away behind. Its shabby plumes were the grey of stone, its snaky body exactly the same. It shrieked at the mage, snapping at him. A brass collar encircled its throat.

"Keep off, you fright," the little man commanded. "You have your mistress to answer to now."

Aeriel rushed forward then, crying, "Eelbird, Eelbird." The eelbird whirled and abruptly subsided, catching sight of her.

"Named them, have you?" inquired the duarough.

Aeriel shook her head, laughing. "Just foolish names. Child's names." She stroked the new gargoyle's matted feathers, its scabrous scales. The eelbird beat its pinions, rubbing against her, gave a weird and loonish cry.

"That one I found in Elver," the duarough was saying. "People there were in great fear of it, calling it a dragon — but where is the other one?"

He shook the little velvet bag, chafing it.

"Oh, will you not come out?" he muttered, groping inside, though for all Aeriel could see, the little sack remained as limp and empty-seeming as before. "There it is."

The little mage gave a sudden cry and yanked free his hand. Aeriel glimpsed a miniature gargoyle, teeth clamped to the mage's thumb, before it loomed suddenly into a great, hairless creature with batlike wings, a tail, lithe limbs halfway between a lizard's and a man's.

"Release me," the duarough cried.

The gargoyle hissed through its teeth. Aeriel hastened to touch it. Its skin was cool and dry. The brass band about its throat gleamed dully.

"Lizard," she murmured. "Monkey-lizard, leave off."

The creature started, releasing the mage, and turned with a hoot of recognition. Its grey double tongue flicked across her hand. Aeriel scratched its cold, pebbly hide.

"I came upon that one in Rani," the little mage said.

Aeriel glanced at the black velvet bag, demanded, "How long have you kept them in there?"

The duarough shrugged, nursing his hand. "Only a daymonth or two."

"They are starving," Aeriel exclaimed. She gazed at the two of them. They were all bone.

"So I discover," the mage replied, flexing his fingers. They did not appear to be bleeding. A moment later, he added, "They would not eat what I offered them."

"Here," said Aeriel, gentling now. She spoke to the gargoyles. "Eat this. Eat these."

Reaching into her pack, she drew out the last remaining apricoks, fed one to each beast in turn, saving the seeds. When they had done, she watched their fallen sides fill out a little, their crusted skin grow more supple and smooth. They circled her, and the other gargoyles. She turned back to the duarough again.

"There is only one left now," she told him, "the one I called Raptor, for it looked like some bird of prey before and an animal with paws behind." She frowned a little. "Where is it now? What has become of it?" She shook her head. "I have no more apricoks."

"Come," the duarough said, putting away the last of his things. He kicked dust over their blue-burning fire, raised the daycloak's hood before stepping out into Solstar's light. "The sibyl will know, and it is still a long way to Orm."

༄༅༈

They traveled north, toward the capital. The dua-rough wore the daycloak now; Aeriel saw him only when their path led through shade. She used the mage's old overcloak to make her pack, wore Hadin's robe, all yellow fire in the shadowless glare of noon.

They took high roads and avoided other travelers. Twice, Aeriel glimpsed below them slave caravans: ragged captives stumbling behind their captors, roped together, their hands bound.

Terror and anguish filled her then. She could almost feel the choking cords herself. I can never live like that again, she thought. If slavers take me, I shall die. Aeriel could not bear to look at the caravans. She and the duarough took other paths.

Solstar was low in the east, nearly setting, when they came to Orm, a city of white mudbrick houses in a low place between three steeps. Talb insisted that the gargoyles secrete themselves in the black velvet bag again. They did so, all five, but only at Aeriel's coaxing.

"We must go as discreetly as possible now," the little mage said. "The White Witch may have called her darkangels home, but she has other agents looking for you. Now tell me of this sibyl you seek."

Aeriel shook her head, tried to clear it, to think of nothing. "I know little of her, only what I have heard. She is a hermitess in the highest temple upon the altar cliffs beyond Orm. She is very old, a priestess to the Unknown-Nameless Ones. Her face is hidden by a veil. All who come before her must offer a gift to her bowl, and she will receive petitioners only by day. She spends the long fortnight in fasting and prayer."

They entered the city then, and the duarough fell silent. Aeriel walked, seemingly alone through the wide stone streets of Orm, the adobe buildings rising to four and five storeys on either side. She spoke no more to the little mage, walking unseen by her side, for he wished his presence to remain unknown.

Some upon the streets, seeing Aeriel's bare feet, thought her a slave. They cried out jeers or offers to her imagined masters. Others, noting the fineness of Hadin's cloak, took her for some foreigner come to buy slaves and cried out invitations to view their wares.

And others, eyeing her wingèd staff, murmured she must be some priestess and left her strictly alone. To none of them did Aeriel pay any heed. Fear made her stiff. Even with the duarough at her side, she was afraid to pause or turn her head — save to those that came too close.

These she turned to look at, and most fell back then, some muttering:

"Green eyes, green eyes," and once one whispered, "Sorceress."

She had to pass very near the slave market in the center of the city, for all the thoroughfares led like wheel spokes to the satrap's palace, across from which the market stood. Aeriel took side streets, trying to skirt it, though she could see the palace roof rising above the other roofs. She had to put her hands over her ears to shut out the noise of bidding and the crowd.

The center of the city fell behind, and at last they

reached Orm's northern edge. Aeriel felt a great weight lifting from her. She could breathe again. White, crumblinng cliffs rose steeply there, dotted with holy places and shrines. Footpaths threaded up the near-vertical slope. Aeriel had to crane to see the sibyl's temple at the top. She and the duarough began to climb.

Halfway up the narrow, twining path, Aeriel heard the little man halt. She stopped as well, a bit breathless —they had been going very hard. Her shadow fell across the mage, and she was able to see him leaning against the cliff, mopping his brow. He waved her on.

"Go on ahead, daughter," he panted. "My frame was not made for such exertions in this thin overland air. Let me rest a little, and I will come after. But you must hurry. Solstar is nearly down."

Aeriel glanced back, and the sun indeed floated low upon the jagged steeps. After a moment's hesitation, she left the little mage and climbed on until at last the path grew so steep she could not see the temple overhead, had to use her staff to help her climb. All Orm stretched out below. She spotted the palace roof, the market square. She struggled over another rise, and found herself before the sibyl's shrine.

It was set into the rock itself, the stone above it carved into the semblance of a roof. Free-standing pillars stood upon a narrow porch of stone, flanking the entry-way. A stone lyonesse with a woman's face and breast lay upon the roof, overlooking a great smoldering bowl, piled high with offerings.

Aeriel stood a moment, not quite knowing what to do. She had never entered a temple before. They had always frightened her. As a child in the syndic's house, she had heard tales of slaves sacrificed upon the altar cliffs of Orm.

She stared at the bowl upon the ground before the temple porch, at the great heap of flowers and fruit, coins of silver, pieces of silk, and studded cups of white zinc-gold. She had no offering.

Then she remembered something she carried. Kneeling, she reached into her pack and drew out the pale green lump of ambergris. She held it out over the smoking heap. Heat rose from there as from smothered coals. She laid the lump upon the other gifts.

"Come into the temple," someone behind her said. "I have been waiting for you."

15

SIBYL

Aeriel whirled, but no one stood before the temple. She saw now that the entryway was a natural opening in the rocks, devoid of doors. A weird wordless crooning began within, very soft.

"Sibyl?" she said. No answer came. The contents of the offering bowl shifted, smoking. The stone lyonesse lay motionless, facing the sun. Handling the ambergris had left Aeriel's hand waxy. She rubbed the sweet-smelling stuff off on one arm. The singing continued. Aeriel went inside.

The interior of the cave was no bigger than a chamber. Light of Solstar streamed in from the door. On the far side of the room lay a slab of stone, dark like obsidian, and smooth. A faint hum seemed to come from it, and a slight, bitter scent.

Before it lay a small firepit, beside which a woman in sackcloth sat, spinning. Her great spindle was dark iron. Her drab wool came from beaten nettles. The woman's face was turned from the sunlight, and it was she who murmured the wordless tune.

"Are you the sibyl?" said Aeriel.

The woman lifted her head. Her face was lined. She wore no veil, only a bandage across her eyes. "What, is someone there?"

Her voice was soft, like paper on sand. The glow of the coals played across her features strangely. Aeriel knelt.

"Sibyl," she said, "I need your help. I have come from Isternes to lay a riddle before you. My name is Aeriel."

"Aeriel?" the old woman whispered. Her hair was unkempt, her fingers stained with nettle juice. "Aeriel that was my fellow in the syndic's house?"

Her thin, calloused hands groped through the air. Aeriel started violently, recognizing the other now. She remembered her years in the syndic's house, in the company of a madwoman of Avaric who told horrific tales of once pushing her sovereign's son into a desert lake as tribute for a lorelei.

"Dirna," Aeriel breathed.

Leathery hands darted over her face. "It is you," the blind woman cried. "My little Aeriel. But what are you doing here, my love? We all heard you had run away — oh, a long time ago."

Aeriel nodded. "Yes. I went back to the steeps where Eoduin was taken. The darkangel returned and carried me away. But what are you doing here? I must speak to the sibyl."

"Oh, I never treated you kindly," Dirna moaned, "but I meant no harm. I was spiteful once, but I serve the temple now. I had to run away, like you." Her spidery fingers left Aeriel's face. "The syndic was in a rage when he discovered you gone, said someone must have helped you."

"No one helped me," answered Aeriel. "Was it you who spoke to me outside?"

Dirna's fingers fluttered. "Did I?" She shook her head, frowning. "I can't recall." Her bandaged eyes seemed to seek Aeriel's. "You know how I forget sometimes...."

"Is the sibyl here?" Aeriel asked.

Again the other shook her head. "Not here — but wait," clutching Aeriel's wrist as the girl made to rise. "She will return. Stay with me a little while."

Aeriel leaned her staff in one corner by the dark stone slab. It was nearly black, but had the look somehow of being clear, as though if only she looked long enough, she might be able to see deep down, as into a well. Still it hummed, almost below her hearing, and the odor that came from it was faintly like tar, or lightning flash. Aeriel sat down again. Dirna sat winding her wool about her spool.

"What is that bandage?" Aeriel asked.

Dirna touched the gauze. "The light of Solstar hurts my eyes," she muttered, "for all that I am blind."

Aeriel gazed about the room. There was nothing to see, not even a bed. The cave was bare. Dirna's hand brushed a stray nettle. She began twisting it.

"But list, I remember now. There was a thing I wanted to tell you. Poor Bomba!"

"What of Bomba?" said Aeriel, looking up.

The other laid her spindle aside. "Are you not hungry, my dear?" she asked dreamily. "It is a long climb up that slope."

Her fingers darting above the firepit, she found a dipper and a cup. A low pan of something lay simmering there. She ladled some and pressed it to Aeriel. The stuff tasted of vinegar, berries, and barley meal. Aeriel set it aside barely touched.

"I am not hungry," she said. "Tell me of Bomba. Is she ill?"

"Not hungry?" Dirna crooned. "After such a climb? Come, drink. You will swoon if you do not eat something. But what was I speaking of?"

Aeriel sighed, sipped from the cup. She toyed with a pebble upon the floor. The hands of the woman across from her darted blindly, searching for something. Dirna was mad, had been mad as long as Aeriel had known her. She sighed again. Pressing her would do no good.

"Oh, yes," the other cried, clutching a handful of dust. She laughed brittlely. "I have remembered now. Of Bomba. I was speaking of Bomba. Your old nurse — Eoduin's nurse. Yes. She's dead."

"What?" cried Aeriel. She had drunk most of the cup by then. Setting it down, she spilled the rest.

"The syndic killed her," the blind woman said, "after you ran away. He said if anyone knew where you had gone, it would be she."

"I told no one that I was going," cried Aeriel. "No one knew."

Quickly, deftly, Dirna unwound the coarse wool from her spindle onto a shuttle. A handloom rested on the floor beside her. She turned to it and began to weave.

"He shut her up in an empty storeroom." Dirna's

fingers darted, passing the shuttle through the warp by touch. The great, coarse square of cloth was nearly done. "Said he'd not let her out till she told where you were."

Aeriel felt a weakness welling up in her. Her head swam. "I don't understand," she murmured. "If he fed her, how . . . ?"

Dirna made a little sound that might have been whimpering. Aeriel could not see her clearly anymore.

"Well, he forgot to give her any water, didn't he?" Dirna hissed. She clicked her tongue. "Bomba was an ample old thing — could have lived a daymonth without a crumb. But not without water. Solstar was barely halfway to zenith when she died. Oh, such a pity, that. He hadn't meant to kill her. She'd been his own nurse before she was Eoduin's."

Aeriel felt dizzy suddenly, and very cold. She shivered hard. Her teeth rattled. Dirna lifted her head.

"Are you cold?" she asked. "There, poor thing, put this on. It's finished now. I've been weaving it for daymonths, since I came here."

Aeriel looked up. Her head felt heavy. Her vision blurred. She saw Dirna lifting the cloth from the loom. She wrapped it tightly about Aeriel's shoulders. The cloth had a rough and tacky feel, seemed almost to adhere to her. Aeriel made weakly to brush it away.

"What?" the other murmured. "Would you refuse old Dirna's shawl? I made it for you."

Aeriel struggled to rise, but her legs would not hold her. She fell heavily against Dirna. The blind woman was wrapping the shawl once more closely about her.

"Are you weary?" she said. "Come, I have a place for you to lie."

Aeriel felt herself half lifted, half dragged, and then a strange, cold touch along her back. The surface beneath her shifted in tremors. A dull humming rose in her ears. Dirna had laid her upon the slab, she realized dimly, trying to struggle, to move. Dirna was bending over her.

"What have you done to me?" Aeriel whispered. She could hardly stir. The shawl gripped her tightly as if it had been sewn to her.

"The drink?" the other said. "They call it stone's blood, to quiet you. You will not sleep. The sibyls drink it to bring them dreams."

"I must see the sibyl," Aeriel gasped.

"Little fool, there is no sibyl here. I killed her and gave her to the stone. Few ever come here, and the sibyl always went veiled. Who would know me from her? Lie still."

Aeriel struggled. The stone on which she lay felt hard and at the same time slippery. Its hum, the tremor in it seemed to be growing stronger. Her hair clung to its surface, as did her desert shift and the fabric of Hadin's robe.

"Bomba, too," Dirna was muttering. "Doddering old ewe. How I hated her. I was the one who was to bring her water."

"Fiend," panted Aeriel. "Harridan — why?" The shawl about her shoulders clutched her till she choked.

Dirna turned away. "Kept you all away from me, didn't she? Called me mad. And you were always her pet. Fussed over you like a hen, from the time you were such a little chit the only word you could cry was 'erryl, erryl!' Some foreign word.

"Would not let Eoduin call you Sissa, said you must have a better name. Then nothing would do but that she call you Aeriel. 'Aeriel!' What manner of name is that? Oh, stop struggling. It won't do you any good. That's the Feasting Stone you lie upon."

Aeriel stopped, staring after the woman with the bandaged eyes.

"Yes," said Dirna. Her lean weathered face cracked into a smile. "The Feasting Stone. The Ancients made it. Who knows what they used it for?" She came back, leaning over Aeriel. "The sibyl is dead, but the Stone still feasts. Offerings laid upon it fall into dust, which after a little time runs through the pores of the rock and disappears. As you will crumble and disappear, my love — soon, soon. And I will watch."

Then the sightless woman reached one leathery hand and pulled the bandage from her eyes.

Her eyes were red, the color of carbuncles. They were smooth as glass, without iris or pupil or white. Dirna stood blinking in the light of Solstar. Aeriel stared. In the desert of Pendar, the White Witch's jackals had had such eyes.

"You are one of the lorelei's creatures," she whispered.

Dirna nodded. "Yes, love. My pretty eyes. The white lady's servant came to me, a year after you ran away, and brought me eyes. He said she had never forgotten me, how I had given her the princeling in the desert, years ago."

Her red eyes glinted, glimmered in the light. They looked as though they were lit within. Dirna clasped her hands, worried them, giggled with delight.

"Her pride, she called me. Her joy. I must serve her again, she said — all I need do, for these pretty eyes, was go to Orm and wait for you. You would be coming, she said. And you would have gargoyles."

She leaned nearer.

"Gargoyles," she said. "Where have you hidden them? You must have five of them by now. But as you see, the sixth is already in my keeping."

She turned, and Aeriel saw a crevice in the wall. The light of Solstar threw it in shadow. She had not noticed it before. Aeriel could scarcely turn her head; her hair was fastened to the rock. The Stone's humming murmured in her ears. Dirna drew a chain from beneath her kirtle, and on it hung a silver pipe.

She put the whistle to her lips and blew a blast so wild and shrill Aeriel could scarcely hear it, though it made her head throb. From beyond the crack, she heard a wail.

"Come out," the red-eyed woman cried. "Come, you horror, or I'll blow a blast to split your ears."

She raised the pipe again, and Aeriel flinched, hearing another shriek from beyond the crack. Then through it crawled a creature grey as stone, so crippled and bony Aeriel could hardly tell it was shaped like a gyrfalcon before, some form of beast behind.

"Raptor," Aeriel whispered. "Gargoyle. Raptor."

The creature hooted at the sight of her, started toward her, then cowered, gibbering, as Dirna blocked its path.

"The sibyl had it," the red-eyed woman said. "She had been feeding it. But the whistle makes it wild. It must obey. The white lady sent it to me, to help me with its fellows, as well as the spindle to make your shawl." She eyed the gargoyle, clicked her tongue. "Poor beast. It's gotten very thin. The last it had to eat was the sibyl's heart."

Aeriel tried to move, to scream, but she had no strength to move, no breath to scream. Something thin and thready was running out of her into the stone.

"Where are its fellows?" Dirna demanded. "The lady wants them."

The gargoyle in the corner yammered and screeched. Hissing, the red-eyed woman turned and seized it by the collar. The silver pin that fastened the brass band gleamed there. Dirna shook it. The raptor writhed, snarling, flexing its talons — but did not strike.

"No, you don't dare," Dirna laughed. "I have the pipe."

Aeriel struggled, fought to rise. Her garments held her to the Stone, but the shawl about her had slipped a trace, and she found she could breathe. The arm on which she had rubbed the ambergris was sliding free, for the fabric did not adhere to it. Her skin on that arm did not bind to the Stone.

Aeriel reached for her staff. It stood against the wall beside the Stone, out of her range. The gargoyle hissed, slinking before Dirna. Aeriel reached with one leg, brushing her walking stick with the ball of her foot.

"Where are the other gargoyles?" Dirna snapped.

Still she held the raptor's collar, her whistle raised. She did not even glance at Aeriel. Aeriel toed her staff. It toppled toward her, falling across her. She grabbed at it, but missed.

"Heron," she cried. "Heron, fly — find Talb! Tell him to keep the gargoyles away."

As the staff fell past her, the heron shimmered. Her form unstiffened suddenly, and flew. Dirna wheeled about. With a snarl of rage, she lunged after the wingèd thing, but the white bird was already through the temple door. Eyes on Dirna, the gargoyle sank into a crouch.

"Little fool," Dirna spat, turning on Aeriel. "So you have given them to someone to keep for you? It does not matter. If they are near enough to hear my pipe, then they will come to me. They must."

She raised the whistle to her lips and blew again. The raptor inching forward behind her flattened itself to the ground with a cry. Aeriel felt her hair tearing as she wrenched her head away, for the note was piercing, deafening — rang until it seemed the mountain must fall.

Then it ceased, and in the silence Aeriel heard the yelp of the gargoyles, very faint and far-seeming. The harridan smiled.

"So, they are coming. Good." She wrapped her arms about herself, laughing. "Ah, the lady will be so pleased. What will she give me in reward? Something rare, surely. Something powerful and fine . . ."

Aeriel heard the scuffle of footsteps. The red-eyed woman turned.

"Eh?" she called out. "What's that — who's there?" Aeriel saw nothing. The hag cast about her. "Are you a servant of my lady? Where are you?"

She gave a cry suddenly, caught her wrist. Clutching the whistle tighter, she flailed empty air. Then seeming to break free all at once, from nothing, she staggered back. The gargoyle in the corner yipped. Dirna groped, struck out at random.

A puff of dust appeared from nowhere, scattered in midair. The harridan shrieked, rubbing her eyes. A pebble skittered across the room. She whirled — then stopped herself, turned back around. She laughed, and closed her eyes.

"Would you blind me?" she said. "Confound me with charms? I was blind once. Did you think I could not find you by the sound of your own breathing — a duarough in a daycloak?"

Abruptly, she sprang, caught hold of nothing, and yanked. A grey cloak came into being in her hand. The duarough, too: he stood before her, in her shadow, his arms half raised, a look of astonishment upon his face. Aeriel tried to cry a warning.

While he was yet in shadow, the duarough's hand darted into his robe, but Dirna was already leaping back. The light of Solstar fell on him, and for an instant the little man remained flesh — then he froze, the color of stone washing over him like a wave, his one hand still hidden in his robe.

Aeriel heard the yelp of gargoyles again, very small

and faint. Dirna stood peering at the statue before her. "Master treasurekeeper," she exclaimed. "After so long, you were not one I ever expected to see again. I thought surely you went with that Estern woman of the king's when she left Avaric."

She tossed the daycloak away from her then, pawing at her eyes.

"I cannot see properly. That dust— if you've ruined my lovely eyes, little fiend, I'll pash you to rubble before Solstar sets."

The sun hung very, very low.

"No," Aeriel whispered. Her strength was vanishing. The tremor of the Stone had grown terribly strong. She felt her garments moldering to dust. "He has not harmed you...."

The hag ignored her. Sitting down, she fished the carbuncles from beneath her lids. Brushing at them, Dirna smoothed them against her palms. Then she began to polish in earnest, using the hem of her sackcloth kirtle.

"Are they scratched? Are they scratched? Soon we will see. I'll make the lady give me a new pair in exchange for the gargoyles. I have earned a new pair."

A shadow fell across her hunched figure. Eyeless now, she did not notice it. Then the two jewels were taken roughly from her. The crouching woman cried out, whirled, groping. The heron skimmed through the temple door, landing near Aeriel.

"I could not find your invisible duarough in that daycloak of his," she said, "so I brought another person who said he was looking for you."

Aeriel felt a rush of unbelief, followed by a wild gladness. A cry escaped her lips. The figure beside Dirna glanced at her, but his face was hard, very pale and drawn, and she could not read it.

His dress was the white garb of Avaric, much mended along the shoulder and dusty with travel. His skin was gold, his black hair fastened behind him in a long horsetail. Five scars threaded across one cheek. His eyes were cold, corundum blue.

"Well, nurse," said Irrylath, holding the withered woman's eyes. "After so long, you were not one I expected to see again. Have you been well? You do not look it. Nor have I been well, these past double-dozen years, ten of them spent in the witch's house, and fourteen more a darkangel — because of you."

"Irrylath?" the eyeless woman whispered. "Irrylath!"

"You know me, then."

Dirna clutched her kirtle's hem. "My little darling. My lovely prince — where are you? I cannot see you." Her hands fluttered desperately, but Irrylath slipped away from her. Dirna whispered, "But you are alive, my sweet. Alive! I thought you drowned in a desert lake."

"You shoved me in."

The eyeless woman cried out, biting one knuckle. "No — no, I never . . ."

She caught herself suddenly, bit off her words. Then she drew deep breath. Her voice grew quieter, more sweet.

"You fell. Don't you remember? I took you to the lake to show you the mudlick." Her hands crept across the floor now, searching for him. "You slipped. I tried to catch you. I held out my hand — don't you recall?"

Irrylath turned the carbuncles over in his palm. His

face had lost its stoniness. His voice was not quite steady when he spoke. "That is not what you once told this girl, who later told me."

Dirna hissed, turning toward Aeriel. "How do you know her?"

Aeriel watched, unable to move. Irrylath's face was all in shadow now, turned from the sun. Only the dim glow from the firepit lit him eerily from below. Aeriel felt almost afraid of him then.

"I am wed to her," he whispered. "She is my wife."

"No!" Dirna shrieked, gargled, muttered in her throat. "No, she is a wicked, clever girl, my love. It's lies she has been telling you."

Irrylath did not reply. His gaze was fixed on Aeriel, his lips slightly parted, as though he might be about to tell her something, but he did not speak. Beside him, Dirna moaned, clawed at her cheeks.

"Give me my eyes."

The young man turned away then, holding the carbuncles clenched in his hands. "You traded my life to the White Witch," he breathed, "for a sip of foul water."

"For our lives!" Dirna cried. "We would have perished in the desert if I had not given you to her. How cruel you have become." The eyeless woman groaned, wringing her hands. "You never used to be so cruel to your old nurse, your Dirna. . . ."

The prince shuddered, staring at her. "You took me from those who might have taught me kindness," he spat, "and gave me to one who taught me other things."

Dirna's hands found him at last. This time he did not pull away.

"Would you have an eye? Here, take it."

He held out his arm. Dirna's fingers groped along it. Just before they found his hand, Irrylath opened it, letting one carbuncle drop. It fell among the coals of the firepit. Dirna cried out.

"Not the fire," she screamed. "The heat will shatter it."

"Fetch it out, then," whispered Irrylath.

Dirna's hand clutched, finding a poker at the firepit's edge. She began stirring it feverishly among the coals — just as Aeriel heard a cracking sound, saw a puff of yellow smoke rise from the pit, smelled sulfur.

"Ruined!" shrieked Dirna. "You have ruined it — my eye."

"There is still one left," the prince reminded her, holding it up. Dirna clawed his hand, but his fingers only tightened. "And one's enough to see by, isn't it?"

He pulled away from her, strode to the temple door, and threw the stone. It glinted red in Solstar's white glare. The sun lay half sunk into the hills. Sailing over the cliff's edge, the carbuncle vanished. Dirna stumbled to the cave's threshold.

"The rocks," she wailed. "I'll never find it among the rocks."

"You might," the prince replied savagely. "Go look for it," and strode past her toward Aeriel.

"A plague on you," the harridan screamed. "A plague on you, to have destroyed my eyes!"

She scrambled after him, one hand searching the floor. Her fingers closed on the iron spindle. She swung it, caught the young man on the back of the head. He cried

out, taken by surprise, and turned, falling to one knee.
Dirna darted past him.

"I will get new eyes," she said. "Did you think to
drag her from the Stone? Too late, my prince. She's
lost — but I will have her eyes before she crumbles."

Dirna had dropped the spindle now, stumbling toward
the back of the cave. Aeriel cried out, fighting the pull of
the Stone. Its hum was louder, the tremor harder. Her
skin felt like powder. Her garments were dust. The
clinging shawl was falling away in shreds.

Dirna's shadow passed over the duarough. In that instant, his arm completed its motion: drawing the black
velvet bag from his robe. Aeriel saw it twitch, heard the
yelp of gargoyles, very faint and far-seeming still. The
raptor cowering in the corner snarled, seemed to be
gaining courage.

The duarough's fingers, momentarily flesh, moved
upon the bag's drawstring — but then the hag's shadow
had passed, and the little mage froze, the color of stone
washing over him again in the light of Solstar.

Aeriel reached desperately for her staff. It lay upon
the floor, beyond the reach of her captured arm. Irrylath
had staggered to his feet. The heron took wing, flew at
the harridan, but the eyeless woman ducked, batting her
away.

Dirna stumbled against the Stone. Her hands groped,
searching for Aeriel. Aeriel cried out, shrinking away
from her, struggling. She felt her skin crumbling, tearing. A warm dampness oozed beneath her shoulder on
the Stone. Her arm, part of her back came free. She
could sit. She could turn.

Aeriel snatched her staff from the floor. Dirna's fingernails snagged her cheek. Aeriel struck out at her, turned her face away. The hag seized the walking stick, reaching with her other hand. Aeriel kicked, caught at her wrist.

Beyond her, she saw the raptor spring — but not at Dirna, at the mage. It seized the velvet bag in its teeth, straining against the stone hand's grip. Then all at once there came a fury of gargoyles: screaming and hooting, snarling and lunging. The little bag shredded to tatters as the grey beasts struggled free.

Dirna cried out. She whirled. Irrylath caught at her arm, but she twisted away. Ducking behind him, she fled the cave. The gargoyles plunged after her, a storm of shrieking and screams.

The harridan sprang from the temple porch. At cliff's edge she halted, whirling. Irrylath's shadow lay on the duarough now, and the little man was once more flesh. Dirna faced them, brandishing something small and silver. The gargoyles checked their headlong rush.

"Stay, monsters," she shouted. "I hold the witch's whistle still. Kill the Avaric prince and his duarough and his bride; then find my eye among the rocks. I serve the white lady, and you must serve me."

She was raising her lean and leathery arm, she was putting the whistle to her lips — when something white and winged skimmed through the temple door. The heron sailed, stroking. Solstar's light shone through her wings. She flew in the face of the harridan, and plucked the pipe from Dirna's hand.

The hag cried out, spun, snatching after it. Cliff's edge

beneath her one heel crumbled, fell into dust. She seemed
to hang in space a moment, then the earth beneath her
other heel gave way. With a cry, she toppled, vanishing
beyond the rim of the altar cliffs. And with a yell like
hounds after their prey, the gargoyles plunged after her
over the edge.

16

SFINX

Everything was very dark.
Aeriel saw nothing and could feel nothing. She hung suspended in a void, so weary she could hardly think. She longed to sleep.

"Aeriel, awake."

Flickers in the darkness now, little flames of golden light.

"Waken, Aeriel," said Marrea.

The maidens encircled her, like lightbearers. Like stars — they who had once been the withered wraiths, the vampyre's brides. They were all so beautiful now.

"We followed your thread," Eoduin told her.

"Am I in deep heaven?" Aeriel asked. She had no body anymore, but she felt heavy still, weighty as dust.

"No," Marrea answered. "We are a long way from there. Deep heaven is full of light."

"But we can go there," another maiden said.

"If you will come."

Aeriel frowned — made to frown, for she found she had no face, no brows to move. She murmured, "Come with you?"

"Yes," the maidens answered. "Yes."

Marrea had not spoken. Aeriel gazed at her. She felt so tired.

"I do not want to come."

"But you must," the others cried. "You must."

"You have no kith, no one to hold you in the world."

"Roshka," muttered Aeriel. "Roshka is my kith."

"You do not know that."

"It is not certain."

"But Dirna said . . . ," she protested.

"Dirna was mad," said Eoduin.

"I promised Erin . . . ," Aeriel began.

"Do you love her more than me?"

The other maidens held out their hands. "We love you, Aeriel."

Still Marrea did not speak. Aeriel resisted the urge to go to them. "Hadin," she whispered, "the princes of Isternes and the Lady love me."

"But Irrylath does not love you."

Aeriel twinged; she felt a sharp, bitter pain where her heart should have been — for she feared they spoke the truth, and she longed to turn away, shut her eyes, shut her ears to their words. But she had no body, no ears or eyes. She could not turn from the maidens or shut them out.

"No," Aeriel whispered at last. She could fight them no more. "He does not love me."

She longed to give up the world then, to go with them, leave the sorrow of that pain, and everything else behind. Almost, she told them "yes" — but stopped herself. Someone was speaking to her, from a very great distance. The maidens started and glanced at one another.

"Do not listen," Eoduin said.

"It is nothing," another told her.

Aeriel felt her body beginning to return. The feel of her own substance was unbearably heavy, smothering. Almost against her will, she began to struggle.

"Someone is calling me," she told the maidens.

"Not so."

"Come with us."

"Quickly, Aeriel."

"No," Marrea broke in suddenly.

Eoduin had drawn very near, touching Aeriel's cheek — she had a cheek now and could feel the touch. "Companion, I very much wish that you would come with us."

Aeriel gazed at her, remembering how she had loved her in childhood, and wanted to go with her. But Marrea moved between them now. Eoduin hesitated, but at last drew reluctantly away.

"Now is not the time," said Marrea.

"But it has been promised us," the maidens cried.

"That we might have our Aeriel."

"Among us."

"Soon."

"Not yet," Marrea answered them. "Nor is this the way. The White Witch is yet in the world. Aeriel may not join our company until that one has been destroyed."

"Let her join us now," Eoduin protested, "and nothing more of the world will matter to her."

But the light and voices of the maidens were growing faint. Someone was speaking to her, shaking her. There was a humming in her ears, a bitter scent. She felt her body completely once again — enfolding her, holding her to earth. She could not have followed the maidens now if she had wanted. Her flesh was numb, cold as cave water.

"Aeriel, Aeriel," the voice was saying. "Come back to me. Come back."

The dark was not utter darkness anymore. The maidens had gone. The surface beneath her shivered slightly. Aeriel heard digging, scratching. Another voice: "Stop. You will ruin that blade."

"Let it be ruined then," the first voice cried. "We must get her free."

"I have a better means."

Aeriel heard a clinging coupled with chinks, as of bright metal ringing on stone. Someone was pulling her, lifting her. The surface beneath her shuddered. Its hold weakened. Then there was a sharp pain and she moaned.

"There. She is still caught there."

The ring of metal once again. She felt a chipping, then a hard, sharp crack. A bitter puff. The humming of the Stone fizzled in a faint crackling flash. Someone was lifting her away from it.

"Aeriel," he said. "Aeriel."

She remembered to breathe. Something brushed her lips, her eyes. She opened them, blinked in surprise. It was Irrylath bending over her. His one hand hovered above her cheek, his lips parted slightly, his eyes half wild. She lay upon the temple floor, no longer on the Stone.

The duarough stood a few paces off, beside the Stone. It crackled still, and then it ceased. Its hum fell silent. A very fine Bernean blade lay in splinters on the floor. The little mage held in his hand the silver hammer she had brought from the undercaves of Pirs.

Irrylath saw her looking at him then. He snatched back his hand, leaning away from her with a start. Aeriel shuddered with the cold. Her skin felt like the shadow of night — save across her shoulders, the backs of her arms: everywhere that she had touched the Stone was fire.

She reached one hand toward Irrylath. She could hardly get her fingers to move, or her lips to part. Did he kiss me? she thought to herself. She almost felt that she would die if he had not.

But he flinched away from her. "No," he whispered, staring at her, as though she frightened him suddenly.

Aeriel put one hand to her head. "I felt something," she murmured.

Some inward part of her protested his denial. He loves me — it must be so. Oh, let him love me, for I want it so. But a great feeling of hopelessness was overcoming her. Had she only imagined his touch? She felt fainting weak.

Irrylath shuddered and pulled away from her. He rose with difficulty, as though leaving her were somehow hard, and turned away. "Not I. It was not I."

Aeriel dragged herself upright and managed to sit. She felt too spent, too defeated for tears. Dark chips of glassy stone lay on the floor. The temple chamber was very dim, for Solstar was down. Talb had put away the silver pick. He knelt beside the firepit now, throwing fuel upon the coals.

Horrible sounds came from the gargoyles, on the rocks below. Aeriel was still shaking. Someone had wrapped her in pale gold cloth, yards and yards of it, very light and fine. It held no heat. The duarough steeped a tea over the coals and made her drink, for she was white with cold.

The pain in her shoulders and along her back was fierce. The little mage tore something into strips and bandaged her arm, which along its underside looked badly scraped. He had no salve. All this time Irrylath stood off, the light of the firepit making hollows of his eyes.

The flames in the pit died down to coals. The little mage left them and went off in search of firewood. Irrylath had taken the bandolyn from her pack, knelt gazing at it. His fingers touched the strings, at first tentatively, and then with great beauty and skill.

Aeriel recognized the melody, the haunting sweet notes almost painful to her ears. That he could be capable of such beauty and yet still hold himself aloof — surely she could never reach him.

"You play so well," Aeriel murmured at last, "much better than I. Why have I not heard you play before?"

Irrylath set down the bandolyn. He did not look at her.

"In the witch's house," he said, "I forgot such things. Only now, since I have been in Isternes, have I begun remembering." He was silent a moment, then he said, almost fiercely, "This was my bandolyn that my mother brought out of Avaric. She had no right to give it to you."

Aeriel looked down, surprised and somehow stung. She was wearing her wedding sari. She recognized it now. She lifted a little bit between her fingers, and looked up again. "Did you bring this with you out of Isternes?" she asked.

Irrylath breathed deep, as though the air were going bad.

"When Hadin told me you had gone," he said, "I set out in a boat to follow you." His words grew steadier now, not quite ragged. "I was becalmed. I nearly starved. But Marelon, the Lithe Serpent of the Sea-of-Dust, found me. She said she had seen you safe ashore in Bern."

Then Aeriel remembered the great plumed head that had risen from the surf and gazed at her. Had it been no dream? She stared at Irrylath. Had he come following her — was he here in Orm on her account? She shook her head. It had not occurred to her before. Her hand was shaking, as she toyed with a pebble at the firepit's edge.

"I got aid in Bern from my cousin, Sabr," Irrylath continued. "The whole country was alive with news of a green-eyed sorceress who had stolen a strange beast from the city of thieves and disappeared through the demon's pass."

"Sabr," Aeriel said, trying to recall where she had heard the name. It came to her, slowly: Nat's words in the Talis inn. "The bandit queen."

Irrylath glanced at her. "She is my father's sister's child, and rules a band of those who fled the plains. Some have been calling her the queen of Avaric, thinking me dead."

Again he was silent, looking away.

"I lost you in Zambul," he murmured. His mouth tightened. His scarred cheek twitched. "Where have you been? I have been in Terrain two daymonths, searching for you."

"I was in Pirs," said Aeriel.

Irrylath drew in his breath. "Why did you go away from Isternes? Did you not guess the witch would learn of it?"

She nodded. "I knew." His fierceness puzzled her. How could her knowing have mattered?

The prince turned back to her. "Why, then? Why did you go? I had you safe in my mother's house."

Aeriel sighed, for sheer weariness. "I had a task." Even that did not matter anymore. The sibyl was dead. Now she would never find the lons of Westernesse before the witch. The lorelei had won. "I came in search of wingèd steeds."

She looked off, then laughed a little, bitterly.

"But I have found only gargoyles instead." She turned to him again. "You cannot defeat six darkangels alone."

Irrylath was gazing at her now as though he did not believe her — did not believe what she had just said, or did not believe she would dare such a task. Was she only a girl in his thinking, still? And what did that matter, now, in any case? The world was lost.

But he only said, "Seven darkangels, if the witch can steal another babe."

A tiny hope flared in Aeriel suddenly. She dared to breathe. "What became of the lons of the West," she asked him, "the ones the icari overthrew?"

But hope sputtered and died as Irrylath shook his head. He spoke with difficulty — she knew how he loathed to recall anything of the witch.

"I do not know," he said distantly. "When I had

captured the lon of Avaric, I was to bring him to her. But he eluded me, in the desert died." Again he shook himself. "The lons were to be brought to her. That is all I know."

Aeriel bowed her head. She was so weary, she ached. But she could not stop herself from asking, "Why did you come? What do you care what should befall me?" She spoke softly, barely above a whisper. "You are my husband in nothing but name. You are neither my lover nor my friend."

She was staring down, could not see his face. When at first he did not reply, she thought it was because he had not heard. But he spoke at last, the words measured.

"Before I came away from Isternes, I told Syllva what you knew I must, that it was I who had been the dark-angel in Avaric that you overthrew."

Aeriel looked up. He had turned his face away.

"To which, she put her hand upon my cheek"— he touched the scars — "just here, and said she had already guessed." His voice grew dark. He gazed upward. "Syllva had known it all along."

Aeriel watched him, finding herself strangely unsurprised. "Of course she knew." How could she not? The Lady was his own mother — how could she not? "Did you think her a fool?"

Irrylath let his breath out, a short, soft hiss, as though her words had unwittingly stung. He seemed to struggle with himself a moment, then turned to face her.

"I told her another thing also," he said, "what I was in the witch's house before she made me her darkangel."

His voice had become utterly steady now, and very

still. Aeriel gazed at him, shaking her head. "What thing?" she murmured. Her despair lightened a trace: all at once something mattered again. What thing? "You were Irrylath."

The prince shook his head and shuddered, as though hating the touch of his own garb against his skin, his own flesh against his bones. He sat leaning away, gazing on her as if she were leagues distant, a world away.

"I was her lover, Aeriel."

Her throat became then dry suddenly. There was no more air in the temple, no more light. She could not find her voice. "What do you mean?" she whispered. "You were a babe, a boy. . . ."

"And then a youth," he said, "as now."

She could not see his face. She could not see him anymore. Everything was in darkness now.

"That is why you cannot love me."

She could hear his breathing, light and difficult.

"I may love no mortal woman while she lives. She holds that power on me yet. It is the White Witch that I dream of, Aeriel. I dream of her still."

Aeriel struggled to rise. She needed her staff to help her stand. She felt giddy, hollow within, as if the Stone had devoured some part of her that would not return. The cold moved through her, like the night.

"Oh," she breathed, "I knew this. Her lover — I knew. The wraiths, they told me once, in Avaric. I was not listening. It was so long ago, I had forgot."

Her skin was bleeding. She felt the blood. She moved away from Irrylath, toward the door, the openness, the night. She could not breathe. She could not bear to think of it anymore. She touched the bandage on her arm. The pain was fire in her skin.

"Ambergris," she breathed. "It hurts."

Aeriel stood upon the narrow porch. Night around her was black, the sky above riddled with stars. Oceanus hung, white-marled and blue above the steeps. She leaned against her staff. Orm spread dark, torchlit, before her. Her bones felt broken at the joints. And she was very cold.

Gradually, she came aware of another light beside the distant fires of Orm. She lifted her head from where she had bowed it against the staff. A blue flame flickered in the offering bowl. It darted over the garlands and treasures. The bolts of silkcloth began to burn.

The flame changed from blue to plum, then rose, growing brighter now. Aeriel saw the cakes and flowers vanish, the cloth consumed. The flame grew amber, yellow, green, then white. The coins of silver, the cups of white zinc-gold began to melt. Upon the crest of the heap, the lump of ambergris bubbled, smoking, its sweet scent filling the air.

Aeriel went to the bowl. The flame stood higher than she did now. She held her hands to the fire, but the great blaze seemed to have no heat. She touched the fire. It swirled about her hand, feeling warm, suffused with energy, but did not burn. She felt something coming back into her now.

Aeriel thrust the heel of her staff into the ground beside the bowl and stepped over the rim. She stood in the middle of the blazing dish. The fire beat around her like burning cloud. It lifted her hair, made her garment billow, but the wedding sari did not burn.

The treasure had formed a pool of liquid silver that swirled, blood-warm about her feet. The bandage upon her arm caught fire. She saw the blood there blacken and burn away. She felt the cold departing from her. The scent of ambergris was all around.

"Are you the sibyl?" someone said.

Aeriel turned and saw the lyonesse with the woman's face upon the temple roof was stirring. She was tawny-colored now, no longer stone. Arching her spine, catlike, she flexed her claws.

"The sibyl is dead," answered Aeriel, surprised that she could still feel surprise.

"You must be the new one, then," the lyonesse said, yawning. "None but those who have drunk the Stone's blood can stand in my fire without burning. Only my sibyls do that. It gives them long life, and dreams."

She yawned again.

"How sleepy I am. It must be an age I have been dozing."

Aeriel drew near her and knelt at the edge of the burning bowl. "Who are you?" she asked.

"I am called the sfinx."

Aeriel felt something, some strange hope stirring. "Are you a lon?"

The lyonesse shook her head. "No, though the Ancients made me. I was their mouthpiece hereabouts, and guarded the Feasting Stone."

"What is the Stone?" said Aeriel.

"A kind of passage," the sfinx replied, "to the Ancients in their cities. Offerings laid upon it travel to them. They studied such things."

"The duarough has destroyed the Stone, to set me free," said Aeriel.

The lyonesse shrugged. "No matter. It served no purpose anymore. The Ancients are all dead or gone away — at least, they have not spoken to me in years upon years."

She studied Aeriel.

"Are you not my sibyl, then? The satrap always sent me one, to tend the light. It is the flame that nourishes me — though it has not burned in a hundred years."

Aeriel began to feel the heat of the fire now, through the cold. Something else had begun to burn in her, too, some hope she dared not name.

"But why does it burn now," she found herself asking, "when it did not before?"

The sfinx tilted her shoulders languidly. "If, as you say, the Stone is destroyed, then that no longer feeds upon the fire's source — but I suppose it burns now because someone has fed one of the other flames with a seed from the tree of the world."

She sighed.

"This flame once had its tree as well, but my sibyl did not tend it well, and it withered." She frowned then, peering out over the cliff. "What is that I see in my city below?"

Aeriel turned, looking, and felt a tremor pass through her. "The slave market," she said.

"Slave market?" the sfinx murmured. "How is it my

satrap now traffics in slaves?" She came down from the roof in a lithe cat-leap. Her leonine brows were furrowed still. "I must see to that." She started forward.

"Wait," said Aeriel, one hand upon her temple now. The heat of the firebowl was making her giddy. "Sfinx, I have begun to feel the fire."

"Then come out," the lyonesse replied.

She did not turn. Her eyes were scanning the city below. Aeriel stepped down from the burning bowl. The night air moved, deliciously cool against her skin. She knew then what it was she hoped.

"I have a riddle," she began, then stopped herself. Her hope of answer had been dashed so many times before, she had to force herself to speak. "I came to ask it of the sibyl, but she is dead."

"A riddle?" said the sfinx, glancing back over one shoulder now. "I am good at riddles. When I was mouth-piece of the Ancients, people came to me to find answers to what they did not know."

Aeriel felt her breath grow short.

"Half the riddle I already know," she said. "It is the second part I need:

"But first there must assemble
   those the icari would claim,
A bride in the temple
   must enter the flame,

Steeds found for the secondborn beyond
   the dust deepsea,
And new arrows reckoned, a wand
   given wings —

> So that when a princess royal
>   shall have tasted of the tree,
> Then far from Esternesse's
>   city, these things:
>
> A gathering of gargoyles,
>   a feasting on the stone,
> The witch of Westernesse's
>   hag overthrown."

"That is Ravenna's rime," the sfinx replied. "A part of it."

Aeriel stared at her. Hope gripped her till she shook. "Can you tell me its meaning?"

The sfinx gazed at her, calmly. "Most riddlers, I have found, already know the answers to what they ask. Who are those the icari would claim?"

"Lons," said Aeriel. "The lost lons of the West."

"And the bride?" the lyonesse asked.

Aeriel stopped a moment, gazed at the temple, the burning beacon, her wedding sari. "I am the bride," she said softly.

"The steeds and the secondborn?"

"The secondborn are Irrylath's half-brothers, the six younger-born sons of the Lady of Isternes. The steeds are the lons again."

"The arrows and the wand?"

Aeriel shook her head. "I do not know what the arrows are: something to wield against the darkangels, I suppose. The wand . . ." Again she stopped. "The wand is my staff."

She turned and saw it, standing where she had planted it beside the bowl. It was different somehow: still dark, slender wood, but seemed to have grown strangely crooked, gnarled like the slim trunk of a tree. Twigs, leaflets had sprung from the knob. Aeriel stared.

"Ambergris," the sfinx remarked, scenting the air. "The dust whales live many thousand years, and what comes of them is marvelous."

Aeriel went forward, touching her staff. It had grown rooted to the soil.

"But the rime," the lyonesse continued. "Who is the princess royal? What is the tree?"

Aeriel stopped herself again. She remembered Roshka, and Dirna's words. "I am the princess royal," she said. "The tree is the lighthouse tree in Bern."

"The tree whose root reaches the heart of the world," the sfinx replied. "Perhaps this tree's root, in time, will do the same."

The branches of the slender tree had grown longer, its bole thicker. Its leaves whispered against one another. Aeriel saw a fruit forming on one bough.

"Are the gargoyles gathered?" the sfinx asked her.

"Yes."

"Has the Stone feasted?"

Aeriel nodded, shuddered. "Yes," though all mark of that upon her body had now been burned away.

"And the witch of Westernesse's hag?"

"Dirna," whispered Aeriel. "Overthrown."

"There is your riddle, then," the lyonesse said. "Look, the satrap has seen the beacon. A procession of torches comes."

Looking below, Aeriel saw a line of lights wending from the palace toward the cliffs. The sfinx arose.

"I will go to meet them," she said.

Aeriel shook her head, reached after her desperately. "But stay," she cried, dismay filling her. "The arrows, the lons — the rime means nothing if I cannot find them...."

The sfinx regarded her a moment then, and Aeriel noticed for the first time that the catwoman's eyes were deep violet. Her heart beat wildly.

"But you have the lons," the sfinx replied. "They came with you."

The lyonesse disappeared in a lithe cat-bound, vanishing down the footpath toward the torches below. A moment later the gargoyles appeared over the precipice: greyling and catwing and mooncalf, eelbird and apelizard and raptor.

They prowled before her on the cliff's edge, hooting and gabbling. Aeriel stared as if she had never seen them before, all wild and haggard in the light. A white bird fluttered from the darkness above and alighted in the branches of the tree. Aeriel left the gargoyles and went to her.

"Wand-given-Wings," she murmured.

The heron sighed. "Ah, at last you have called me by my right name."

Aeriel asked, "Did ever you carry a green-eyed girl child . . . ?"

"Out of Pirs?" the heron finished for her, nodded. "Yes, once. Years ago. Her mother conjured me. I was to take the babe to a certain family in the north, but a darkangel pursued me, and she slipped from my grasp. I could not find her when I returned."

"Slavers found her," said Aeriel. "I was taken to Terrain."

An apricok was growing on the bough. The heron bent and plucked it, giving it to Aeriel. She turned and called softly.

"Raptor. Raptor, come to me."

The last of the gargoyles came then, and she fed it the golden-red fruit. Some of its haggardness left it. As with the others, it soon looked less starved. Aeriel found herself thinking of the sfinx's words. The sfinx had called the riddle solved. Solved? Aeriel clenched her teeth.

The vital lines — the arrows and the lons — they still meant nothing to her. Nothing! Frustration seized her. To have come so *close*. She held the clean seed in her hand. Turning now in dismay, she flung it into the fire, then drew the rest of the heart-shaped seeds from her pack and flung them in as well.

"I do not know why I have been keeping these," she said, "or why the keeper bade me save them."

But the words were no more than half spoken when the gargoyles hooted and howled. First the raptor, then the others sprang past her into the flame. Aeriel cried out, starting forward, then stopped herself, for she saw they stood as she had done, and did not seem to feel the heat.

The gargoyles' collars began to melt, the brass running down their grey hides like golden blood. But the silver pins that held the bands were not melting. Instead, they were growing bright with the heat. Then the collars were gone, dissolved. The gargoyles shook their heads, and six silver pins flew, falling like glowing stars upon the ground beyond the bowl.

The apricok seeds floated upon the molten treasure and did not burn. They had begun to swell, like grain in broth. Each gargoyle took into its mouth one seed, each now the size of two doubled fists and exactly the shape of a gilded heart. The scent of ambergris rose on the night.

The gargoyles swallowed them whole, without chewing, then lapped at the running silver as though it were milk. Aeriel saw them beginning to change. Their limbs altering, their fur and their feathers growing sleek; their pebbly hides or scales lay smooth.

Then Greyling came down from the bowl, stepping from the fire, and was no longer Greyling, but a black she-wolf with silver throat and belly and legs.

"Bernalon," whispered Aeriel.

"I am she," the lon replied, "and we are the ones that you have sought."

Catwing followed, a winged panther, pale with shadowy silver spots.

"Zambulon," said Aeriel.

"The White Witch overthrew us, one by one, using her sons," the pale cat said.

A great stag, all color of bronze, with eyes and hooves and antlers of gold came forth.

"Mooncalf," cried Aeriel, then caught herself. "Pirsalon."

"She tore out our hearts and put collars on us to strangle our strength, and our thoughts, and our speech," he said.

A copper-colored paradise bird with a snake's tail, dark green, emerged.

"Eelbird," said Aeriel. "Elverlon."

"But you have given us new hearts," she said, "new blood, and taken the witch's collars away."

A long-limbed, wingèd salamander that looked almost manlike came forth. His hide was as black as Erin's skin, all speckled with reddish spots.

"Ranilon," said Aeriel.

"The world is not lost while we live," he said. "We will gladly go with you to Isternes, to serve as steeds against the witch."

Aeriel felt buoyed up, breathed in the night. A deep joy began to well in her, infusing her. I have found them, she thought. I did not fail, and the lorelei has not yet won.

Catching movement then from one corner of her eye, she turned and saw Irrylath standing in the temple door. His face seemed haunted in the flame's pure light. He stared at her as if he did not know her, and at the lons.

She saw the duarough too now, kneeling beside one of the silver pins. Still it glowed. He tapped it with the blunt side of his pick, shaping it. His strokes became surer and more expert as the glowing pin flattened, razor-edged.

"Strange metal, that," he murmured, "very hard and keen. Ancients' silver, I think they call it. No mortal fire could melt it, they say. Hot enough now, though, to reckon. One might make arrowheads of these."

The last of the lons emerged from the fire, a tawny gryphon, formed like a gyrfalcon before and a great cat behind.

"Terralon," laughed Aeriel. She felt heady now, flushed with triumph. All things seemed possible.

"We must hold a council of war in Isternes," the gryphon said.

"And there are the free lons yet to be gathered," said Bernalon. "Marelon, and Pendarlon, and more."

The white bird upon the knotted tree rose. "I will bid them come to you in Esternesse," she answered. Then spreading her wings, she sailed over the cliff's edge, away over the steeps. Aeriel gazed after the line of her flight, ghost-pale against the night-shadowed hills.

"Haste, haste," the bird-of-paradise said. "We, too, must fly."

Aeriel drew a little away, reined in her exultation now. "There is a young girl in Pirs," she began. "I promised to return for her."

"The witch has already called her sons home," the panther warned. "There will be war."

"We must make plans to assail her, and soon," Pirsalon added. "Before the White Witch steals another babe to give her seven darkangels again."

Irrylath had come down from the temple porch. Aeriel could feel him in the darkness behind. The steady cling, cling of the duarough's hammer, making weapons, filled the night. Irrylath halted. Aeriel turned, and then drew back startled, for the prince was holding out his hand.

"Come, Aeriel," he said softly. "Our task is only just begun. We must return to Isternes, and hold a conclave of the lons."

Slowly, Aeriel went to him, eyeing him carefully, for still he gazed at her, as though she were some strange, astonishing thing. There was blood in his hair where Dirna's spindle had struck him. Without thinking, she reached to touch it — and to her astonishment, he did not draw away, nor turn from her gaze.

"We must go by way of Pirs," she found herself telling him, "for Roshka and Erin are waiting for me."

"Climb on my back," the gryphon said, and Irrylath lifted her, setting her between the Terralon's great buff-colored wings. Aeriel searched her husband's face, but he was not looking at her now, though he no longer shrank from her.

"Go on," she heard the duarough say, pausing a moment at his work. "Just leave me a mount and I'll follow you, as soon as I have finished these."

The arrowheads gleamed silvery-white. The panther of Zambul went and sat beside Talb. The little mage's hammer rang. Irrylath sprang onto the back of the paradise-bird. Aeriel sat watching him. Perhaps you cannot love me yet, she thought. But at least we can work together now, until our task is done. Afterwards, who knows?

The gryphon rose into the air, followed by the salamander and the prince's cockatrice. The wingless Stag and Wolf flung themselves over the cliff, plunging in bounds no mortal creature could have made. Aeriel gripped her mount's soft, close fur as they wheeled away over torchlit Orm. The sky spanning vast and starlit before them, they sped eastward, toward Isternes.

POUL ANDERSON
Winner of 7 Hugos and 3 Nebulas